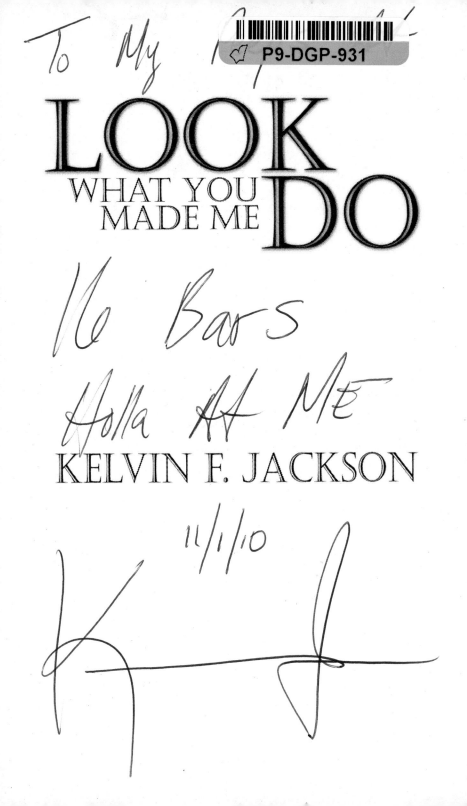

To My [...]

LOOK
WHAT YOU
MADE ME
DO

16 Bars

Holla At Me

KELVIN F. JACKSON

11/1/10

BIG STAXXX ENTERTAINMENT 8972 Quioccasin Road Suite 128
Richmond, VA 23229 copyright© 2010 Kelvin F. Jackson

ISBN-13 978-0-9842971-0-8 ISBN-10 0-9842971-0-3

Cover Design/Graphics: Marion Designs
Editor: Kelvin F. Jackson

This is a work of fiction. Any references or similarities to actual
events, real people, living or dead or to locals are intended to
give the novel a sense of reality. Any similarity in names,
characters, places and incidents is entirely coincidental.

KELVINJACKSONTHEAUTHOR.COM
For bulk sales call 804-252-8760

   Or e-mail:kfjacksonxxx@gmail.com

Printed in the United States of America

(804) 252-2340

ACKNOWLEDGEMENTS

First and foremost I would like to give thanks and all the glory to my LORD AND SAVIOR JESUS CHRIST. Without him and his grace in my life none of these blessings would be possible.

Next I want to thank my parents Joe and Linda Jackson for their support and always being there when I needed them. To my son Jean, I love you more than words can express. To my baby sister Tinesha Jackson I am so proud of you...hopefully now you can be proud of your big brother as well.

BIG SHOUT OUTS to my hood Wyandanch AKA CRIMEDANCH Long Island NY. Had it not been for my foundation and the mindset formed in those streets and the motivation to be a GO-GETTA, once again... this would not be possible. And to Tawanna-Lyons-Stokes my typist thank you sooo much!

To all my families of Jackson's, Drapers, Reid's, Turners, Hairston's, Armistead's, Lewis, Thompson's, Reynolds, Evans, Seabury's, Quinones, Smiths, and Rivas', which are far too many to name individually, thank you for your ongoing support.

To all my ladies and dedicated book buyers and readers; I DO THIS FOR YOU!

To all my peoples on lock that need that heat to help you pass the time; I DO THIS FOR YOU! To all my college students on the grind getting that education: I DO THIS FOR YOU!

And most of all the dreamers who dare to step out on faith with proper planning to something different....I-DO-THIS-FOR-YOU!!!!

Chapter 1

It was 2:30 in the morning and she had finally pacified her two year old son Jayonne to sleep. Musiq Soulchild's CD was spinning on her stereo system and Teach me how to love was playing at a low volume. As Dez sat on the side of her bed off the last of her blunt, she heard voices whispering outside of her bedroom window.

She looked over at Jayonne sleeping quietly in his crib as she put out her blunt, reached over and grabbed the AK47 propped on the wall next to her bed. She knew the day that she unwillingly inherited her cousin Hova's enterprise that this day would soon come. She grabbed the remote and turned up the stereo.

When she turned off the light in the bedroom she sat on the floor next to the bed facing the bedroom door and braced the stock of the assault rifle against the wall to cushion the recoil. It had been three months since the Feds had arrested Hova and left her holding 3 kilo's and $47,000 in her house where he kept his stash. Dez was well known as Hov's favorite Cousin and felt obligated to hold him down because he'd done so much for her and Jayonne.

Mainly moving her out of the hood.

Well now the hood had come to her safe haven and it was time to teach motherfuckers a lesson. Don't Fuck with Destiny! Dez figured that they'd probably got into the front door easily enough because she always kept it unlocked when she was home. She felt that if you couldn't feel safe at home, you couldn't feel safe anywhere. The two masked gunmen approaching her bedroom door were caught off guard by the music and too stupid to realize there was something strange about the front door being unlocked.

"I didn't hear music when we passed by the window, but I did smell weed smoke. You think she is in there getting some dick?" questioned BG.

"I don't know but I'd like to fuck that fine ass bitch! After we take her money, I might take that pussy too!" said Jake.

"But what if she is in there with somebody?"

"Then we'll just have to smoke whoever the fuck it is!"

As they made their way to the bedroom door the light in the hallway alerted Dez to exactly how close they were to the door by the shadows of their feet. Her heart hammered in her chest as she loaded a round into the chamber anticipating her bedroom door being kicked in. As her eyes narrowed in anger she was thinking these bastards want to violate my home and threaten me and my baby's life? Time for them to die! She looked over at Jayonne sleeping in his crib and said "mommy loves you" as the bedroom door came crashing in.

TEACH ME HOW TO LOVE *show me the way to surrender my heart-Girl I'm So lost*-Blared on the stereo. The light from the hallway filled one side of the room, but Destiny was off to the side of the empty bed in the shadows unseen. They stood with guns pointed at the empty bed confused looking like target practice dummies. Destiny pulled the trigger and the small room turned into Vietnam. "Brrrraat! Braat! Brrrrraat!" screamed the chopper ripping both men literally in half with two sweeps.

The shorter of the two went the quickest and was dead before he hit the ground. As he lay on the carpeted floor his eyes were stuck open from shock beneath the black ski mask. There were large smoking holes and splattered blood stains on the wall where BG had been standing. As Dez slowly walked forward and stood over BG holding the assault rifle pointed at his head, she noticed his eyes were still open. She removed the .380 from her double D honey complexion tits and put 2 slugs between his eyes. But Jake wasn't as fortunate. When Destiny approached Jakes bullet ridden body sprawled on the floor, he was still breathing short shallow breaths as blood gushed out of 2 huge holes in his abdomen. Jake looked at her gorgeous body that he had lusted over on many occasions. Destiny stood 5 foot 6 inches tall with straight jet black shoulder length hair. Her complexion, cinnamon smooth and perfect smile made her easily possible video vixen material. She held the .380 in one hand and squatted slowly in her bra and panties to remove the ski mask. Once she removed the mask and saw who she already assumed it was, her stomach started to flutter as anger consumed her.

"I knew it was you, you bastard! How could you deceive Hova like this?" Asked Dez.

Jake lay there twisted with his eyes begging for mercy. But mercy was the furthest thing from Destiny's mind.

"Hova practically raised you!" she said with fury. She continued "You ate his food. You drove his cars. And now you come to kill his cousin taking care of him and try to rob him. I know you would have killed me and my baby Jake. All because he told me to cut back on how much work I gave you!"

Jake began to slowly shake his head no, just when Dez realized she heard crying in the background under the sound of the music which was still playing loudly. She looked over her shoulder to see Jayonne's tear stained face staring at BG's dead body. Her baby standing in his crib in pajamas looking at a dead man brought her back to reality.

She jumped up hiding her pistol behind her back, walked over picked up the remote and turned off the stereo/CD player. As she walked over to pick up her son out of his crib, for the first time she noticed the strong smell of gunpowder that encompassed the bedroom.

"Shhh baby its ok. Mommy is right here," she said as she picked him up out of the crib and took him into the bedroom. She stopped by Jake and noticed that he had moved on to his next existence. Rushing to her closet she opened the door and removed 2 duffel bags off of the top shelf. She threw them on the bed and threw on her " SUGA $TAXXX " sweat suit that she quickly snatched off a hanger. She pushed open the clothes hanging in the closet so she could get to the large safe on the floor. Realizing that her time was limited she quickly spun the dial and yanked the door of the safe open. Dez filled one duffel bag with the contents of the safe which contained what was left after paying Hov's lawyer $50,000 and flipping the work 3 times. She tossed the bag containing $107,000, give or take a few hundred on the bed and filled the other bag with clothes for her and Jayonne. She grabbed her purple haze and box of blunts out of her night stand. She would definitely need something to calm her nerves.

On her way out of the bedroom she stopped and observed the bloody carnage that lay in what was once her safe haven. She looked at Jake and remembered all the times that he and Hova had come to her crib in the suburbs handle business. He'd to work up the courage to try to spit game and she would shoot him down every time. But she was always able to see qualities in people that others couldn't and she felt for a long time that Jake was a snake. You would have to be a snake for your father, one of the richest gangsters in Brooklyn to not fuck with you. When she thought about Icon who was Jakes father, she felt a chill shoot through her. She had heard of some of the gruesome murders his name had been tied to and knew that by killing his son, even in self-defense was almost a definite death sentence. She pushed those thoughts to the back of her mind as she grabbed her bags and her baby and pushed her way out of the door into the warm, late night air. As she tucked her hair which had fallen in her face behind her ear, she noticed a few of her neighbors standing out on their porches. Dez knew the assault rifle was probably loud enough to wake the dead. Especially in such a quiet, secluded neighborhood. She ignored them as she put Jayonne in the car seat of the still new 07 Denali that Hova had put in her name. She slid into the familiar plush coach leather seats and pushed the button for the automatic ignition. She took one last look at her home in East Meadow long island as she backed out of the driveway. She had no doubt in her mind that from this day forward her life would never be the same.

Chapter 2

Young Benny A.K.A Benzino pulled up in front of the upscale Barber shop known as Butta Cutz in his brand new chocolate S550 Mercedes, sitting on 22 inch chrome factory rims. It was a normal summer Brooklyn morning a little after eleven and the sun brought the hood to life. As Benzino slid off of his tan leather Gucci interior, he looked like a million cash. He hated that he had to deliver the grim message to his boss, but due to their relationship he figured that he was the best one to do so. Benzino was six foot six and Timberland boot black with muscles that were clearly defined under his wife beater. He was considered handsome by the ladies, wearing his signature clean shaven head and ice flooded Cartier glasses.

"What up big B," he stated to Byron, which was one of the barbers as he entered the shop.

"What's crackin Zino? How is that new car treating yo u?"

"She treating me aight. Is the bossman in the back?"

"Yeah it's packed back there. They been playin since yesterday afternoon."

Byron could tell by Benzino's demeanor that something was wrong. He usually spoke to everybody. Especially the cuties that did braids. But not today. When he received the call from the friend of a friend that Jake had been ID'd as one of the two victims found slaughtered in a house out in long island, he figured Jakes griminess had finally caught up to him. When Benzino entered the backroom which was something like a small casino, it was like walking back in time to the late 60's. As he slowly walked across the money green carpet towards the large poker table in the rear of the room, a smooth Jazz tune played at a low volume through the speakers. It sounded like a familiar Billie Holiday tune. Thick clouds of blue smoke from expensive cigars hovered above the gentlemen sitting at the table. He walked past the black jack table and nodded to the dealer acknowledging her presence. Passing by the Crap table which was heavily crowded with expensive jewelry studded high rollers, he dropped his head looking over the top of his glasses and winked at the pit boss which was his younger sister named Columbia. As he approached the Poker table however, the amazement of witnessing this particular group of men struck him all at once. Then he remembered that this was the first weekend of the month. These were some of the richest Gangsters to ever run the streets of NY. They had made their millions in the 60's and 70's and had built everlasting bonds that were unbreakable. In this game it was a minimum bet of $1000, which in reality was just a drop in the bucket. Nothing to men who owned multimillion dollar corporations and hid unthinkable sums in Swiss Bank accounts. As Benzino approached the table he noticed the large pile of poker chips sitting in the middle of the table and knew this was a heavy hand.

"I'll call your 5 and raise you 10," stated Glenn Cove George from Long Island. There were intense poker faces around the table as all attention turned to Icon. It was his time to bet or fold.

"Shit, you gotta make me a believer! I'll call your 10 and raise you another 10," stated Icon raising the pot to $85,000.

"I fold," stated the other 3 players almost in unison.

Icon locked eyes with his long time friend George and a slow smile spread across his lips. At 58 years old the only thing that gave any indication of his age was his salt and pepper goatee. He stood 5ft 11 in, but the bullet of a coward 20 years earlier had put him in a wheelchair. A coward that was soon after found with all of his limbs severed.

"Three Jack's and a pair of 10's," said George as he spread his cards on the table and smiled at Icon.

11

Icon's smile left his face and he dropped his head feigning defeat. But as George reached for the pot Icon spread his hand on the table showing 3 aces and 2 kings.

"Damn Z thought you had finally beat me one," stated Icon and let out a healthy laugh that displayed his perfectly white teeth. In the middle of his laughter he feels a large hand resting on his shoulder. He looks over his shoulder to see a discouraged and seemingly uptight Benzino. He knew instantly that something was terribly wrong just by the expression of his non blood related son. Benzino was always known to be the one with the smile, besides his sister Columbia, that could brighten Icons day.

"What's wrong with you son?"asked Icon

"I need to speak with you in private."

"I'll be right back fella's. Play this hand without me." The cards were being dealt as Benzino and Icon made their way off to a remote corner. Benzino didn't beat around the bush because he knew Icon hated bullshit. "Jake is dead. He was found in a house with BG this morning out in Long Island at about 4 o'clock. My sources say they were shot up pretty bad, but that's all I know about what happened."

Icon sat stone faced, obviously adsorbing the news that he just heard. His first thought was good, it's finally over, but almost instantly a vision appeared in his mind and he was overcome with guilt and shame. He reflected on the first time he laid eyes on Jake as his wife Glenda held him after giving birth. He had walked over and taken him out of her arms and felt proud as he thought about the gift that God had blessed him with. He planned to teach him all he knew and groom him to one day run his empire. But that had never come to pass being that Glenda was dead set against Jake being involved in a life of crime. Her overprotection had turned him into what Icon had feared the most. A momma's boy with a gangster for a father. At 14 years old when Glenda could no longer control Jake he began to run with sneaker and clothes hustlers and doing petty stick-ups which led to a series of short stints in Juvenile detention centers. He had a cold streak in him which was his father's blood and that made him dangerous. But his simple-mindedness, curly hair, and hazel eyes, he had all undoubtedly traited from his mother. Jake had been given a few chances as well as the benefit of the doubt, all because he was his only son. But he proved time and time again that he was a fuck-up. So naturally Icon had disowned him. As a single tear escaped Icon left eye, he thought about how this news was probably gonna push his wife over the edge losing her only son.

"Find out who did this," Icon stated as he firmly grabbed Benzino's wrist. "And make sure they receive nothing less than the same fate."

Chapter 3

Destiny and Jayonne maneuvered through the crowded Washington DC Greyhound Bus Terminal. Jayonne was wide awake as to be expected considering he had the benefit of getting some sleep on the ride down 95 south. Dez had only made one stop and that was to fill up the truck at a rest area on the Jersey Turnpike. They arrived at the Red Roof Inn off the Silver Spring exit in Maryland, at about 8:15 that morning. During the ride down she tried to clear her head so she could plan her next steps, but it was next to impossible trying to stop the constant replay of the bloody massacre. She looked at the blunt in the ashtray that she had rolled in the rest stop, and figured that was a good place to start. She looked in the backseat, saw that her son was asleep in his car seat and fired up. Dez cracked the sunroof on the Denali so the smoke wouldn't choke her sleeping son and took a deep pull letting the purple haze fill her lungs. Dam! She thought as the tears, soon began to roll down her beautiful face. Why did them motherfuckers have to try me? Why the fuck did Hova have to get locked up and leave me under so much pressure? But it wasn't long before she sucked it up, thinking that she had to be strong. She had to pull herself together because the future of her and her son depended on it! Once they had settled in the Red Roof she began to make moves. Between the four spots Hova had left operating, she had over $36,000 in the streets. She knew that they would soon be looking to get in touch with her so she could send Hova's pick-up people through to pick up money and hit the spot off with another package. The weed had calmed her nerves and made her sleepy, but she had business to tend to. She could sleep later. After she completed dialing the number from the telephone in the hotel room a cell phone rang in a Brooklyn brownstone.

Dez smiled as the familiar Duffel bag Boy ring tone played in her ear from Vito's phone. She looked over at the duffel bag sitting in front of the TV containing over $100,000 and considered the irony.

"Who dis?" Vito answered not recognizing the area code.

"What's up V? This is Destiny and I'm in a situation. I'm out of town and I need you to do what you do."

Even though she knew the cat would soon be out of the bag, she kept the details to a minimum. Vito was one of the fellas on Hova's team who had kept it 100 since he got knocked. He was a seasoned hustler, born and raised on the streets of Brownsville. 5ft 11inches tall with a medium brown complexion, this slim niggah was also known as a gunclappin ladiesman.

"What's up lovely what you need from a fella?" said Vito in a sly seductive tone. She smiled again knowing that he was truly on her side and told him what she needed him to do. He agreed and told her to hit him back later that afternoon. She agreed and ended the conversation. She had laid down on the king size bed next to her son and immediately fell asleep when he laid his arm around her neck.

She had awakened at 12oclock check out time and after a quick shower got back on 95 south head toward DC. As much as she hated the idea she knew that she had to ditch the truck. After all it was in her real name. Once Dez and Jayonne ditched the truck at Tysons Corner they jumped into a taxi and headed to the bus terminal. Now they stood in line waiting to purchase tickets to a small town in Tennessee called Johnson City. She had a cousin named Lashay that had moved down there a couple of years earlier to attend college at Eastern Tennessee State University. She planned to catch the Greyhound into town, get a hotel room and call Lashay a couple of days later.

As she reached the ticket counter she noticed a uniformed officer eyeing her suspiciously. Her facial expression read nonchalance as she smiled at him, but she felt her heart rate quicken and sweat beginning to role from her armpit. She realized that she fit the profile of so many young girls who had been caught transporting drugs to various destinations by way of Greyhound. Dez figured that her smile disarmed the officer whose attention had turned to a young kid in a designer hoodie, over-sized baseball cap and a neck full of jewelry. She purchased her ticket and quickly headed to her gate feeling the heavy weight and burden of the money she was carrying. When she reached the gate she felt someone approach her.

"Excuse me miss, do you need some assistance?" inquired a clean shaven gentleman in a marine service uniform. He was a cutie Destiny noticed off the bat and something about that uniform and his presence comforted her. She handed him the bag with the clothes.

"Thank you. I've been struggling with these bags all day," she stated smiling.

"What gate are you going to? I'm headed to gate 11."

"So are we," she said thinking that maybe she had found a travel companion. As they walked toward their gate and she carried Jayonne on her hip, he smiled brightly at the man carrying their bag. Destiny immediately noticed the almost instantaneous bond.

"Excuse me for being so rude. My name is Donovan and I guess you could tell by the uniform and the large green army bag I'm returning from a tour of duty over in Iraq. I've been away from the states for 2 years "he said as the bus driver made the call for passengers to start boarding. They approached the driver and handed him their tickets.

"You change buses in Richmond," said the driver as he ripped their ticket stubs and returned them. They both boarded the fairly empty bus together, but to Destiny's disappointment after he put her bag in the overhead compartment he moved on further towards the back of the bus to find an empty seat.

"Thank you," she replied as he walked away through the isle.

"Oh please, the pleasure was all mine miss..." he said glancing over his shoulder, remembering that she never told him her name.

"I'm sorry Dez-I mean my name is Destiny." Sweet, sweet Destiny he thought as he smiled at her and headed for his seat. Dez put the other bag on the floor in front of her and sat Jayonne in the seat by the window. She looked over at her son standing in his chair, hands on the back of the seat, and smiling towards the back of the bus. She ignored it until he started to giggle uncontrollably. She looked back only to see Donovan making crazy faces that he stopped and looked out the window whistling like he was innocent as soon as she turned around. But as the bus began to back-up out of the terminal Dez turned Jayonne around and sat him down in the seat for safety reasons. She put on his seatbelt and looked at him as he stared up at her with big beautiful, full of life innocent eyes. She felt ashamed and terribly irresponsible as a parent as she thought, what have I gotten us into?

"Ma ma-toys, wanna pay with toys," said Jayonne in a tone that broke her heart.

"No toys now baby. But I'll get you all new toys soon, I promise."

"New toys!" he said smiling and clapping his hands in wide eyed excitement.

As the bus left the terminal she pushed the button to let her seat back and got comfortable for the two hour ride from DC to Richmond Virginia. By the time the passenger coach had made it to 95 south she was fast asleep.

Chapter 4

"Just doesn't add up. Her neighbors said she was quiet and polite and went to work every day," said detective Bennet from the Nassau County homicide division.

"Yep, but they also said that she had a cousin or brother and his friend that would stop by at least twice a week. Said even though they acted polite enough, they dressed like common street thugs,"added Detective Whitney.

Whitney and Bennet had just finished questioning the neighbors which was standard procedure in a homicide investigation. They entered the front yard lifting the yellow police do not cross tape and entered the house after a few steps. The familiar stench of putrid death was all too familiar. As they walked slowly down the same hallway as Jake and BG had earlier that morning they heard the sounds of uniformed officer's voices and transmissions from their radios. Entering the bedroom they immediately noticed the 2 covered corpses with large pools of halfway dried blood surrounding them. They had gotten some information but weren't ready for what they were about to witness.

"Holy fuckin Christ!" stated detective Whitney as he pulled back the tarp from over BG. Half of his chest was non-existent and his neck was only a few strands of cartilage that connected his head to the rest of his body.

"Looks like he was hit with cannon!" said Bennet.

"Close. An AK47 was taken out of here by evidence. They found 16 spents shells and our guess is these two caught most of em'. We also had to pry pistols from the hands of each one of these guys. Looks like she got to them before they got to her," said the uniformed officer leading the investigation.

"What's with the smaller holes in this guy's head?" asked Bennet knealing over BG.

"Another missing piece of the puzzle. We found 2 empty .380 caliber shells, but no sign of a weapon. We're still looking but we believe she took it with her," said the uniformed officer.

Whitney was already headed over to check on the other corpse who had apparently been ID'd earlier by the drivers license in his wallet as Jake Wallace. He had immediately recognized the name from his earlier years working in a police department in Brooklyn. Detective Whitney remembered the name because Jake stayed in so much shit as well as who his father was. He had arrested him on a few occasions and figured that his appearance couldn't have changed that much over 8 years.

"Prepare yourself," one uniformed officer explained.

"He is tore up real good. Looks like she took out most of his midsection."

When he pulled back the covering over Jake he turned and emptied the contents of his stomach on the floor. Some of the vomit splashed onto a few officers shoes.

"I told you pal. Gee's are you gonna be ok?"

By the time the uniformed cop had finished his sentence, Detective Whitney was already headed towards the front door to get some air. But Bennet had begun to ask questions.

"Any leads on the suspect?"

"One of the neighbors said they saw her and her son leave outta here soon after they heard the shots in a big black SUV with chrome rims. The Passat in the driveway belongs to her."

"So how much distance you estimate she's put between herself and this place?"

"There's no telling. We didn't get the info about the truck until recently. We are looking for it, but she could be anywhere."

No one had heard Detective Whitney come back into the room.

"I don't know where she is, but I certainly hope we find her before this guys father does. He's one mean, cripple son of a bitch, whose name was tied to over 27 unsolved murder investigations when I worked in Brooklyn. One thing I know for sure he is not gonna take this lightly.

Chapter 5

The sun was shining brightly through the window of MDC Federal holding facility in Brooklyn as BET played on the elevated television set. The two tables in the day area were both surrounded with inmates' playing cards.

"How many you got?"asked Hova's spades partner.

"Niggah I'm looking at like 6 maybe 7, what you got?"

"Sheeit, enough to put the wheels on this bitch and roll out. Let's take a 10!"

As they began to play the hand somebody turned the channel to Eyewitness News. Hova looked at the screen when dudes starting beefing over changing the channel from BET.

"Hold up! Hold up! Leave it there, that looks like my cousin Destiny's crib!," he shouted fearing the worst as Murder in Long Island was posted across the bottom of the screen. Hova listened in horror as the serious faced Caucasian woman reported the story.

"Good afternoon Chuck. In this seemingly quiet home behind me, two men were brutally slaughtered at around 3 am this morning. Officers at the scene said neighbors reported hearing what sounded like a machine gun go off inside this house at approximately 2:30 morning. Authorities have identified one of the two men as Jake Wallace from the Brownsville section of Brooklyn. They have also recovered multiple weapons which will be submitted as evidence. The suspect, who we are still saying is unknown was believed to escape the murder scene with a small child in a black SUV..."

Hova didn't need to hear anymore before he dropped his cards and ran to the phone. His mind was racing. He didn't want to believe what he already knew. The gun was definitely the AK and the other motherfucker was undoubtedly that bitch niggah BG. He was thinking about his little cousin Destiny and where could she possibly be. He had taught her well, but he was thinking that she was probably scared to fucking death! As the phone rang he sent up a silent prayer as he covered his eyes with his hand and tilted his head backwards. The phone rang 4 times calling his girlfriend Veesha.

"Come on, come on answer the fuckin-Hello! V! Hello!" he said as she answered on the fifth ring.

"You have a collect call from-Hova-push 5 to accept or push-"

"What's up baby I didn't think you were gonna call till later. But I'm glad you-"

"Listen, this is an emergency! Click over and call Dez on 3-way!"

"Honey what's wrong? Is everything-"

"Please, just click the fuck over and call my cousin."

Veesha knew from the tone he used with her which she had heard before but never directed toward her, that she should do what he said immediately. She clicked over dialed the number and clicked back. They both sat and listened as Destiny's phone went to voicemail.

"This is Destiny...say it baby...and dis is oney,"chimed in Jayonne, "and we can't take your call right now but if you leave..."

"Hang up and try it again," Hova told Veesha.

She did and got the same result. But this time he left a message.

"Look Dez I just saw the news. Dam this shit is crazy! Call V just to let me know yall are safe. You know we can't talk on these phones or communicate through this mail because it's all monitored, but I got some emergency people to make sure you ok. Don't worry we gonna get through this together. Hold your head and give oney a kiss for me from uncle Hova."

He paused for a second realizing what Dez had probably gone through and said,"I'm sorry cuz. I love you."

Veesha guessed it was the end of the call and hung up.

"What's going on baby?" Veesha asked in a timid voice.

"I'm sorry ma," he said realizing he barked on her and probably scared the shit out of her.

"I need you to get up here as soon as possible. I really don't want to go into detail on this phone. Can you come and see poppa in the morning?"

"Yes daddy. I'll be there as soon as visitation starts." Hova ended the call telling Veesha he needed to make another call and get his thoughts together. He also promised to call her again later that night. Deciding to put the call on hold until he gathered his thoughts, he headed off to his cell. At 5ft 9 inches tall and 230lbs of pure muscle, his presence was truly intimidating. But his fair skin complexion and spinning 360 waves made him a magnet for the ladies. As he was entering the cell his man Cormega came walking up to him.

"Yo son what happened? I saw you watching the news. Was that ya man Jake the Jake they was talking about?" questioned Mega.

"Yeah fam but he was on some bullshit if he got laced in that crib," said Hov.

"What do you mean?" pushed Mega digging for info.

Hova seen it for what it was and deaded the conversation. He refused to give a niggah some info to get to the crib off him.

"Look I gotta go lay it down. I ain't feeling so hot right now," he said and went in his cell leaving Mega standing there. He laid down on his bunk and thought about what all of this meant. He didn't want to seem selfish but it first meant that everything that he had left at Destiny's was in danger of being lost. Secondly it meant that his closest cousin, the only other person in the world he trusted with so much, was on the run for murder in self defense and also that his right hand man had tried to cross him. But most of all he thought about what

Icon and his people would do now that his son had been killed. Hova knew it was his responsibility to protect Destiny and Jayonne. But he also knew that it wouldn't be easy to hide Dez from someone as powerful and with as many connections as Icon. Icon was relentless in pursuit of righting what he considered to be wrong in matters relating to him. For that reason alone he prayed that God would answer his request to protect Destiny and Jayonne.

Chapter 6

A playground full of happy ghetto children were enjoying the sunny summer city day when the all black van pulled up to a tire screeching halt in front of the project building. As the six intimidating figures exited the sliding side door of the van, the atmosphere as well as the smiling and playful faces on the playground changed. The fear and apprehension even spread to the young hustlers and cuties sitting out on the benches. The hood had a way of understanding clear and present danger. All six were suited head to toe in black army fatigues, black boots and skull caps, and black shades. As they made their way into the building Vito was just coming out of the sparks apartment collecting the $7,200 that Destiny had asked him to go pick-up. Sparks had asked where Jake was because it was his week to make the rounds. But he didn't think anything was out of order, because since Hova got knocked, only Jake or Vito handled his affairs. However Sparks was upset that Vito didn't have a new package for him.

"So when we gonna get right? You know how my flow is," said Sparks. Vito had looked around the apartment at all of Sparks workers sitting around smoking blunts and playing video games on the large plasma flat screen hanging on the paint peeling walls. The blood red 3 piece custom made leather sofa set, with dice reading 7-11 on the back of the shorter sofa, and 4-5-6 on the white dice with red dots on the longer sofa, looked fashionably out of place. There was one kid getting his hair braided sitting on the floor between a pair of the most deliciously creamy thighs Vito had ever seen. Vito followed the legs up to some coochie cutting short-shorts and then further up to the beautiful chinky eyed straight haired Puerto Rican cutey's face.

She caught him getting an eyeful and smiled seductively. Vito smiled back thinking if you wasn't 15 shorty, I'd burn yo ass up. As Vito was leaving the apartment he told Sparks "keep your phone on so you can come down and meet me, aight."

"No doubt peoples. Just hit me soon!"

Vito had no idea that would the the last time he saw Hova's soldier alive. But now as he watched the Death Squad pass by him on the project steps he knew that something horrific was about to pop off. It had been a while since he had heard of something serious enough for Icon to send out his goons, but he knew for sure that where they went death always followed close behind. The last place he thought they would be heading was Sparks apartment. By the time Vito reached the ground floor and was heading out of the building, Benzino was kicking in the front door of young Spark's apartment.

"BOCK-BOCK!" was the sound of Sparks 40 cal, hitting Zino twice in his vest. But Zino took it like a champ, as he had practiced and prepared for such an event. But the smallest of the six figures in black entered behind Benzino and with pantherlike speed and precision threw a razor-sharp hunting knife that lodged in Sparks forearm causing him to scream out in agony as he dropped his weapon. The young kid getting his hair braided jumped up and tried to run out of the apartment and was snatched up in a choke hold. The pretty Puerto Rican screamed and jumped on the guys back that put braids in a choke hold. Another knife appeared. The room went silent as the Puerto Rican girl was brutally snatched off the guys back by her hair like a rag doll and had her throat cut viciously from ear to ear. As she lay on the floor bucking and kicking trying to catch her breath, which would never happen, blood flowed rapidly from the gaping hole between her chin and her chest. The coldness and savagery of the killing filled the others in the room with shock and fear. The room fell silent as pretty legs breathed her last breath.

"Which one of you is Sparks?" said Benzino in a calm but menacing tone.

"I'm Sparks," he said with his face twisted in pain from the knife lodged in his arm. Benzino walked over to where Sparks was sitting on the floor rocking and holding his arm.

"Look, as you can see I'm not here to play games. I know you work for Hova and I also know Hova is locked up. But Hova has a cousin named Destiny that is right now on someone's most wanted list. We have reason to believe that you have contact with her because she has been overseeing Hova's affairs. So what we want to know is how do you get in touch with her when you need more work?"

"Man I don't know who or what- AAAH FUCK! Wait! Please stop! Stop!" screamed Sparks as Zino grabbed the handle of the knife in his arm and began to twist it.

"Stop fucking with me young blood! Tell me something!" said Zino smiling calmly.

"I only dealt with Jake and Vito I swear, and Vito just left from here collecting the money from the last package Jake dropped off! That's all I know I swear on my mother!"

Benzino took in the information he just received and processed it. This Vito cat must have communication with Destiny he thought. Time to find Vito.

"How do I find this Vito cat?" asked Zino.

"He is supposed to call me back when he get right and I'm suppose to meet him," said Sparks.

"Where's your phone?"

"It's the Nextel over there on the counter next to the refrigerator."

Benzino looked at two of the guys that came in with him and gave them a nod. Acknowledging the official no witnesses sign, they produced 2 nine millimeters equipped with silencers and went around the apartment killing every occupant with 2 shots in the head execution style. After the smallest of the 6 figures in black grabbed Sparks' phone, they exited the apartment leaving a mess to clean up, and a ton of paperwork for crime scene and homicide. There weren't many situations where the Death Squad didn't get their man. Or in this case woman. Now they were waiting for a phone call that would hopefully bring them closer to completing their mission.

Chapter 7

Destiny's eyes sprung open when she heard Jayonne's voice.

"Mommy! Mommy!" She looked to her side where he had been sitting. Nothing. She looked around the empty bus which looked abnormally large. "Mommy! Mommy!" she heard again as she looked towards the front of the bus where she heard her son's voice coming from. She reached between her tits and removed her .380 as she saw her son being taken off the bus by a figure in black. She jumped up frantically and started running towards the front of the bus. It seemed the faster she moved the further the front of the bus became. When she finally made it to the front of the door she jumped off the bus into a huge crowded terminal.

"Mommy!"

They were about 30 ft away, but the crowd was so thick. She had to get to him. She began to push through the crowd fiercely.

"Move! Excuse me motherfucker! Move goddammit, I got to get my baby!!"

The way the man in black was carrying Jayonne she could see her son's face and look directly into his scared eyes. Her heart jack-hammered and blood rushed to her head as she continued to force her way towards her baby. But it seemed the more she persisted, the further away they moved. 'I'm coming baby! Move out my motherfuckin way!" she screamed. They turned a corner up ahead and she lost sight of them. Oh god no no! She thought pushing, trying to maintain eye contact. Why the fuck is this place so crowded she thought. When she turned the corner Destiny became overwhelmed and filled with fear as she saw them heading towards the exit. The man carrying Jayonne looked back quickly, smiled, then turned and continued running towards the exit. She locked eyes with her baby again and saw he was crying.

"Maaahhhhmmmmy!"Jayonne cried out as the man in black pushed his way out of the terminal. Destiny let off a shot in air.

"Pop!" The crowd went crazy screaming and trying to run for cover. She saw an opening and ran for the door. She watched as Jayonne was pulling away yelling for her out of the window of a black van.

"Nooooo!" screamed Destiny as she began to run after the van. But it was no use as she watched it pull into traffic. Even though the van was pulling further away it seemed like she could hear him more and more clearly...

"Mommy!" Mommy!" screamed Jayonne in Destiny's ear trying to wake her up.

"Wha! Wha!" she turned to see her son and snatched him up in her arms. She held him tightly as she saw the last passenger, a preppy white girl exiting the bus. It was a dream. Oh god no, it was a nightmare! She looked back to see if Donovan was there but he had apparently already got off the bus. She looked out of the window and saw that they were at their next stop. It was just then that she realized how tight she was holding onto her son. She looked at him with his head back giggling with laughter. What would I do without my baby she thought. She gathered her bags and her son and exited the bus. It was nowhere near as crowded as the terminal in her nightmare. Destiny and Jayonne headed over to the ticket counter to find out what gate the bus for Tennessee was leaving from.

"It leaves from gate 18 at 7:45," said the girl at the counter with the bad weave.

"OK, thank you. Where can I get something to eat for me and my son?"

"There is a restaurant up at the front of the terminal that sells chicken and burgers. They are pretty reasonable too," said ticket girl.

Destiny nodded a thank you and spun off. As she was walking she passed by a magazine stand. She saw Donovan thumbing through an ESSENCE magazine and was about to go over and ask why he left her sleeping on the bus but decided against it. He wasn't obligated to do anything she thought. Dez made her way to the food court restaurant and brought them something to eat. As they were eating she decided it was probably a good idea to check her phone messages. She turned on her phone as she watched her baby repeatedly stick a French fry in ketchup and suck it off. The first thing she noticed was the time. Dam it's only 5 o'clock. That's almost 3 hours waiting time. Dez noticed that she had "4 new messages." As she began to review them she noticed that the first 2 were from Hova. As she listened to his voice she had mixed emotions but she genuinely felt that he had her best interest at heart. But then again, she thought how do you purposely put someone in harm's way that you claim to love? She knew Hova fully understood the risk of keeping money and drugs in her house. But for that fact so did she. She was just as responsible for her circumstances as he was. The other two were from one of her good friends named LaLa. LaLa still stayed in the projects and the sound in her voice was another cause of concern for Destiny.

"Man something real serious is going down in the PJ's. I just saw them bring 5 covered stretchers out of I building headed to the morgue," LaLa had said.

But LaLa was such a drama queen! She only called when it was bad news or gossip. Destiny then remembered that she needed to call Vito. She decided that she would give him at least another hour, just to make sure that he was able to handle everything he needed to. She wanted to call Veesha so when they finished eating she went and purchased a phone card. Veesha answered on the first ring.

"Hello?" Veesha answered suspiciously not recognizing the "804" area code.

"What's up V? I just got Hova's message. I guess you already heard what happened."

"Actually no, but I guess it's pretty serious if he didn't want to tell me over the phone. You know all of those calls are recorded."

"Well Jake and somebody else broke into my crib last night to rob me. I killed both of them sonofabitches in self-defense," said Destiny.

"Oh my fuckin God! You did what? Dam girl are you alright?"

"I'm still a little shaken up and I think my baby may be traumatized by what he saw, but to protect myself and my son I would do it again in a fuckin heartbeat." Veesha couldn't believe what she was hearing. This wasn't sweet little Destiny.

"Look girl you have to get somewhere safe until we can work this out. I gotta go see Hova in the morning. Will you call me back tomorrow afternoon?"

"Yeah I'm on the move right now. I had to ditch Hova's truck in DC but tell him everything else is safe," she stated looking at Jayonne sitting on the duffel bag.

"Just stay safe and call me tomorrow, ok."

"Aight V, bye."

Destiny hung up the phone and let out a deep breath. She had been leary of Veesha as well. She always wondered why Hova didn't even trust his so called girl enough to keep his work there. Well she soon found out after Hova got locked up. Destiny occasionally visited her Aunt Gwen which was Hova's moms because it seemed like when he got locked up, her breast cancer took a turn for the worst. But when Destiny saw Veesha get out of Tiffany's pink Escalade, she knew some shady shit was poppin off. Tiffany was a red bone stripper/hustler that had a pussy eatin game that was known to turn out the most strictly dickly of the cocktakers. Before she made that call back to Veesha she would have to weigh the fact that if Hova didn't really trust her...why should she.

Chapter 8

The smells of Curry Goat, a popular Jamaican dish, filled the small takeout establishment on Hillside Avenue in Queens. It was half filled with heavy island accented cats engaged in various conversations. Halfway through the meal that he was eating ,Vito looked at his ICETEK watch which was flooded icey sickness!

"Dam!" he stated seeing that the Dred already had him waiting an hour and a half.

This muthafucka procrastinating is fuckin up my rhythm, he was thinking as he looked out of the front window to see if there was a sign of Dred. He had put the money that he got from Sparks with his own money and headed to Queens to cop two bricks. He wondered where that sneaky ass niggah Jake was at and why Destiny had called him to take care of what it was clearly Jakes week to handle. He pushed the thought to the back of his mind as his connect walked through the front door of the restaurant that his family owned.

"Got Dam Dred! Where da fuck you had to go for that shit? Jamaica?" Vito asked sarcastically.

"You got joke eh? Me wan mek shur ya get ta bes ting. Is a lotta brown coke floatin roun rite now and me know ya no want dat," said Dred. Vito thought about it and was glad Dred went the extra mile. He dam sure didn't want that brown shit.

"Ereting already in place. You good to roll, star," said Dred going back to work behind the serving counter. Vito had to admit that they ran a tight operation and realistically he wouldn't want to do business anywhere else. Dred had even put the 2 bricks in the stash box of Vito's pearl white custom convertible 760 Bemer. Hova was conservative. Nice watch, decent pinky ring, no chains. But Vito was just the opposite. As he strode arrogantly out of the restaurant; neck, wrist, and earlobe on heavy shine status; rockin a t-shirt and faded denim jeans with rhinestones from the "$TAXXX Officials" collection, he pushed the button on his keychain to autostart the Bemer. He slid in his whip, hit the highway and was back in Brooklyn in twenty five minutes. By the time he made it from the car to his kitchen where he was about to put his cook game down, his phone had rung 8 times. He broke the seals on the bricks and took out a brand new box of Arm and Hammer. As he weighed out 200 grams of blow and 50 grams of baking soda he glanced at his icetek and thought, what is taking Destiny so long? She should have hit me back by now. As he was adding water and heading to the stove with the pot his phone rang again. This time it was his man Looch.

"What da deal family?" said Vito answering his phone.

"Yo what up? I just heard about Jake. What the fuck happened?!"

"Whatchu mean? I just heard about Jake? I ain't hear shit."

"Word? I heard him and his boy BG got bodied out in LI trying to run up in somebody's crib. Whoever it was clapped em; did em dirty too." Vito took the pot off the stove and set it on the countertop.

"Where? When? This the first I've heard of it."

"My sister said she saw some shit on the news earlier. I'm still getting different stories. But the word is they have a suspect" said Looch.Vito was trippin. Something wasn't adding up.

"Look my niggah I got some BI (business) to handle. Get back at me later" said Vito.

"Hold up peoples, I need a little something. A Nina Ross," said Looch meaning 9 ounces.

"Aight I got that for you too. I'm in the lab right now, gimme like an hour and a half."

"Aight don't forget me!" said Looch.

"Don't worry I gotchu! One."

Dam Jake is Dead? Well that answered why Destiny had him making Jake's rounds. Why didn't she tell me? He thought suspiciously. But he had young sparks waiting, or so he thought so he got back to the business at hand. Forty-five minutes later he was done cooking up half a bird and put the call through to young sparks. On the other end of the call Benzino was looking at the screen when "V" and a phone number popped up. He looked at his sister Columbia and Icon who were both sitting in Icon's illustrious office in the rear of the barbershop.

"This is the call we've been waiting for. He's apparently been communicating with the girl," said Benzino.

"Yes, I have some knowledge of this Vito character. From my understanding he was also involved with Jake" said Icon. Benzino waited for the phone to stop ringing. When it stopped ringing he handed it to Columbia.

"You remember how we rehearsed it right?" Benzino asked Columbia. She smiled her beautiful smile. Columbia was the epitome of a dark chocolate sistah. Her features were those of an African Queen. She unlike her brother was short, about 5'-2", with natural thick Jet black hair that almost touched her abnormally round ass. If the tennis stars Venus and Serena Williams would have been triplets, Columbia would have been a darker mix between the two of them. But Icon had given her her nickname because she reminded him of a fine uncut cup of his favorite coffee. Columbian of course.

"Yeah I got it, just gimme me the phone," she said. Vito's phone rang on the other end. When he saw it was Sparks calling back he answered immediately.

"What up youngblood? You ready to make moves?" asked Vito.

"Um hey," Columbia said in her sweetest young girl voice, "Sparks is using the bathroom right now. But he told me if his peoples call to tell you he will be at the cleaners on Pitkin Ave," said Columbia.

"Aight shorty, tell him I got one more stop and I'll be there in about 15 minutes."

"OK. I'll tell him-bye" she said ending the call as quickly as possible. Vito hung up the phone and headed out the door. He had a nagging feeling about the whole mood of the day. He had his Desert Eagle posted up in his stash box which made him feel a little more comfortable. As he got in his Bemer and pulled away from the parking space, he waved to his neighbor who was a retired Golddigger. Nancy was in her early fifties but she still had traces of the pocket draining beauty she once had been. Vito remembered when he was younger and Nancy hung out with his moms. In his young mind he would fantasize about freakin with her. Now he just felt sorry for her as she sat on the front steps with old played out jewelry and a low-cut shirt that advertised way too much saggy tit. He swung through to hit off his boy Looch and tried to pump him for some more info, but he still hadn't heard anything new. Ten minutes after taking care of Looch, he turned onto Pitkin Avenue and headed towards the cleaners. He was slowly approaching the front of the cleaners and looking for Sparks when he heard the sound of an engine accelerating quickly. Vito turned to look out of his drivers side window just as the black van slammed into the Bemer. The crushing impact broke Vito's left shoulder and caused his face and head to slam against the passenger side door. The airbag exploded out of the steering wheel. He was still trying to regain his bearings when he felt himself being snatched from his vehicle out of the passenger side door.

"What the fuck-"Vito mumbled as Benzino tossed him effortlessly over his shoulder. He attempted to see through his blood covered eyes but it was useless. The pain in his left-side was overwhelming. When he hit the floor of the van pain exploded in his left shoulder and the intensity caused him to lose consciousness.

Chapter 9

Vito was awakened by the strong scent of smelling salts. He was in a dreamlike state as he sat in the middle of a large room tied to a chair. The light in the room was abnormally bright and he attempted to focus on the other figures in the room. Vito felt a mild throbbing pain in the side of his head and his shoulder. He focused on the man the closest to him with the syringe full of a clear liquid.

"Morphine," said Icon's personal doctor. "Takes away the pain. Sure does make you feel goooood huh?"

Suddenly things started to return to Vito's memory. The crash. The airbag. Benzino dragging him out of his car. Vito knew of Benzino but didn't know him personally. He knew that he was Icon's top dog and he knew how much resentment that Jake had for him because he felt that should be his spot. Vito looked at his shoulder and saw a bone protruding out of his skin.

"Oooh shit," Vito slurred in a low voice.

"Yes. Oh shit is correct," said Benzino coming into his view and knealing in front of him." Look we are truly sorry that you got caught up in the middle of this Vito, but the word I got after checking you out was that you might not be easy to coerce to cooperate."

"Well you heard right. What the fuck is going on? Why am I tied up?"

"Ahhh, a man who likes to get right down to business. I like that," said Icon slowly rolling up to where Vito was sitting.

"Well I know you are aware of my son Jakes murder."

"So what's that got to do with me?"

"The girl that killed him, her name is Destiny and we know that you've been in contact with her. What I want to know is where is she?" asked Icon. Vito couldn't believe what he was hearing. Hova's cousin Destiny had killed Jake? Why? How? Vito thought back to their phone conversation. I'm in a situation. I'm outta town and I need you to do what you do. So this was the situation? Benzino saw that Vito was thinking.

"Before you start to play Mr. Save-a-hoe, you might want to know that I went through your phone and called the Red Roof Inn. They confirmed that a Miss Destiny Love checked-out at 12:00. So don't play games with us. It's not in your best interest," said Zino.

Vito knew what kind of people he was dealing with. But Destiny was his girl and Hova was his muthafuckin man! He tried to push the envelope by lying by omission.

"Man I talked to her, but I don't know where the fuck she at. I know my peoples and if she killed Jake she dam sure had a good reason." Icon thought about that statement.

"Being that as it may, one of my family members has been murdered. Someone has to answer for it" concluded Icon.

Vito attempted to gain his bearings and take inventory of his surroundings. He observed that the room wasn't that large and that there was only one window. Another quick scan registered there were four people in the room. Even in his present state Vito was in survival mode looking for an escape. His eyes fell on Columbia.

"Your friend, the young guy sparks. He was pretty quick on the trigger. Too bad he couldn't move fast enough to avoid these," said Columbia opening her jacket revealing a set of 4 razor sharp knives.

"What do you mean?" he paused. "Hold up! Your voice, you were the one on the phone what did you do to my lil man?" asked Vito.

"Let's just say we put a stop to one of the drug problems in the PJ's," added Columbia smiling deviously.

"Well look, I can't help you so you just gotta do whatever you gotta do. Fuck ya'll muthafuckas!"

Columbia looked at Icon who gave her an affirming nod. With the same speed and precision that she had used in Sparks apartment, she launched one of her deathly sharp knives. It caught Vito in his throat and lodged in his Adams apple. There was no blood. His eyes sprang open momentarily and his head dropped signaling his death.

"Clean up and get him out of here," said Icon already rolling towards the door way. Then he stopped and said "Find that fuckin girl!"

* * *

During the long layover waiting for the next bus to leave going to Tennessee, Jayonne found himself a playmate. She was a cute little girl with two thick pigtails that was missing one of her teeth. She was traveling with her mother who was also a single mother heading to Knoxville Tennessee. The stress and the impact of what she had done was beginning to wear down on her. So much so that Destiny had even considered calling and turning herself in and hoping for leniency. But what would happen to Jayonne? His sorry ass father, who had never been a part of his life, didn't even come into the equation. Lucky as was his nickname, should have been named Bad Luck as far as she was concerned. She really wanted to smoke a blunt, take a shot of something strong, anything to medicate her stress and emotions. She looked over at her son playing contently.

"Could you keep an eye on him and my bags while I make a phone call?" she asked Knoxville.

"O.K., but we only have 15 minutes before the bus starts boarding." Aw shit, she thought. She couldn't believe that she had lost track of time like that.

"I'll be quick as possible, I promise," said Destiny getting up and heading to the phone. As she walked over to

41

the payphone she put her hand into her sweat pants pocket to pull out her phone card. Shit.

She couldn't find it. As she was heading over to the ticket counter to buy another one she saw Donovan coming into the terminal from the street. Dam, he must still be waiting for his ride. By the time she purchased the phone card and made it back to the row of pay phones they were all full. She waited impatiently until one was open. She punched in the phone card number and Vito's cell phone number which she knew by heart and within seconds was listening to his ringtone.

"My, My, My Miss Destiny. You've been one hard young lady to catch up to," said Icon answering Vito's phone.

Destiny was hesitant and alarmed but attempted to keep her cool, recognizing the voice on the phone did not belong to Vito.

"Who is this?!" she stated also beginning to get angry.

"This is Jake's father; I believe you know who I am. There's been a lot of commotion because of you-"

"Fuck you! If that snake of a son that your wife should have swallowed or you should have shot on the mattress wouldn't have invaded my home, that bastard wouldn't be dead!" She said in a low whisper now with hot tears of resentment flowing down her cheeks. Icon had to admit that she did have a point. "That may be accurate, but a lot of people are dying because of you. Now if you just get on the bus at the Greyhound in Richmond and come on back to N.Y. maybe we can work this out." Icon knowing where she was caught her off guard, but then she remembered caller ID.

"I'm sorry but I don't trust you. Just like I didn't trust your son!"

"O.K. young lady but understand this. You can run but you can't hide. Anywhere you and that son of yours goes just look over your shoulder and my presence won't be far behind," stated Icon in a threatening tone.

"Well that's just a chance that I will just have to take!" she said and hung up the phone.

When she turned around her son was staring up at her with big curious eyes. She looked over to where it had been crowded only minutes earlier to see her two bags and the last of the passengers going through the gate to load the bus. She snatched up Jayonne and headed over to her bags that the terminal police were approaching because they were unattended.

"These are mine, thank you," she said grabbing her bags and headed for her bus. She handed the driver her ticket as she struggled with her bags and got on the crowded bus. She looked at the sea of faces, all nationalities as she made her way through the isle. She finally found a seat, put her bags in the overhead and sat down holding her son. She looked out of the window and saw the sun was setting. A lot of people are dying because of you, Icon had said. Destiny wondered if Vito was dead and as soon as the thought entered her mind she knew he was. It was at that moment that she knew she had to disconnect herself from everything. As she held her son tighter and the bus pulled out of the terminal those words continued to echo in her head...A lot of people are dyin.

Chapter 10

The Greyhound pulled into Downtown Johnson City terminal on Market Street at approximately 6:45 am the following morning. There was a light drizzle falling causing the streets to be covered by a fine mist. Destiny had fallen asleep after the first couple of stops and had been awake since about five. A significant amount of passengers had exited the bus so there were a scattered amount of seats as she looked over her shoulder to see how many passengers were left on the bus. She saw that the girl going to Knoxville was sleeping soundly. Destiny made her way to the bus exit after waking up Jayonne and grabbing her bags. She was happy to see that there were few taxicabs sitting around waiting on customers. She noticed a couple pawnshops and a few other two story buildings that looked like they were constructed very early in the 1900's. As she was heading towards the taxi a money green 05' Cadillac STS spun slowly into the parking lot. AS the Players Anthem by Big Boi and Pimp C exploded from the cars sound system it pulled up right next to the bus. When the young cat that was driving got out in a plain white t-shirt, Evisu jeans, Bathing Ape kicks and a watch that could have blinded the sun, her heart skipped a beat. It wasn't that she was impressed by the materialistic elements, but more his swagger. They locked eyes and it was something strangely familiar about him. Even a half asleep Jayonne smiled at him.

"Sup Shawty?" he said to her showing a mouthful of gold and diamond fronts.

"Hi," she said shyly which really wasn't her.

"What's up lil bro? I see you've met Destiny,"said Donovan coming off the bus with his green bag.

OH shit, she thought. That's why he looked familiar. He's Donovan's brother! She didn't even know Donovan was on the same bus as her. He must have been asleep in the back where she couldn't see him.

"Wuzzup Shawty? You and lil-man need a ride somewhere?" asked Donovan's brother Buck.

She thought about it and keeping her anonymity in tact. Then she considered that she was in a new state and a new town where she knew nobody except for her cousin who didn't even know she was in town. It would be nice to know somebody!

"Yeah, we are just moving into town, but we aren't suppose to move into our apartment for a couple of days! Could you take us to a nice safe hotel?"

And that was it as Jayonne reached out his arms to Donovan, indicating that he wanted him to carry him, which was totally out of character for him. The only person he did that for was Hova. They all got into the Caddy, and for the first time since this all began Destiny was optimistic for her future.

Chapter 11

"Darron Archer-Visit!" came the C.O.'s voice over the loud speaker. Hova was at the table in the middle of what his opponent assumed was an intense chess game. But he was really biding his time until Veesha came.

"Dam fam, it don't look like we gon finish this one," said his opponent, an older Domincan cat from Washington Heights.

Hova gave the perception that he was intensely studying the board. He looked up, winked at the Dominican, and smiled. "CHECKMATE!" said Hova moving his Knight and getting up from the table. Hova was a clever chess player. As a matter of fact he was clever in almost all areas. When he was younger his mother was extremely proud of her son when he was promoted from the first grade to the third grade. He continued to remain on the honor roll with his grades up until eight grade, when he started smoking weed. But his grades only dropped as low as B minuses due to the fact that he refused to be part of any group considered unintelligent. He got into the game at 15 working for older cats, not much older though, that had a section of his projects on lockdown.

One day he had knocked off a two thousand dollar pack and the cats he was working for had gone out of town to All-Star NBA weekend. He was use to only having $500 packs. The projects had been jumping and nobody had any work. He went to school with a Spanish cat who told him that he be dippin in his pop's shit, who sold Major Weight. Hova rode his bike over to the neighborhood where his Spanish friend lived and just as he hoped the cat was out in the park smoking weed like he always was. Hova told Miguel he had $1800 and he needed a serious hook-up. Nobody had ever come to Miguel with that kind of money so he got a little too excited.

Miguel brought Hova a sandwich zip lock bag with 8 plates that looked like sugar cookies that he couldn't close the bag over. Hova had never brought weight before, but he knew that Miguel had gone overboard and his pops was probably going to kill him! On his way back from Miguel's he stopped at the corner bodega and brought the same size and color bottles that the people he worked for used and headed to his crib. He had bagged up the $2000 that he had initially made, off half of one of the 8 plates, hit the hood and made the money back before they even returned from the trip to All-Star weekend. But he was smart. He knew that he wasn't in a position where he could just jump out and start his own spot.

So even though the dudes that Hova worked for noticed that it was taking him longer to move what they gave him, he was still one of their most reliable workers. By the time Hova had finished moving everything that he had got from Miguel, at the age of 16 he had just under 30 grand. That was ten years ago. He continued to work for the older cats for about three more months all the while plotting his next move. Hova's right hand man Pistol Pete had a cousin named Buffy that came to N.Y. every summer to visit from California.

Buffy was a gorgeous young Cali beauty. Long Beach lovely, and her and Hova had kept this long distance love affair, since they were 14. Hova, always the thinker and keeping his ear to the street heard that kilo's were going for 10 grand a piece compared to the 21 g's that they were going for at the time in NY. So Christmas vacation Hova and Pistol Pete flew out to Cali to see Buffy and make a move. After those first 3 bricks Hova never looked back. He was now worth 2 to 3 million dollars easy. That was not including the new house out in West Orange, New Jersey where the mother of his 2 daughters, Mika and Reka lived with his fiancé' that was soon to give birth to his son, named Lisa.

He still had over 50 bricks buried in the backyard under the above ground pool for extreme emergencies. What he had going on with Destiny was really for Destiny. He really did love his cousin and had no idea that things would turn out the way they did. Back in the present as Hova checked himself out in the mirror in his cell he thought about Veesha who he was about to go see, on his visit. She was in fact someone he did have feelings for, but that wasn't his main purpose for having her on his team. She was a good fuck, a great steak, and a fashionable arm piece for the hood.

Definitely not wifey material.

She even believed that she was slick enough to creep wit that pussy lickin bitch and it not get back to him. But it was all part of the game.

He had got a fresh cut last night, not because he needed one, but just to be fresh ta def. As he walked down the hall he gritted on the C.O.'s. He hated all police. He just looked at CO's as police that popped cell doors. The visiting room was fairly empty this morning he thought as he entered and made his way down to where the officer told him that his visitor was waiting. He always planned his visits out carefully to make sure that Lisa and Veesha wouldn't bump heads in the visiting room. But when he reached the area where he had to sit down at the dividing glass and pick-up the phone, he felt his blood turn cold by the sight of the other person sitting opposite him.

"Mr. Archer, AKA Hova. How is the federal system treating you?" asked Icon clean as can be in his tailored Armani Suit and Stacey Adams footwear. Benzino was standing behind Icon smiling, but still a quite intimidating presence.

"Man what the fuck ya'll motherfuckers want? Where is my Shorty Veesha?

"Well, we told her that we had some business to discuss and she understood the importance of the matter at hand. She did ask us to tell you to call her later," said Icon.

"Look I know why ya'll here and I don't know where Dez is and if ya'll fuck with my cousin and her son-"

"Tough talk from a man on the other side of the glass," said Benzino getting agitated and moving forward as if he could actually get through the bulletproof glass himself.

Icon nudged Zino with his elbow and said "Yeah that Vito character was tough too wasn't he?" He looked back at Hova now, not smiling," but now he's dancing with the devil."

Hova's eye narrowed in anger.

"Come the fuck on man! What ya'll niggahs do to my man V? Vito ain't have nothing to do with this shit man. Dam!"

Hova knew all too well the caliber of the characters that he was dealing with and the many, many vicious murders that Icon's name had been connected to over the years. He also now knew that Vito was dead. Dam, first Jake now Vito. Shit was happening too fast.

"The body count won't stop until I find her Hova. My wife is grieving and has to bury her only child in two days. Six people dead and much too much of my valuable time is being invested in this bullshit and my patience is wearing very thin."

"What do you mean six people?" "You will hear about the others soon enough-" "Man I'm outta here I don't have time to dance with you right now," Hova said getting up and about to leave the visit.

"You're mother, a very sick woman. Am I correct?" stated Benzino.

That stopped Hova in his tracks. He directed his words at both men.

"Let me tell you the realest shit I ever spoke. If ya'll motherfuckers even speak about my moms again, on everything I love ya'll would breathe 2 days tops, before you took your last breath in this existence," said Hova calmly and hung up the phone leaving the visitation room.

Even though neither man said anything, Hova's words had an unerring affect on both of them. Maybe it was the fact that neither had had their lives threatened before. Or maybe it was that they both felt he might very well make good on his promise.

Chapter 12

Detective Whitney entered the noisy Brooklyn police station and had a Deja'vu. The multiple phones ringing and various bookings and interrogations going on simultaneously left nothing to be desired from his old job. He definitely preferred the quiet squad room he had become accustomed to. The smell of stale coffee that hung in the air mixed with the cloud of cigarette smoke that seemed to constantly hover at the top of the large station house was the complete opposite of his current smoke-free work environment. Whitney watched as young and old were brought in and out for various criminal offenses. There was one thing that was clearly different in what he saw amongst the current criminals. He was surprised by the alarming number of females, mostly very young that had become a new face of crime. They were still babies he thought to himself. Two officers were taking out a chain gang of guys, handcuffed and shackled, apparently headed to court when Whitney approached the main desk.

"Hey, good afternoon. I'm here to see O'Connor in homicide. He's expecting me." The husky woman had her head down in paper work. She lifted her head to respond to the familiar voice. The two that had a not so good history locked eyes.

"Oh hey Laura, long time. How have you been," he asked not really wanting to know. "Harry Whitney the heartbreaker. Love em and leave em they use to call you right?"

"Look that was a long time ago; I never meant to hurt you."

"Yeah whatever," she said picking up the phone and dialing. Then into the phone "A Steve-Harry Whitney out here, says you're expecting him. OK I'll send him back." Whitney had went out with a bunch of guys and a couple of girl cops after work one evening and had a couple of drinks too many. He had actually believed that he was doing her a favor by screwing her brains loose. But it ended up back firing in his face and made him a new enemy.

"Go ahead, he's waiting on you," she said dismissively and went back to her paperwork. He got the fuck away from her as quick as possible and headed to O'Connor's office. He passed by a white dope fiend chick with huge fake tits that poked her tongue out at him in a suggestive manner.

"Not in this lifetime," he said passing her by and entering O'Connor's office.

"Harry, how the hell are ya?" said O'Connor extending his hand out over his desk.

"Oh you know the routine-police reports and body bags. Homicide work doesn't change much." Whitney took a seat across from O'Connor who had sat down and was puffing on a Marlboro.

"So you got a look at Icon's kid, huh?" asked O'Connor.

"Yeah he was fucked up real good to. He was literally held together by a string."

"Well there has been some pretty gruesome activity on this end as well. Yesterday squad zipped up five young kids in the projects. All of them killed execution style except a young girl. She was cut ear to ear with an extremely sharp knife. Didn't rip. Cut her like butter."

"Wow! Do you think that the killings were related to the Wallace case?" asked Whitney waving off the smoke in the small office.

"Hard to tell. You know anything tied to the infamous Icon never leaves any witnesses. So it does fir his M.O... It's just trying to put the pieces of the puzzle together that's difficult."

O'Connor's door swung open and a young up and coming homicide cop came in holding a folder. He walked over to O'Connor's desk and tossed the folder on it. "This is from this morning-the body found in the dumpster by the old lady over off of Flatbush Ave."

O'Connor opened the folder and looked at Vito's dead body, beginning to swell with decay.

"Did you ID this guy?" asked O'Connor.

"Nah not yet, but we've got some guys over in narcotics that want to check him out. He still had on all of his jewelry-expensive looking stuff too. More n likely a dealer is what we make of it."

"He looks broken up pretty bad. And it looks like someone tried to give him surgery on his adams apple," said Whitney now looking at the photo's.

"Looks like the work of a sharp knife," said the young cop.

"So right there we have a link between the two incidents," said O'Connor. "With the knife," O'Connor said to the young cop "Tell narcotics to get out and put some pressure on a few of their snitches-ask some questions. I've already got a couple of my guys digging up what they can find on the girl so far we know she grew up in Bed-Stuy."

"Alright Steve, I'll get back to you after homicide checks this guy out," said the young cop leaving out of O'Connor's office.

"Well since all of this started under your jurisdiction, I figure we have a joint investigation," said O'Connor.

"Yeah, just like old times," said Whitney unenthusiastically." Just keep big Laura off me.....please!"

Chapter 13

The funeral procession crept slowly through the entrance of the large cemetery led by a snow white hearst carrying Jake's lifeless body. Following closely behind in the triple black brand new Rolls Royce Phantom was Timothy Wallace aka Icon and his estranged grieving wife Glenda. The procession extended approximately two miles long with brand new cars and trucks, all makes and models. The license plates read from all across the country. Florida to California, and from Arizona to Illinois. There were a few that had been friends and acquaintances of Jakes, but for the most part they came out of respect for Icon. The past couple of days had been difficult on Icon. As much as he didn't want to, he was obligated to go through the process with his wife making arrangements to bury their son. As he sat in the car with her now eyes puffy and red from heartache, he was glad that at least this part was almost over.

But he knew all too well that he would have no serenity at home until Destiny was dead. He had heard from his sources inside the police department that there was an all out search going on to find her, but as of now they were clueless. He really hadn't had time to check in with Zino to see what kind of progress that he was making, but as far as he knew after the bus station in Richmond, her trail had went cold. As they came to a stop next to Jakes final resting place Icon curiously eyed the freshly dug hole and the pile of dirt that lay next to it. As his personal limousine driver got out and removed his wheelchair from the trunk, Icon pushed the button which activated the system that aided him in exiting his vehicle. The right rear door raised Lamborghini style. The entire right side of the rear seat which made like a recliner lifted and extended out of the back door. Icon emerged slowly out into the early afternoon sunlight in all black custom tailored Armani and slid almost effortlessly into his awaiting wheelchair. Benzino, who had been driving behind Icon in the Benz with Columbia and her daughter, approached the wheelchair as soon as Icon was seated.

"I'll take it from here," Benzino said to the limo driver. The large group of mourners exited their vehicles and began to make their way towards the gravesite. Glenda walked up beside her husband Icon and they watched as Jake's casket was slowly removed from the hearse by the pallbearers. Icon was watching her closely. She had gone through a wide range of emotions over the past couple of hours. The first incident was when five different girls all who had claimed that Jake was their man got into an all out titties-flying, free for all scrap right in front of the casket. She was infuriated and extremely embarrassed as they all had to be forcefully removed from the church.

Next was when a few of Jake's friends that came to view the body began to leave bottles of liquor and different kinds of weed in his casket to take with him on his final journey home. It wasn't until she realized what was going on that she got up from the front row and began to remove the bottles of Cristal and Hennessy. Bags of cush and haze. She was appalled at what she believed to be a circus. After all the time and effort she had put into seeing to it that her son have a dignified and honorable send off these people were making it a mockery! But when she finally lost it was when they started to close her baby, her only child in his casket and she realized that it was the last time she would ever see him on this earth. Icon tried to restrain her but he in his condition was no match for adrenaline pumped Glenda. All she saw was Jake in his crib. Jake on his tricycle. Jake enthusiastic about his first day of school with his Spiderman backpack headed out the door to meet his little friends. And that was when she became overwhelmed by her thoughts and emotions...and jumped in the casket!

"Take me with my baby lord! Please take me with my baby!" she had screamed.

And now as she stood graveside she realized that she truly had turned this into a three ring circus.

Columbia kept her distance with her daughter and stood with Icon's entourage. She knew the resentment that Glenda held towards her but in all actuality, she gave less than a fuck. She knew exactly what Jakes death meant and was happy someone else had done it first. After the preacher told some more lies about Jake, the casket was lowered, flowers were tossed, Glenda closely watched the weed and Hennessy dudes, a final prayer was said sending off his spirit, and it was over.

On the ride back home to Icon's mansion he attempted to console his wife.

"Maybe we should take a trip. Get away so you can clear-"

"Don't you patronize me you bastard. I know you are glad my baby's gone!" spat Glenda. The limo driver immediately raised the partition separating the back from the front. Icon took the insult in stride, no matter how much truth rang to it.

"Come on now. How are you gonna say something like that? He was my blood."

"When I wouldn't let you turn him into you, you disowned him. You have put more time into raising your so called cousin's kids than you did with Jake."

"That was because you guarded him like he was a piece of fuckin glass!" stated Icon starting to become angry. But Glenda was feeling herself and forgot who she was talking too.

"And the nerve of you to have that young black bitch and her daughter-Your fuckin daughter at my sons funeral. I wish it was you in that goddam casket-"

Icon's large left hand backhand slapped Glenda into remembering the killer she was dealing with. Her hand few up to her mouth, but she could already feel her lip swelling and tasted blood in her mouth. She backed away in the corner wide eyed with fear as tears began to fall from her hazel eyes. He spoke with venom.

"Now you understand this. I know you are hurting and devastated right now and contrary to what you may think and what sometimes my actions may show. I love you. You were there to nurse me back to health and wipe my fuckin ass when I couldn't do it myself. But you understand this because I am only going to tell it to you one time. If you ever, and I do mean ever wish death on me again, I will personally put two slugs right here!" he said touching the center of her forehead.

She knew he meant it and they rode the rest of the way home in silence

* * *

"Bye-bye babygirl" Benzino said to his 14 month old niece as Columbia got out of the Mercedes. Aliyah, Columbia's daughter, smiled her beautiful smile as her uncle kissed her cheek and tickled her stomach.

"Don't worry. Her spoiled little behind is going to be spending a lot of time with you. Just keep it up," said Columbia.

"And I'll enjoy every minute of her," said Zino.

"You wanna come up and talk for a while. Your niece would love your company."

"Nah, I'm sorry sis-I've got to check on few things. You know the routine." She knew the routine all too well. He was Icon's next in charge.

"Alright. I guess I'll see you at work tomorrow night," said Columbia holding her daughter and closing the passenger side door.

Columbia turned to see the doorman in his immaculate red uniform smiling and holding the door open for her.

"Hi Andre" she said as she entered the Park Avenue high-rise building. Columbia loved the illustrious and extravagant living arrangements that Icon had set up to accommodate her. She always got curious stares from the other occupants of the exclusive residence, but for the last year and a half her entire charismatic existence was a mystery.

"Good evening Ms. Quentin. And how is the little misses?" inquired the doorman. They exchanged a few more pleasantries, then Columbia took the elevator up to her layout on the ninth floor. Not to her surprise by the time that they made it inside her enormous spread her daughter Aliyah was sound asleep. She was grateful, because that gave her the perfect opportunity to make herself a drink and gather her thoughts. The funeral had been stressful for Columbia as well. It wasn't often that she had to tolerate being in the company of Icon's wife, but she truly hated the icey stars that Glenda gave her.

It had been 11 years since that fateful night. She and Benzino had been arguing over the TV when their father, a large dark skinned Dominican named Killer came into their bedroom and rushed them into the closet. The fear in his eyes as well as the tears when he told her and Benzino, "No matter what you hear going on out here, stay put!" told them both that something was terribly wrong. Then as his lips quivered, they heard their father speak the last words that he would ever say to them," Remember, daddy will always love you." Ten seconds later they heard the pounding of Icon's henchman at their apartment door.

Their father opened the door for the men and attempted to reason with them over something that involved a shooting in some gambling hall. What his children didn't know was that the monkey that Killer had been carrying on his back, called Heroin, had convinced him that he and an associate could pull off robbing one of Icon's gambling spots. That had ended up being the worst decision of his life. After executing Killer and his wife who had been in the shower, Icon's henchman made a thorough search of the apartment and found Columbia and Benzino balled up hiding under some clothes in the closet. Had any of Icon's other goons besides Simpson been in charge of the assassins, Benzino and Columbia would have been killed with their parents. But Simpson didn't believe in killing kids and had come up in an orphanage. He wished that childhood experience on no one.

He also immediately noticed the fight that they had put up against the men and realized with the right grooming, the potential that they had. When he first took them he didn't mention it to Icon. It took a year and a half to get Columbia over the trauma of losing her parents, but for Benzino it only took 6 months. In his mind he reasoned that the less he resisted, the easier his life would be. He had quickly realized the increase in the amount and quality of the food that they were being given compared to what they were use to. And that was the least of the benefits. Eventually they both took a liking to the Asian martial arts trained assassins that they had been paired up with. By the time Icon learned of what Simpson had done he was furious that Simpson had violated his number one rule of leaving no witnesses. He was skeptical up until he took the trip with Simpson to the Orient where Columbia and Benzino were being raised and learning the culture. At the initial introduction, the then 17 year old Columbia and 19 year old Benzino bowed respectfully. Icon was impressed by the size and strength of the young male and the quickness, grace, and beauty of Columbia. Six months later they were bought back to the states and put to work under Icon's employ. They were supposed to be his cousins children from North Carolina, and Icon being who he was, there were no questions asked.

They quickly began to grow on Icon and he in return bestowed on them more trust and responsibilities. It soon became that they were filling each others voids. With Jake being the disappointment that he was, and Benzino idolizing Icon as a father figure, it came natural to school young Benzino. Columbia on the other hand was like most girls who had that void of a father figure, supporter, comforter. To Icon who wasn't particularly attracted to dark complexion women, she was mindblowing. During their first sexual encounter she had been the initiator.

The aggressor.

He felt a slight pinge of guilt, but her sexual prowess had awakened a part of him that Glenda hadn't seen or been able to pull out of him since the tragic shooting

. Now as Columbia stood looking out over Midtown Manhattan from the full length picture window at the breathtaking view, she sipped a fine white wine and absorbed the Melodic Crooning of the talented Alicia Keys at a low volume. She viewed the traumatization that her and her brother had been subjected to as necessary. All a part of Gods plan. The experience of living in China had molded her thinking and the teachings in discipline were truly a gift. Yes she did love Icon more than anything this world could offer and she would truly do anything for him. That was one of many reasons she gave him Aliyah. And now that Jake was dead, Aliyah was the sole blood descendant and heir to Icon's empire. Columbia smiled wickedly as she pondered the possibilities.

Chapter 14

The dock where the ships came in to port were buzzing with activity as Benzino pulled up to the Oceanside warehouse. Forklifts were moving pallets of merchandise off the ship and the smells of propane gas and sea water filled the air. Benzino had went and parked his car and jumped into his work truck, the latest Navigator. The warehouse was one of Icon's best income producers, but the idea had originated with Benzino. During the time Benzino had spent in China he made some interesting friendships. One of those friendships was with a cat named Mao Chin who attended one of many martial arts academies that Zino studied under in the beginning. Benzino would later find out that Chin's father was a major player in the Chinese Mafia. But this relationship was also a well thought out piece of the puzzle orchestrated by Simpson. Once Benzino returned to the states he and Chin kept in touch. The urban street clothing industry was on blast with lines like Phat Farm, Rockawear, and $Taxxx Officials, all being manufactured in sweat shops in Asian countries at extremely low labor wages. Benzino had a business planner draw up a proposal which he presented to Icon. Pleased with Benzino's efforts, initiative, and prospective profit margins, Icon financed the venture. The warehouse, the size of a football field was importing clothing as well as an extensive line of electronics equipment and black market items from China. Now as he exited the Navigator smelling like Issey cologne, he was greeted by Mao's cousin Lu.

"Zino, I've been waiting on you. How are things?" asked Lu.

"Things are pretty good, Do you have some good news for me?"

"Yes, yes I do. As a matter of fact let's go to your office and discuss business."

The medium build Chinaman in the long black trench coat followed Benzino to a large office just off the inside of the entrance. El Salvadorian and Mexican illegal immigrants busily worked the brightly lit, newly constructed warehouse. Benzino's office was extravagantly decorated in fine cherry wood and original paintings from some of the orients most accomplished artists.

"I talked to cousin chin this morning. He said production is going well and these first 500 boxes are just the tip of the iceberg," said Lu.

"Yes we spoke yesterday, I am aware of our progress. So where is the merchandise?"

"Have one of your employees bring in one of those boxes of Airforce 1's." Benzino made the call and two minutes later there was a knock at the office door.

"Where do you want this boss," asked the burly Mexican carrying the large box.

"Set it down over here in front of the desk. Thank you...close the door on your way out. Gracias," said Benzino thanking him in Spanish.

Lu took a box cutter out of his pocket, split the tape that was holding the box closed and pulled the flaps open. He removed the top layer of Nike sneaker boxes to reveal several small packages wrapped in plastic. The 12x12 inch vacuum sealed cubes contained the most potent marijuana to ever enter the United States. Lu took the box cutter and split open one of the packages. He removed three of the compressed buds and passed them to Benzino. He closely observed the multi-colored greenery. The golds, the purples, the oranges, the reds and whites.

"This is beautiful," he stated bringing the buds up to his nose.

"Yeah Chin, you outdid yourself on this one," he added commending his Asian comrade that wasn't present.

Benzino knew that Icon had been done with the drug trade for a long time and he would definitely disagree with him bringing any kind of dirt around his legitimate businesses. But Benzino rationalized and justified his actions by the affirmation, its only weed. But this was just a test run. Chin had over 300,000 pounds that were ready to be shipped and another 200,000 soon to be harvested in his specialized laboratories. Benzino had already instructed the crew handling this shipment to put these particular boxes in a special area and they were not to be disturbed. He walked over to one of the paintings on the wall in his office, ran his hand along the backside of the frame, and pushed a switch. The picture slid effortlessly to the side on a hidden track making a hissing sound. Once the safe was revealed he stepped up to the retinal and fingerprint scanner which would identify who he was and grant him access to the safe. Once his identity was confirmed by the computerized scanner, he pulled open the safe door. He turned and smiled at Lu.

"Ah, Chinese technology," Zino said jokingly.

Inside the safe was brightly lit. There was a metal briefcase in the center surrounded by stacks upon stacks off crispy new bank wrapped hundred dollar bills. Benzino removed the briefcase that had been previously counted and handed it to Lu. As Lu set it on the desk and began open it Benzino said," Please don't insult me Lu. It's all there." Lu closed the briefcase and said, "Sorry, no disrespect intended." Lu exited the office and the warehouse with promises of being in touch soon. Benzino immediately began to make his calls to the people who were eagerly waiting. He called 40 ounce Rich out in Long Island and Booya from the Polo grounds. Jimmy Simmons out in Charlotte NC and Stubby AKA Gerald Mitchell out in Akron Ohio. Eddie Jackson out in Memphis. And this was just the beginning. He knew for sure that these cats would get the job done. After placing his calls he sat in his leather office chair and put his feet up on his desk.

The Dynasty continues!

* * *

"Don't you want a receipt?" asked the girl in the flower shop as she handed Donovan a dozen long stem roses.

"No thank you" he said showing her his Denzel smile. He left the flower shop feeling nervous but hopeful as he climbed into his rental. It had been 2 long years since he'd seen the love of his life named Lucy. They had been a couple for 3 years and had plans on marrying when he returned. But he never expected to be gone for such a long period of time. In the beginning they wrote each other twice a week faithfully. But that only lasted for 8 months. Her letters and support kept him grounded and sane in the midst of the madness and all of the senseless killings that he witnessed. When she stopped writing it was like his semblance of sanity slowly began to unravel. When things heated up and soldiers started dieing everyday, something inside his mind began to change and realistically, having his thoughts anywhere but on his immediate surroundings was extremely detrimental to his survival. When the wave of random acts of terror intensified directed towards the troops, the only thing that mattered was survival! He would never forget that ungodly hot day when they were patrolling the streets in the city of Bagdad. The convoy that rolled through the crowded streets wasn't unfamiliar to the Iraqi people. The convoy that was about two miles long had stopped for some unknown disturbance up ahead. The young girl who was smiling innocently when she approached the hummer filled with soldiers was carrying what appeared to be a tray of ice water. The gesture seemed genuine considering the intense heat and humidity. When the guy Donovan knew to be Chad reached out off the back of the hummer to grab the tray, the explosives that had been attached to the young girl detonated turning the scene into chaos. The young girl, Chad, and all the occupants of the jeep exploded into thousands of pieces of flying blood and flesh. Two hummers were flipped upside down and an entire storefront was destroyed. In the smoke, desert dust, and fire people were running about screaming in Arabic and crying. Then the assault riffles of the Iraqi rebels attacked the convoy! In the mayhem Donovan lost it and cut down everything that was not wearing American soldier fatigues. His face was stained with the blood of war. The blood of people he knew and didn't know.

And he could taste it!

"Don! Come on, Don this way!" he heard above the ringing in his ears when he had stopped firing his assault rifle.

When Donovan snapped back out of his reverie he was turning onto the country road that led to Lucy's house. He'd only been home two days and had been trying to muster up the courage to make the trip. As he drove he looked out off to the left at the rolling countryside. He reminisced of the time when they would take walks and talk about their plans for the future. Soon the cows and horses of Lucy's family's farm came into view. Donovan began to feel hopeful as he turned onto the long dirt drive way that led to her house.

Chapter 15

Back in Brooklyn, the loud salsa music shook apartment windows and bounced off the buildings as the shiny black Suburban with the 30 day tags pulled up in front of the apartment building. Little Spanish kids ran up beside the truck, dancing to the music of the man who always gave them money and brought them ice cream off the ice cream truck. When the 6ft 11 inch massive presence of a man, at 300 pounds, emerged from the vehicle, he was shown all the love from the children that he was known to give.

He rocked a 40 inch ice flooded cable, with "chulo" as a medallion, heavy with diamonds the same color as his beloved Puerto Rican flag. He was a mean looking sonofabitch with a scar that ran from just below his right ear to the right side of his mouth. The children that he knew so well followed him not noticing that he really wasn't paying them any attention. He was walking almost in a trance.

"Chulo! Chulo! Uncle," said a little boy's distinctive voice that caught his attention. Chulo turned to see his young nephew Amari following behind him amongst the group of children. Amari looked sad as much of the rest of the family members mourning their loss.

"Mommy won't stop crying," he said to Chulo, after Chulo picked up the small child.

"I know little amigo. Mommy is going through a tough time right now," he said to his nephew kissing him on his cheek.

As he walked into the building carrying Amari he felt the weight of the twin .44 caliber long barrel cannons that were stuck in the waist of his size 46 Blak Label Jeans. Chulo had coke spots on 141st and 142nd streets and Broadway Uptown in Harlem and a large crew of Dominican workers that feared and respected him. But for the past two days he had been pumping the projects around his old neighborhood in Brooklyn for information on how his beautiful 15 year old niece Angel had been so brutally murdered in the projects. Chulo's sister Gina had been a wreck trying to explain how her daughter had been cut from ear to ear and left dead in an apartment with her boyfriend and his friends.

Sure Chulo knew that Angel was growing up a little too fast and he really didn't like the interest that she took in black guys, but that was no reason for her to die like that. He sold weight to a couple of cats in Brooklyn, but none in those particular projects. He'd spread some money around trying to squeeze out some info, but so far all he had gotten was something about a black van and six dudes. But that was it. Once he reached the apartment door he could smell the good food cooking inside.

Since they found out about Angel, the whole family had come together to try and keep Gina from losing it. His mother's cooking always had an effect on him and as he headed towards the kitchen his stomach started to growl. His man Booya from the Polo Grounds told him that he had some exclusive tree's coming in supposedly from China. That was just what he needed right now to calm his nerves. As he looked at his sister and mother a wave of anger consumed his body. Gina sat there staring off into space, hair disheveled, with rings around her swollen red eyes, mumbling incoherently.

"Mi Angel-Mi Angel" Gina repeated. Chulo's sister Josette saw him enter the kitchen and slowly shook her head. Gina never acknowledged his presence.

"Still nothing," Chulo said to the table. "But ears are open. Something will come." Becoming frustrated with the scene he was witnessing, he walked out of the kitchen and placed a call on his cell phone. The person he called didn't answer. He knew if anyone could produce information on something this person surely could.

* * *

Hova's lawyer finally came through. The courtroom was fairly empty as Hova and Mr. Robitowitz approached the presiding judge, The Honorable Harold H. Mcginley for a bond hearing. The prosecuting attorney for the United States had stated her reasons at the initial arraignment why she believed Mr. Archer should be denied bail until his trial. But $50,000 and a few greased judicial palms later, Mr. Robitowitz had finally pulled the strings to get him into court. Noone but Hova's fiancé and his lawyer knew what they were working on. He wanted to surprise everyone, especially Destiny if things worked out and at that time he was going to tell her that the money she had was really her money.

The feds had shaken him up pretty good, and he was lucky that the confidential informant only caught him up on powder Cocaine charges. If the 4 kilo's that he had sold would have been crack, he would have been history! As he stood in his orange jumpsuit bound by handcuffs and shackles he looked over his shoulder to see his fiancé Lisa sitting among the other onlookers. She looked professional in her tan and cream colored business suit and three inch pumps. Her long hair was pulled up in a bun as she usually wore it in her position as a bank Manager and her conservative glasses gave her the appearance of being well educated, which she was. Her MBA in finance more than made up for her slightly above average looks. Her medium brown clear skin and facial features, had nothing on the red bone with slanted eyes, sexy Veesha, but Lisa was a Tigress in the bedroom with a snapper that was on one-thousand. And not to mention Hova couldn't have asked for a better mother for his children.

"Mr. Robitowitz, what amount would your client be able to come up with to post bond. As you know these are some very serious charges?" emphasized the judge.

"At the moment, Mr. Archers fiancé is here and has access to $75,000," Mr. Robitowitz lied knowing she told him $150,000.

"Your honor, the United States request nothing under 2 million for a charge as severe as the sale of 4 kilo's of cocaine," stated the US District Attorney.

Damn, Hova thought. At 10% that's $200,000, which is $50,000 more than he was prepared for, but he could still pull it off. Hova's lawyer played golf and took vacations with the judge, who he'd already given $15,000 of the fifty Hova had given him.

"We'll set bail at 1 million dollars bond," said the Judge, which was the amount originally agreed upon by him and Hova's lawyer the day before. The DA looked like she wanted to protest but the decision had been made. Hova turned to his fiancé who winked at him and smiled knowing he was on his way home after being locked up for the past 3 months. She was 5 months pregnant with their son, but she was still horny as a goat! He was quickly ushered out of the courtroom as the next case was called and Mr. Robitowitz walked over to meet with Lisa to arrange the transfer of the funds. Four hours later Hova walked out of the Federal Detention Center to see Lisa waiting by their Mercedes Benz station wagon.

"What's up baby? Dam you feel good!" he said hugging her lightly as not to squeeze the baby.

"Oh I'm so glad to have you from behind that dam glass," she said with her arms around his neck. And then they kissed. A long slow I miss you baby out in public kiss.

"We better get to the crib before I catch another charge right here," he said smiling as they hesitantly separated. They got in the car and slowly pulled out into traffic. He had already been expecting it, but it took him about ten minutes into the ride before he could pinpoint his tail. He wasn't sure if they were undercover agents following him just because, or if it was Icon's people. He had no doubt that Icon was probably one of the first people besides the ones present in the courtroom to know that he had bonded out. Icon had eyes and ears everywhere. But that little slick threat that they had made left a sour taste in his mouth. Hova had always looked at Icon with nothing but respect up until now. He looked in the rearview but tried to do it inconspicuously as not to alarm Lisa.

"Babe I'm hungry and I really would like some good food now that I'm out of that hell hole."

"I've got a whole refrigerator full of food at the house. But if you just wanna grab something now that's cool. What did you have in mind?"

Hova could hear the disappointment in her voice knowing that she wanted to get him home and take advantage of him. He saw the look on her face and knew she was feeling unattractive because of how much weight she had put on in the three months that he was away. He leaned over and started to nibble on her neck and earlobe which made her giggle and put a huge smile on her lips.

"My nerves were so bad about the bond hearing this morning that I didn't eat breakfast or lunch," he lied.

"I just want a quick bite and you can make me a nice big dinner tonight."

"I know the girls have been wanting their daddy. They are gonna be so surprised to see you," said Lisa.

"Man did I miss by babies. But listen, some crazy shit has popped off ever the past couple of days and from what I can see its getting crazier by the day." Hova noticed a seafood takeout up ahead.

"Pull over right up here," he stated still watching his followers in the rearview mirror.

As the Dodge Charger with the black and the white dudes in suits rolled past the Benz wagon, they kept looking forward but turned two blocks up ahead. Definitely the alphabet boys. In all actuality he would much rather have had them keeping tabs on him than Icon's people.

"What do you mean some crazy shit Darron? As if this case isn't enough."

"I'll explain it to you when we get home. Right now lets just grab something to eat."

And that ended the conversation. But not the suspicious looks from Lisa. She knew the possibilities and possible consequences of getting involved with Hova a long time ago and even though it was irrational for a woman of her education and upbringing, she was down for her man in every sense of the statement.

Chapter 16

Donovan saw that there were no cars in Lucy's driveway but noticed the unusually out of place black pick-up truck with the confederate flag and shotgun rack in the back window. He didn't think much of it. Lucy's father always had different people doing some sort of work on or around the house. Both of her parents worked for a large local chemical company for the past 20 plus years. Lucy had an older brother and sister who had both moved out of the ranch house a few years ago before he left for the military. Lucy did have plans at one time of attending college, but since he had lost contact with her, he wasn't sure what she was doing with herself.

When he got out of the car carrying the flowers, once again he took in the familiar surroundings. He walked up the red brick sidewalk leading to the front door that was bordered with perfectly trimmed shrubbery. Donovan pressed the lighted doorbell button and heard the chiming tone that had been forever etched in his memory. He had rang this same doorbell too many times to remember. Not getting a response, he pressed the doorbell again. After waiting for about two minutes he decided that he would go to the back door. Someone had to be here.

The truck was in the driveway.

Taking the grassy way around the large house, which he knew Lucy's room window was on, he set out to knock on her window. Maybe she was sleep. Donovan was carrying the flowers and walking lightly when he noticed her window was open.

He heard voices.

No.

Another step closer.

He heard noises!

As he approached the window, his facial expression changed. Every nerve in his body told him not to look in the open window. Screamed don't look. He pulled back the curtain and his heart stopped...Then began to pound in his chest. Her build had been approximately 140 pounds as he remembered her. He would be surprised now if the girl he watched now getting fucked in her ass and smoking crack with the bony crazed looking white man, weighed 100 pounds. He watched this horrific vision too long and the last thing he remembered was her and the white man turning and looking at him shocked. And then they smiled at him.

Donovan became dizzy and suddenly he was back in Bagdad. The sounds of war and gunfire surrounded him as he ran into a building with his squadron to flush out Iraqi militia forces. He penetrated enemy territory weapon blazing. Kill or be killed was the only all consuming thought. As he crept carefully down dark hallways sweat pouring in buckets, he was cautious, every sense on alert. The first enemy to attack him was on him quickly. Came seemingly from nowhere. Too close on him to maneuver the weapon to get off a shot. The knife in his boot came to mind. His assailant was determined. On is back screaming something Donovan couldn't comprehend. He was reaching. Awkward position. Just two more inches and he could grab the knife. One...last...stretch. He grabbed it! He swung blindly and the horrific cry let out by the assailant let him know he hit his mark. Then he plunged the knife again... and again.

He felt the assailant lose his hold and fall to the floor. But before Donovan could gather his bearings there was another just as fierce as the first. Fighting for dear life and what they believed in. But the knife found its mark on this one effortlessly. The jagged edge plunged in his back and neck tearing with jagged edges. The chest, the neck repeatedly. Blood was flying everywhere. So much blood, and he tasted it! Coming out of his blind rage he let the lifeless white man fall to the ground with multiple stab wounds. He looked across the room at his beloved Lucy, sprawled out on the beige but quickly turning crimson carpet. Donovans hands and face were covered with blood. He looked at his hands, one holding a knife caked with thick blood and flesh as if he'd never seen them before.

Once again, something had snapped. He went unknowingly to that place that he wanted so desperately to avoid which had become a part of his subconscious. As he calmly climbed back out of Lucy's window, he noticed the long stem roses lying on the ground next to the window. His mind told him that he had done the right thing. It was obvious that her drug addiction was a major factor in what had happened between them and the termination of their relationship. As promising as Lucy's future been, he couldn't let her continue to exist as a crackhead, could he? Never, he thought as he hosed off the blood of her and her...her trick! Once he had cleaned up the best he could, he walked back to his rental car with the flowers, in much the same way he had when he arrived. When he made it home he scrubbed up, removing all blood and remains from the brutal slaying, then he disposed of the clothing as to destroy all evidence. His M16 he couldn't very well carry on a day to day basis. But the knife. Yes, the knife he would keep at all times.

* * *

Destiny and her baby were well rested. The two days of winding down from all of the excitement had done her a world of good. As she watched Jayonne attentively sitting on the bed watching cartoons, she had an overwhelming urge to grab and tickle him.

"No mommy! No!" he screamed out giggling hysterically with laughter as she held him down and tickled his midsection.

As she watched him laugh and smile she was reminded of her reason for living. And he was it. She had killed to protect herself and her baby and would do it again. But today was the day that she had to make moves. AS much as she didn't want to bring drama into her cousins life she really didn't have any place else to turn. Lashay was doing well for herself in school, 4.0 GPA, and well on her way to a degree in Journalism. None of the kids in the family were dumb and if Hova hadn't chosen the life over education, he might have ended up at Howard University like he had planned. The birth of Jayonne changed the course of Destiny's life. She also had college in her future, but pregnancy in her Jr. year at Boys and Girls High school affected her choice dramatically. She picked up Jayonne who was laughing still, out of breath gave him a kiss on his check and sat him back down to watch TV.

She thought about the money that she wouldn't be able to collect. Dam she thought, that's a lotta cheese down the tubes! With Vito and Jake both dead and Hova locked up, nobody was gonna be looking for somebody to pay that paper to. She realized that there wasn't anything that she could do about it and figured the next best thing to do would be to put the money that she did have in a safe place. Having over a hundred g's sitting around in a duffel bag was just too risky. She thought back to how close she came at the bus station to the police searching her bag. Then she thought about Donovan, who Jayonne had taken such a liking to.

He was really a nice guy, but something about him was...well different. She could sense that there was a troubled soul behind that winning smile. They both Donovan and Buck had been courteous by giving her and her baby a ride to Hampton Inn. She figured maybe it was that southern hospitality stuff as she scrolled through her cell phone and found her cousin Lashay's number. The hotel room was nice, but she was use to having her own. She knew the police would be looking for her, but she was more concerned about the father of that sorry sonofabitch that she had killed. She had already begun to scan the classifieds and apartment locators looking for a new home. She noted that there were many apartment complexes with vacancies and the drastic difference in rental pricing. She wasn't sure what type of areas that they were in, but she was sure her cousin could keep her out of bad living areas. She dialed her cousins number and Destiny's number that had been programmed into her phone registered on the incoming call screen.

"Dez? What's up cousin?" Lashay asked excitedly.

"Hey Shay. Well, I kinda had to leave town and I'm in a fucked up situation."

"What's wrong girl? You know we fam, I'll do whatever to help you out."

Destiny knew that Shay had her back, it was just good to hear it confirmed.

"Well right now I'm at the Hampton Inn next to the Waffle house right up the street from your school."

"Hold up. You mean my cousin is right here in Tennessee? Get the fuck outta here! I'm hollering at my peoples getting some trees, but I'm only five minutes away. How long you been here?" asked Lashay surprised.

"Look I'm in room 117 and I'll give you all the details when you get here," Destiny paused and continued " grab me a sack too."

"Say no more, I'm on my way!" Lashay said ending the call. Destiny pushed the end button and thought about what she had just done. She had now made her cousin who was out of state getting her education, a part of her mess. What if they somehow tracked her down? What if she was implicated by the authorities as harbering a fugitive? She could be locked up and lose out on the education that she had so desperately pursued. Lose her financial Aid. Now as she thought about it, she was doing the same thing that Hova had done to her by putting her in a compromising position. But she would tell

Lashay everything and leave it up to her to make her own decision. She wouldn't leave out any of the possible consequences. But deep down she knew Shay would still do whatever was in her power to help her and her son. She went over to the duffel bag and took out $3000. She planned to tell Shay almost everything. Even though they had always been close Destiny knew that it probably wasn't a good idea to put out how much cash she had in her possession. Jayonne being no stranger to money jumped up.

"Toys mommy?! New toys?" he asked jumping up and down excitedly on the bed. She looked at him remembering that he had to leave behind all of his toys and that she had promised him she would buy him some and said "yes baby. Today we will try to get you some new toys."

Ten minutes later there was a knock on Destiny's room door. She was still somewhat nervous, with good reason. As she walked across maroon carpeting her heart rate quickened slightly. But when she looked through the peephole and saw Lashay, she let out a sigh of relief, undid the chain-lock and the deadbolt, and opened the door. What a sight for sore eyes. Lashay was the definition of a Brooklyn shorty. Her burgundy shoulder length weave matched her red complexion perfectly. She had on low rider jeans that slightly exposed her white thong and a short white t-shirt that exposed her flat stomach and belly button ring. The shirt said "SPOILED" in rhinestones. The first thing that hit, Dez was the mixed aroma of Hydro and Chanel perfume.

"Hey girl," said Shay throwing her arms around her cousin. Jayonne's eyes popped wide open and he screamed "Auntie Shay!" getting up running over to where they were standing.

"Oney!" Shay screamed picking him up and spinning him around burying his face with wet kisses. He loved it. He was a fiend for affection. For the next twenty minutes they smoked as Destiny elaborately reinacted the events that brought her there.

Lashay was speechless for a minute.

"Well it looks like today we are apartment hunting and toy shopping. I know some really good complexes too. There is only one thing that I have to do. I had an alarm put on my car 2 weeks ago and it's been acting up. So we gotta stop by this audio shop and then we can do whatever," said Shay.

Not long after they were in Shay's fire engine red Volkswagen Jetta. It was a light drizzle falling but the sun was trying to shine through the clouds. Destiny was beginning to enjoy her reunion with somewhat normal life.

Chapter 17

Justin's was packed as Icon, Benzino, and Columbia entered the world renowned restaurant owned by Sean "P-Diddy" Combs.

"Your regular table is waiting sir," said the drop dead gorgeous waitress. All eyes were on the trio. They were well known but that wasn't the reason for the attention. The mystery, the history and the power that encompassed Icon and his entourage was a main source of gossip among the who's who. Among Icon's vast expanse of business ventures was a large independently owned Entertainment Company/record label titled ELITE. It was run by his long time associate and business partner Simpson. Columbia among other titles was in a charge of artist development and project coordinator, on the days when she actually worked in the offices. She was actually very good at what she did and respected in the industry for her no nonsense professionalism. With beauty like hers in a male dominated industry, she couldn't carry it any other way.

"So that was an interesting service this morning, you think?" Icon inquired feigning sarcasm.

"I'm sorry that you had had to be subjected to such embarrassment," said Columbia sympathetically. The waitress returned, took their drink orders and left.

"Actually I had to refrain from laughing a couple of time. It was rather amusing," stated Icon solemnly.

Benzino curiously eyed a group of young ladies, obviously models, as they entered and sat a couple of tables over. One obviously knowing who he was gave him a seductive smile and an inviting wink. He returned the gesture. A few minutes later the waitress returned with their drinks.

"Well the main reason I asked you to meet for dinner with me on such short notice is to show you this," he said removing a picture from inside of his suit jacket and handing it to Benzino.

He was immediately unnerved by the photograph. As he looked at the picture that Destiny and Jayonne had taken at the Sears portrait studio, he was stunned once again by her beauty. Benzino was unusually quiet as he passed the picture to Columbia to observe.

"I figure it would help our efforts if we could match a face with the name and know what the person looked like that we are trying to find," said Icon.

"She is a very pretty girl. Hard to believe she did it," said Columbia. Both Icon and Benzino had to smile at her irony. She herself was the definition of beauty and murder.

"Anything new on her whereabouts since Richmond?" asked Zino.

"Not as of now, but my contacts inside the department know how important it is to me that I find her before they do." There was momentary silence.

"We do have another piece of the puzzle that could possibly complicate matters. My people also tell me that Mr. Archer got a bond this morning. We have to be cautious because a lot of this revolves around him," said Icon.

"Fuck him!" Benzino whispered through gritted teeth.

"He was real tough talk behind that glass in jail. I wanna see if he really gangsta like his rap game!" he continued.

"Calm down son. You'll get your chance in due time. I understand he's got a house somewhere in Jersey and I'm working on exactly where. But for now we must keep our focus on finding the girl and her son before the cops," said Icon.

Columbia was quiet as she usually was. She was studying the portrait, burning the visual imprint in her mind.

Not much for the talk as she was for making moves when it was time to handle business. She was sipping on a vintage flowery white wine when she saw him approaching the table.

"Sean! Long time no see!" Icon said to Diddy.

"I just came back from overseas, heard you were in the building and came to pay my respects. I heard you lost your son," said Sean.

"Yes. And it's been tough, but I'm managing. Thanks for your concern."

"How are you Miss Columbia? Still beautiful as ever," his smile flirtatious.

"Good. Working hard trying to take our label to the next level like yours," she said smiling but serious.

She was thinking, That Karen Steffans chick put a bad bone on you, but I still might give you a shot!

"What's up playa? You suppose to get at me," Diddy said to Zino.

"You know the hustle playboy. But look for my call in the near future!"

"Look it was good to see ya'll again. Enjoy your meal and drinks. This one is on me," said Diddy and disappeared into the back.

"TAKE-THAT   TAKE-THAT," Benzino humorously recollected in his mind of the hitmakers platinum success remixes.

They conversed some about other business ventures and plans of possibly taking a vacation to the beaches of Rio in the near future. After their dinner Benzino stood.

"I hate to take off, but I have a very important meeting with a-um distributor that has the potential to be very profitable," said Zino.

"That's my protégé. Mind on his money and money on his mind" said Icon. He had no idea what Benzino had in mind for distribution. And realistically he couldn't care if Benzino was going to West Hell the way Columbia was eyeing him. He knew it didn't take much alcohol to get her feeling frisky, and the half bottle that she had consumed had her ready.

"I'm going with you," Columbia said to Icon smiling and in an almost child-like voice.

"Is Louisa with Aliyah?" Icon said to Columbia.

"Wouldn't leave her with anyone else," said Columbia of her babysitter.

"Alright you two, I'm gone" said Zino kissing his sister in her forehead. Ten minutes later Columbia and Icon were in the phantom headed to their private hideaway out in the Hamptons. Icon considered the episode with his wife Glenda earlier and looked at the beautiful woman sitting next to him who had also bore his child. And he asked himself, why do I deal with bullshit?

* * *

Hova was lying in the middle of his living room floor on the plush white carpeting watching the 60 inch plasma flat screen. On each side of his chest lay one of his daughters sleeping, exhausted and content, finally having their daddy at home. His fiance' was in the Master bedroom still recovering from the Fuck-A-Thon that lasted for two hours before they picked up the girls from the babysitters. As he watched *AMERICAN GANGSTER* and the consequences behind living a criminal lifestyle, he was forced to take an analytical look at his own life. Right now he was in a situation that could very well remove him from his family for a long period of time.

Sure they would be well off financially but was it worth being away from his little girls. His son on the way. His loving caring wife. As he looked at his daughters he thought-hell fucking no! But in all actuality it was too late to consider this. Hindsight is 20/20! He had no clue where Destiny was and no idea where to start looking. If only she knew that he was out. That she could come and stay with him in Jersey. He looked at his cell phone ringing again on vibrate and saw Veesha calling for the 152nd time. When she went to go visit and he wasn't there she probably flipped! He would eventually get at her, maybe in a week or so. She wasn't going anywhere if he chose to still fuck with her. She was an official dimed out gold-digger. But she was fucking with that bitch Tiffany, who was also known to get bitches to set niggah's up to get robbed. Nah, as much as he hated to admit it he was gonna have to let V go.

"Oh, ya'll look so cute," said a half sleepy Lisa standing over Hova and his sleeping daughters.

She was a wonderful sight to him, standing there, swollen belly, hair looking a mess. It was good to be home.

"Yeah we played airplane, helicopter and chase daddy. They should be out for the night," he said getting up and grabbing his phone. He picked up one of his daughters, who stirred a little but didn't wake up and Lisa picked up the other. They took them upstairs to their bedroom and tucked them in. His fiancé went to use the bathroom and he headed downstairs to the kitchen. He feels his phone vibrating again and takes it out to look at it. He thinks it's Veesha again and is a bit apprehensive when he sees the name on the screen. NOT Veesha, he thinks.

"Hova, compadre. What's good my friend," says the familiar voice that he hadn't heard in awhile.

"Chulo? What the fuck homey? Long time no hear from," he said excitedly to his old acquaintance.

Miguel had introduced Hova to Chulo years ago and Hova would deal with Chulo when he didn't make the trip out to California to cop. Chulo had been working for Miguel's father back then. Now he ran blocks in Spanish Harlem.

"Things got a little hot for me uptown, so I went over to the DR(Dominican Republic) for six months. But I left my phone with my peoples and told them if you call for them to call me ASAP."

"Funny thing you should call. I ran into a situation. Got jammed up. I was in MDC for three months and just bonded out this morning."

"Dam Hov, you good? You know I got birth certificates, socials, licenses. We could change your whole game up" said Chulo seriously.

Hova gave a little chuckle because he had already given this some consideration. But that would automatically negatively affect the lives of his whole family. Lisa had worked too hard to get where she was to be subjected to that.

"Nah fam, I'm good. So what made you get at me. I know you didn't call just to say hi," said Hova.

"Look bro. Some fucked up shit happened to my niece. My sister's daughter. I really need to talk to you in person. I know you got eyes and ears in the projects and if anybody I know can help me out, it's you."

"How fucked up? You mean FUCKED UP-FUCKED UP?!

"Bro, she was my fuckin heart!" he said fighting back tears. Something in Hova's gut told him that he could help his friend. But whatever was going on was somehow linked to his situation with Destiny and Jayonne.

"Alright bro, why don't you meet me downtown Manhattan sometime tomorrow morning. Let's say about eleven," said Hova.

"Alright bro, done deal. I call you around ten to see exactly where we will meet. Look I really appreciate this Hov. I will be forever grateful."

After Hova hung up, the thought about what Icon had said about a lot of people dieing resurfaced in his consciousness. He also knew that Chulo had a sister that lived near the projects that he had workers in. He didn't know exactly what had happened, but one thing Hova didn't believe in was coincidences.

Chapter 18

Two of the most feared narcotics undercovers slowly cruised through the projects looking for their guy. Robocop and The Terminator as the duo were known as, had immediately recognized the body of Damien Daniels, well known on the streets as Vito. They had been working undercover for the past five years and hustlers knew, if you took a chance slinging when these two were on the clock, you really didn't value your freedom. Even the fastest dudes in the hood couldn't get away from these cops in foot pursuit. It was like they never ran out of wind. And by the time they wore you down from chasing you so long, almost the whole police department had you surrounded in back-up. It was also known if you made them chase you more than seven city blocks, it came with an automatic beat down when you got caught, courtesy of NYPD. But now they were on a mission to find an individual who they knew had direct dealings with Vito. When they pulled up in front of the Chinese restaurant where they knew Looch hung out, all of the guys on the corner began to walk away in different directions O'Connor had asked for their help in coming up with some leads on these two particular murder investigations, that he was sure was what turned into a double-homicide home invasion, gone wrong out in Long Island.

The two white officers made eye contact with Looch who was talking to a young girl in an outfit that left very little to the imagination. Robocop then sent a text message telling him to meet them at an abandoned building, which was there usual meeting spot. Looch gave the undercovers information in return for immunity for himself and his workers on the block. Ten minutes later Looch entered the condemned construction, cautiously observing the surroundings to see if anyone was watching.

As he walked across the accumulated debris, dirt and broken glass, his breath was taken away by the overwhelming stench of piss from various animals and addicts. It was still fairly early in the day and it was possible a few fiends could be sleeping in corners from the night before. That was the last thing that he needed. Somebody seeing him talking to the infamous Terminator and Robocop in an abandoned building.

"Looch old buddy?" said Robocop approaching. "Stackin them one's homeboy?"

"Yeah, raking in that scrilla-bubblin that cake, this morning?" added Terminator, both making a weak attempt at sarcastic humor.

"I'm just trying to get by," Looch said nervously.

They both slowly approached him. Not large men, but intimidating all the same. Something moved in a corner and they all jumped. Robocop drew his weapon and they watched as the large rat disappeared into a hole in the wall.

"Your main supplier, the one you've been makin buy's from, Vito. When was the last time you seen him," asked Terminator, with their attention back on Looch.

"About 3 days ago. The same day that crazy shit happened in J building."

"Do you know of any ties that Vito had to the kid Sparks who's apartment that bloodbath happened in?" inquired Robocop.

"Looch pondered the question. He wondered if they thought Vito was behind the massacre at Sparks's apartment. Looch knew that it was Hova's spot, but he also knew Vito was on Hova's team.

"Ya'll think Vito had something to do with that shit in J building?" asked Looch. Looch didn't even see the right hook coming as Robocop punched him in his mouth. Looch dropped like a bag of rocks landing flat on his ass holding his mouth. Terminator bent over him inches from his face.

"You don't ask the fuckin question asshole!" said Terminator, black coffee breath assauting Looch's nostrils.

"Sparks worked for Hova, but Hova is locked up. I know Vito and Hova were connected but I don't know how exactly," said Looch with blood-strained teeth. Robocop removed the picture of Vito's dead body, on the slab at the morgue. Looch looked at the picture in wide eyed horror as it landed in his lap.

"Oh shit! What the fuck happened to him?!" The picture was vivid in detail, displaying Vito's mangled shoulder, gash in his adams-apple, and swelling from the body sitting overnight.

"You think that's something, look at these, "said Terminator dropping the other five pictures in his lap of the execution in Sparks apartment. Looch looked at each visually graphic lifeless body in each photograph. The fact that he had known or seen each person in the pictures made it that much worse. Personal.

"We need some information. Something. This ain't the type of shit you want going on around here. This shit here makes it hot for everybody.....Even you! We know somebody had to see something."

Now they were asking him to literally play with his life. His family's lives. Sure he had heard about the black van. Shit, everybody in the projects had seen it come and go. But he also knew who the people in that van were rumored to being connected to. Things had a way, that he learned from a few other peoples mistakes, of mysteriously happening to people who spoke about Icon's supposed Death Squad. That was a line that he was not willing to cross.

"Let me look into some things-ask around a little and see what I can turn up," he lied.

He remembered the last time that the black van had came out. It was about four years ago. At that time the body count had been three. Mrs. Williamson had said she wasn't scared of no one. She wasn't gonna have this kind of stuff going on in her neighborhood. No way. Wouldn't tolerate it. Saw five people in black outfits get out of a black van and go to the apartment where the people had been found dead.

She talked to the newspeople.

Talked to the uniformed cops.

Talked to the homicide detectives.

Less that twenty four hours later she was talking to nobody, because they found her the next morning in her apartment hanging from her ceiling with her tongue cut out. The message was blatantly clear. Looch looked at the pictures again, of the scene in Sparks' apartment and Vito on the slab at the morgue.

"Yep, I'll look into it and get back at you," he said lying through his bloody teeth!

* * *

As the snow white drop top Porsche gets caught by the traffic light on 42nd street and 8th avenue in front of the Port Authority Bus Terminal, NEYO'S hit-single, Do You knocks from the custom sound system. Eyes and heads turn to see the beautiful Columbia, wearing white Chanel shades, with her hair pulled up into a ponytail. As she moves her head to the music. She smells the pretzels, hot dogs, and peanuts being sold by the street corner vendors. The light changes to green and she pulls off headed to the offices of ELITE records. The sun is shining bright and the cabbies are driving crazy as usual, but she can drive with the best of them. She made it home about five this morning, which she slept most of the ride back into the city on Icon's lap in the back of the Phantom, and was still able to catch a couple hours before she headed out to work. She always thoroughly enjoyed herself when she spent time with Icon.

The sex was great, which she really hadn't expected, but it was his personality and sense of humor, along with the mentoring and wisdom that he passed on to her in conversation. He didn't think anything like anyone she had ever met. She thought of one of the topics they discussed last night. He had went into detail about how The Russian Mafia had infiltrated the United States and were growing in strength and influence at an alarming rate. He broke down how the Communistic infrastructure in Russia had collapsed and the affect that it had had on that Country as a whole. He spoke knowledgably of how The Nuclear Arms race was evolving and how the advancement of Northern Korea and Japan played a major part. She had always been inquisitive and eager to learn new things. As she was driving she caught a run where all the lights changed to green changed in sequence. She dipped from lane to lane like she was driving in nascar, and soon swung into a familiar parking garage on 51st. She was a sight to behold stepping out of her most recent birthday present from Icon and taking the parking ticket from the attendant.

She was wearing Jimmy Choo footwear, a form fitting outfit by a new Italian designer, and carrying Birken Bag that was all coordinated to a tee. Her natural beauty shined effortlessly like the sun as she walked up the crowded Manhattan street heading towards ELITE. She would have slept in this morning but there was an important meeting with the A&R's, Road Managers, and talent scouts concerning acts that were in the development stages and potentially new groups and artist that the company was considering signing. It was tedious work organizing budgets for studio sessions and travel expenses, and she wanted to make sure that her people under her, including interns, were doing their jobs and pulling their weight. She entered the building, her heels clicking across the floor and raised her Chanel glasses so that they sat on top of her head. She nodded to security who greeted her with respectful smiles and entered the elevator. When the doors opened on the 15th floor, the place was buzzing with the kind of activity that the video watchers and I-Pod listeners never saw.

"Morning Ms. Columbia," said the attractive receptionist who was the first person you saw representing ELITE records.

"Good morning Mona. Is everyone waiting on me?" asked Columbia who was running a little late.

"Most of the people scheduled to attend the meeting are waiting in Conference room C," Mona added.

"Thank you. Call and let them know that I'll be there in five minutes," said Columbia heading down the long hallway leading to her office.

Phones were ringing as energetic people moved about with purpose. Pictures of various artists signed to the label lined the many corridors of the company. She saw that most of the smaller offices were empty because the employees who had offices, rather than cubicles, were waiting in conference room C. She entered her executive suite, closed the door and removed the tie that held her hair up in the ponytail. Walking behind her cherry wood desk, she removed a brush from her bag and pushed a button on her phone. She turned the phone on intercom as she retrieved her messages. Kanye's people. Rick Ross's people. Jim Jones's people over at KOCH. She would return all of these calls, but not at the moment. Just as she was about to end her voice mail another message came through. She froze. Pushed the button to play in again. She listened closely to the voice that sounded like it was in the middle of a snowstorm. Or a wind tunnel.

"Uh-issss-ahhh...uh-issss-ahhh," said the extremely distorted voice on the voicemail. She listened to the weird and disturbing message two more times before she brushed her hair out and headed to the meeting. She had a very strange feeling about the message, but she pushed that possibility as far as she could to the back of her mind, slammed the door shut, and locked it!

"Sorry I'm late. Got caught up in traffic," she stated as assumed her position as administrator of the meeting.

They were all seated, fifteen in total around the large oakwood table, many with laptops and Blackberry's handy to store and retrieve information. One of the head budget coordinators initiated the meeting.

"We are right on schedule and a little under our projected budget for this month with just under $200,000 spent in studio time. These are the studios that we have been using and their billing statements," said the efficient young man with a smile, handing Columbia the documentation. She reviewed them, saw that they were stamped Copy and kept them for her records.

"Very good coming in under budget. Keep up the good work."

"We've got three acts flying in this week. Two R&B female groups. One from Houston Texas. The other from Detroit. And we've got an MC from Tennessee. All of them have a lot of potential and an established following in their areas," stated a talent scout.

"Are these the groups that we listened to in my office last week?" asked Columbia.

"Yes. You were excited about the girls from Houston's demo."

"I remember. Make sure I get a memo for day and time. I want to check them out personally as well," added Columbia.

A few more talent scouts checked in stating their progress, and the meeting proceeded.

"J.J. is doing well on his promotional tour. They love his voice out on the west coast as well as through the central

United States. He definitely is set to do big numbers," said JJ's road manager referring to record and CD sales.

"And Sharon Reid is being received like the next coming of Mariah Carey. Her two hot singles are keeping her tour dates sold out," stated Tanya Woods, Sharon's road manager and close friend.

Columbia was attentive throughout the meeting and noted all the progress that was being made, but it was something about that staticky unnerving message that wouldn't leave her alone. And that made her very uncomfortable.

Chapter 19

Hova sat in the passenger seat patiently waiting for Lisa to come out of the Newark Airport main terminal. He had been cautiously observing his surroundings since they left the house to drop off the girls at the daycare. He felt comfortable as they pulled into the airport, that he wasn't being followed this morning. Now he watched Lisa coming from Avis where she had just rented him a vehicle so he could handle his business. Lisa slowly lowered her pregnant self into the driver's seat of the Mercedes, pussy lips still swollen from the Fuckfest the night before. Hova looked at her and smiled as if to say, you asked for it.

"Here you go baby. I got a black mustang for a week. We can extend the time periodically if we need to. All I have to do is call because it's on the Platinum Visa," said Lisa handing him the keys to the rental.

"Thanks babygirl."

He leaned over and kissed her on the cheek.

"I don't know what I'd do without you."

The Benz pulled out into traffic, leaving the passenger drop-off and headed towards the area that Avis kept its rentals. Ten minutes later after they parted company, Hova was on Route 9 headed towards the Holland Tunnel. He was deep in thought trying to figure out where Destiny may have run away to. He knew that he would have to contact Veesha today, if for no other reason to see if she called with her whereabouts. She could literally be anywhere in the country. Hova arrived at the Holland Tunnel toll booth and was glad to see that traffic was moving freely this morning. He liked the feel of the mustang, but he really missed driving his truck. When he exited the tunnel on the N.Y. side he called Chulo.

"Hova, what's up? I'm on the Westside highway headed downtown. Where you at?"

"I'm downtown. Meet me at the heliport parking lot by Chelsea piers," said Hova.

"Be there in ten, fifteen minutes depending on traffic," responded Chulo.

"Aight, one," said Hova ending the call. After he finished talking to Chulo, he placed the call that he knew he would eventually have to make, After dialing Veesha's number, she answered on the 3rd ring.

"Dam Hova. You fucked up boo," she said sleepily, just waking up. He wanted to say something slick, but then he thought about it. He needed this slimeball bitch right now, so he played it cool.

"Nah, it ain't like that shorty. I had some real important business to tend to. Why you buggin? You knew I was gonna get at you."

"Do you know how stupid I felt when I went to visit you and they said that you had bailed out?" she asked.

"Keeping it on the hush was necessary. You remember how them dudes came up there with that bullshit the other day when you came to visit," said Hova speaking about Icon and Benzino.

Veesha shifted uncomfortably in the bed she was in.

"I know. I know," a slight pause, "Did you hear about what happened at Sparks apartment in the projects," asked Veesha.

"Nah, I was gonna call my little man in a few. What happened? Was they over there wiling out wit dem guns again?

"He dead boo. And whoever killed him, killed everybody in the apartment." The news hit Hova like a cinderblock dropped out of a helicopter!

"How? Who? Why? Aw fuck," Hova said reflecting on how close he and Sparks had become.

Now Hova's blood began to boil. So this was what Icon was referring to when he made a statement about so many people dying. He was silent on the phone. He thought that he heard something in the background while talking to Veesha, but ignored it.

"Your cousin Des never called back. Have you spoken to her, I know she must be scared to death," said Veesha.

"I still haven't heard from her. I gotta be careful how I go about contacting her though. I know the police and possibly the Feds may be looking for her because of the murder and the assault rifle. Not to mention them motherfuckers that probably killed my peoples. Dam! Jake, Vito, and now Sparks. I gotta get at them mothefuckers before they catch up to my cousin," said Hova.

"Just be careful baby. I was real mad at you yesterday," said Veesha stroking Benzino's cock to an erection ,"but after sleeping on it and thinking shit over, I understand that somethings don't always work out as planned. So when am I gonna see you?" She said in a whiny voice. Benzino smiled at Veesha coaching her through the conversation.

When Benzino's call came through to Veesha's cell phone, his timing couldn't have been more perfect. He had gotten her number a couple weeks earlier at a club, and she was so drunk and high off of the E-pills, that she probably hadn't even remembered. When he saw her at the jail when he and Icon went to see Hova and she didn't show any sign of recognition he knew she was too twisted to remember him. So when his call came through yesterday after the CO that had been trying to get with her, told her that Hova was picked up by a pregnant woman in a white Mercedes Benz wagon, she felt played and was ready for some getback. Nothing more dangerous than a trifling bitch scorned!

"I gotta holla at my man about some things and check up on my other peoples , but as soon as I see what's going on and try to get some more info on what's been happening, I promise I'm gon come holla," he lied.

"I miss you. You know you owe me," she said studying Zino's dick close up, gripping it tightly in her hand. Hova actually felt a twinge of guilt and considered really going to check her. But he really didn't like how he heard that she was carrying it when he was locked up. Sloppy drunk in the club and getting dropped off the next day by the hood lesbo? Not feeling it, he thought. But of course he had not been honest with her either.

"Aight. I'm gonna call you later on," he said thinking his next stop after getting with Chulo would be to change up his phone number. He ended the call and headed towards the heliport near chelsea. Hova had taken a few of the expensive helicopter tours over N.Y.C's Manhattan Island. He remembered one particular tour one night when he was really feeling himself and his liquor, and was trying to impress a cutey that was visiting the big city from Chicago.

"I think I'm gonna buy one of these in a year or two," he'd said to the pilot as they took off.

"This model would run you oh say 1.7 give or take a few hundred grand," answered the pilot as if to say that Hova could never afford something like that.

Hova had let it go at the time, but now as he pulled into the heliport parking lot he smiled knowing he could cop a few of that model if he chose to.

Hova pulled up next to Chulo, standing next to his suburban who had just ended a phone call. It had been a while since Hova had last seen Chulo, but he was always use to seeing the big man smiling. Now as he looked at the big man, he could tell that he was hurting. But also along with the hurt he saw something else. There was definite presence of a rage and fury that Hova was sure, that whoever was on the receiving end of it, was going to have a bad fucking day!

Look What You Made Me do

* * *

Federal Agents Haugen and Moran entered Richmond Bus terminal wearing their signature blue suits and everyone who had even talked about committing a crime, including the Greyhound employees were shook. They had just completed the journey from Washington DC, where they had thoroughly inspected Hova's abandoned Denali for evidence and clues that might lead them to find Destiny. Yesterday when they initially started following Hova after he was bailed out, they were hoping that he would lead them to his cousin, who was wanted on much more serious charges. They already knew that they had a solid case against Darron Archer. Enough to put him away for at least fifteen years. That had been Jakes work. The four kilo sale had been a bit of misdirection to keep Hova off balance to who the real confidential informant was, which was Jake. What Hova or Destiny didn't know was that in addition to double homicide and weapons charges, Destiny also had a sealed indictment for conspiracy to distribute 2 kilo's of crack cocaine. Also the work of Jake. The agents on the case were furious, that because of Jake Wallace's stupidity and greed, they had lost their star witness and was terribly close to fucking up their whole case. They had a file 10 inches thick on the seemingly untouchable Timothy Wallace A.K.A. Icon. They knew if they had any intention of getting the conviction against Destiny, they had better get to her before Icon and his people did. After showing around the picture of Destiny and reviewing the DC terminals security tapes, their leads had brought them to Richmond, where they were now approaching ticket girl.

"G-Good afternoon," responded the nervous ticket girl.

"No need to be nervous. We just have a couple of questions and we'll let you get back to your job," said agent Moran.

They removed a digital picture printout from the surveillance cameras at the DC terminal and showed them to ticket girl.

"Yeah, I remember them. They were here a couple of days ago," she said.

"Well she's involved in some serious business and her and that little boy of hers are in a great deal of danger. If you remember where they were going you may save both of their lives," said Agent Moran.

"They were going to Tennessee. Someplace called Johnson City."

* * *

Buck was deep in thought as he cruised up N. Roan street headed to his place of business. He had learned from his and Donovan's father, who was doing a 30 year bid in the Tennessee Department of corrections, that a life of crime of any extended period, especially in the drug trade, almost always guaranteed a stay in somebody's prison. When Buck was younger he had a thing for installing radios, amplifiers, car alarms and tinting windows. His father had seen the bigger picture and also as an opportunity to start a business that Buck and hopefully Donovan would be a part of. So he had invested in a small stereo and rim shop. It started off well and soon business was booming. Buck quickly made a name for himself and the quality of his work, which brought him a customer base that spanned a 30 mile radius that encompassed the tri-city area.

But Donovan had chosen a different path. One that included following the steps of their grandfather who was a highly decorated soldier and spending lots of time with his childhood sweetheart Lucy. But when Buck's father had fallen in one of the biggest drug busts in Johnson City's history, all of his assets were seized and the shop was shut down . Buck found himself between a rock and a hard place. He was determined to keep his dream alive. He had heard about loans and grants offered to minorities and all kinds of money that was available from the government to start or expand a business. It was tedious work but he was determined. He went to the library and went online.

He found addresses and contact numbers for the SBA (small business administration) and found out step by step what he needed to do. He knew what he wanted to do and his persistence and lack of procrastination secured him a $10,000 loan repayable at low interest because he was a minority and a $15,000 grant that he didn't have to pay back. From there he leased a building and never looked back. Last year his stereo shop cleared over $300,000 in profits alone. He had five employees and now as he pulled into the shop one of his guys was just finishing up a detail job on a new Maxima with 22 inch rims purchased at the shop.

"What's up Robby?" Buck asked, stepping out of the Caddy into the sunshine.

"Just finishing up here. We got two stereo jobs and one alarm system to install in the garage for this morning. About 5 sets of rims sold for this afternoon. Same ol' same. Business as usual," said a well paid and happy Robby.

Buck entered his showroom which was elaborately furnished with all the latest in car stereo equipment, accessories, and wide variety of the hottest rims on the market. He was walking past one of the salesmen when he stopped him.

"What's up Buck? I needa holla atcha," said Eric.

"Come on back here in my office," said Buck.

After walking past the speaker room and down a short hallway they reached his office and went inside. There was a newspaper on Bucks desk facedown, but he didn't pay it any attention.

"What's on your mind E?"

"Well first-that cutey you be fuckin with, Lashay, came in yesterday. She was having some problems with her alarm we installed-minor stuff. I fixed her right up and she told me to tell you to call her."

Buck smiled as he thought about the cutey from uptop that he had been trying to get with. Not only was she beautiful and sexy, but she had a head on her shoulders and she was pursuing her education.

"I know she was looking good too, wasn't she?" asked Buck.

"Yeah she was, but she had this other chick with her. God-dam this honey was bangin! From their conversation I take it she just got into town. I'd like to get a chance to crack on that!," said Eric.

"Why didn't you?"

"Man this is my place of business. You know I don't do that," answered E reaching for the newspaper on the desk and flipping it over, "Did you see this?"

Buck read the headline with a puzzled look on his face. Once recognition hit home that it was is brothers ex-girlfriend and some other guy that had been brutally knifed to death he looked at E and said "Aw shit."

Chapter 20

Donovan was sitting in the living room watching Hell Date, when his mother walked in and had the newspaper under her arm.

"Honey?" she said nervously.

"Hey ma," said Donovan getting up and giving her a kiss on the cheek."

" How's my favorite girl?"

Mrs. Anderson was a God fearing church woman who loved her sons dearly. She had always been concerned about the paths that they would take after the incarceration of their father. She was extremely happy to see both of her boys turn out to be fine young men. Sure Buck was a little too street, but he had made some good decisions as well as had a good head on his shoulders. Not to mention that that head had put her in a beautiful home as well as pay for her brand new Lincoln in the driveway that was the envy of all her members at the church. But something about her oldest son was different now that he had returned home from the war. When Donovan had left going to Iraq he was a genuinely happy spirit. But when he walked through the door the other day after Buck had picked him up from the bus station, his mother could tell this wasn't the same person who left going off to Iraq. Sure he was the same man in physical appearance. Same easy smile. But there had always been a light, somewhat of a sparkle in his eyes that seemed to come from deep within his soul. She no longer saw that light.

"Have you seen the paper today?" asked Mrs. Anderson

"No ma'am. I've been running errands and trying to get my affairs back in order. Why do you ask?"

Donovan's mother slowly removed the paper from under her arm and handed it to him. She watched him read the headline and cover story.

"This is very sad. I feel terrible for her family," said Donovan with not much emotion.

She observed him for a moment reflecting on how much in love he had been with Lucy. She remembered watching them so happily together and thinking that she was looking at her future daughter in law. Donovan and Lucy had spent so much time on Ma Anderson's couch watching DVD movies, that at one time she was surprised when she came home from work in the evening and saw that they weren't there. She had expected more from him than I feel terrible for her family.

"Is this the first that you've heard of this? Have you called or gone by to see her or the family since you've been home?"

"Nah ma. Her message was pretty clear when she didn't respond to my communication. I mean of course I'll pay my respects to the family, out of respect for the family. And maybe all the death that I've seen and barely escaped over the past year has got me somewhat numb," he paused "I really don't know. But it does disturb me deeply."

"I don't know if anyone said anything to you about her battle with drugs while you were away. The last time that I'd seen her was at Wal-Mart and she looked just terrible. Nothing like the Lucy I'd known. I'm not sure, but the rumor around the church was that it was that crack mess. That stuff is the devil manifesting himself in this existence I tell you. Anyway, her parents put her into a rehab for a couple of months, but as soon as she got out, she was back with that group f undesirables that she had started hanging with and from what I hear, worse that she was before," a tear ran down Mrs. Anderson cheek, which was soon followed by another, and another," she had come by a
couple of times to borrow money. She was such a pitiful sight, but she didn't deserve to-"

Mrs. Anderson laid her head on her son's chest and wept silently. As she did Donovan replayed the vision of what he had seen through Lucy's window in his mind, and he stared out of the window stone-faced. Lucy had been weak falling victim to drugs. In his mind there was no excuse or justification, and therefore no remorse in the hand that fate had ultimately dealt her. They had promised each other that they would be each others strength. She broke that promise. No, he didn't consider that his presence was her strength. That if he wouldn't have gone off to enlist in the marines and helped his brother run his business, that maybe none of this would have happened. Then he had a thought.

"Wait a minute mom. What about all the times that I asked you in letters if you had seen or heard from Lucy. You told me no, ma. Why would you deliberately lie to me?" Donavan asked somewhat becoming angry.

Mrs. Anderson walked away from her son and went over and looked out of the window. She had hoped that she would never have to explain to Donovan why she chose not to tell him about Lucy's battle with drugs. But the truth was out and she had to come clean. She walked back over to the couch where he had been sitting and sat down.

"Come over here and sit down baby," she said in an even tone. He sat beside her. She continued," Donovan you are my first born and I love you dearly. I believe you know that, as well as I would never do anything to intentionally hurt you. All I ever wanted for you in this life is happiness. For a long time with your father I had happiness. A happiness that made me go to bed every night looking forward to the joy of the next day and our future. But your father began to make some bad choices. When he got laid off from his job it was devastating. He could have
made the choice to work two jobs. I even told him I was willing to work two jobs. But no!" she sad becoming emotional again.

"He started selling drugs and got turned out by that drug game-and...and I thought that my love and dedication could change him," she said, pain filled tears flowing. Donovan watched her with concern. He knew the depression that she went through when his father got locked up. "You were focused on laying a positive foundation for your life. I didn't want you running back here trying to change somebody who wasn't willing to change her life for herself. In my mind, I was protecting you and guarding your best interests. If you are upset with me I deserve and accept that," she looked at the newspaper on the table. "But I never expected I'd have to tell you after something like-like that," she said pointing to the newspaper.

Donovan sat there and absorbed everything his mother had said and thought that she was probably right. If he had known about Lucy's smoking Crack he would have surely went AWOL attempting to save her. He stood up and kissed his mother on the forehead.

"No mom, I'm not mad at you. I understand your intentions and apologize for questioning you. I had not right to do that after all you've done to be a mother and father to me and Buck," he said sincerely.

"Do you want to ride with me out to give my condolences to Lucy's family later on?" Donovan had absolutely no intention on returning to the ranch house. It wasn't that he was concerned about returning to the scene of the crime. He was sore that he'd thoroughly destroyed any incriminating evidence or links that may lead back to tie him into the crime. He had made sure of that. But it was al of the old memories of times spent together in the past that he didn't want to recall.

"Let me think about it mom. I have a lot of mixed emotions that I am doing battle with right now. If I change my mind I'll let you know," said Donovan knowing he would never return there.

Donovan made his way down the steps to the ground level and out of the back door to the patio. He looked at the large inground pool with the diving board on the far end. He inhaled deeply filling his lungs with fresh air and exhaled slowly attempting to clear his thoughts. He didn't feel like a cold or cruel person, but his actions clearly displayed that something in his rational thought process was fucked up bigtime! He looked down at his hands. The hands that even scrubbed clean would forever be stained with the blood of his one and only true love. It all hit him at once that she really gone. Gone forever. And he began to weep.

* * *

Lashay and Destiny had spent the whole day together, yesterday. They had first gone to get Lashay's alarm fixed at some guy's shop named Buck that by now Destiny had grown tired of hearing about. He got Bank. He a cutey. If he act right I might let him Fuck. Same old Shay, Destiny thought. But she did make this guy sound like he had it going on. Prosperous businessman, not a drug dealer, and he seemed to be a nice guy? Even he sounded interesting, enough was enough! They had then set out to find Destiny and Jayonne a place that they could call home. Destiny was quickly becoming tired of fast food. Lashay had offered that they come and stay with her, but Destiny shot down that suggestion immediately. Lashay shared a two bedroom apartment, just off campus with a roommate. Destiny had no intention on her or her son sleeping on anyones floor, couch, or sharing a bed. Especially one she did not know who
slept in. Lashay wasn't a slut by a longshot, but she wasn't an Angel either. She remembered Lashay had been the victim of her own naiveness in high school in situations reguarding alcohol and some popular dude. But it seemed as though those heartbreaks and times of ridicule made Shay a stronger and more ambitious person. She had been tagged with a few degrading titles in high school, but she turned that negative

energy into fuel that led her to a full paid scholarship to college. In her mind back then she had believed those guys that told her they loved her. She longed to hear those words from somebody. Anybody. She had cried to Destiny when Hova screamed on her saying that she was embarrassing the family. So now when she returned home and rolled through the streets of Brooklyn she held her head high. When she strutted through the projects and smiled at the same girls that called her names, who had three and four kids, on welfare and forever doomed to smoking blunts in the PJ's, inside she knew who had the last laugh. They had looked at six different places, all two and three bedrooms, so Jayonne could have his own. They finally found the perfect spot. A three bedroom townhouse on the outskirts of town in a beautiful gated community. They had planned to put the lease in Lashay's mane because at the time it wouldn't be wise to use Destiny's or a fictious name. When the rental agent told them the lease was $850 a month, Lashay looked at Destiny as if to say" can you handle that?" Destiny said that she had a nice chunk of change but wasn't specific on her price range. Lashay had a 720 credit score which she had worked hard to establish and really didn't want to fuck up. The area was upscale with beautiful manicured landscaping, 24 hour security patrol, swimming pool and fitness center, as well as childcare all provided right on the premises. Destiny had smiled and nodded her approval and Lashay filled out the application so they could start the credit check and references. Lashay had no doubt that everything would go
through especially with the small success of her on-line magazine that she'd started six months ago. It was still in it's beginning stages but the traffic from her My Space and Black Planet links provided her with a noticeable income. After the approval, the rental agent told Lashay that it would take 48 hours to process the paperwork and she could come and pick-up the keys anytime after that. When they left they went

straight to Toys-R-Us, where they spent two hours and $760 and not all on Jayonne. Once Lashay had dropped her off at the hotel after stating she had some errands to run, she knew that she would probably not get a better time to move forward with her plan of putting the money somewhere safe. Once Destiny put a restless Jayonne to sleep she removed the phone book from the nightstand next to the bed and opened it up to the yellow pages. After she located a nearby Bank Of America which she knew was large enough to have safe deposit box accessibility, she called to verify what was necessary to open one. She had her son's birth certificate which she kept with her at all times and the customer service rep told her that would be fine. After waking her son up and reducing the amount that she was putting in the safe deposit box to $90,000, Destiny and Jayonne left in a taxi headed towards the bank. When she entered the bank with the duffel bag she received suspicious glares from bank employees and customers. A black woman, even with a child, carrying a duffel bag into a bank, was enough to make everybody nervous. After a few seconds she was quickly approached by a bank representative.

"Good afternoon Miss, may I help you with something?" The young man in a shirt and tie inquired.

"Yes, I am interested in renting a safe deposit box. I called a little while ago and spoke to a," she removed a piece of paper from her purse and looked at it, "Mrs. Williams. She told me the documentation required to rent one and I have it all here."

The bank rep looked at her, Jayonne, and the duffel bag, in that order and wondered what could she possibly have in that bag that she needed to put it in a safe deposit box, Destiny became frustrated.

"If you have a problem with my skin color I can take my business else...

"Hold on, hold on please young lady," cut in Mrs. Williams."

Please come with me and I will take care of everything.

Twenty-five minutes later Destiny left the bank with her funds secure and headed back to the hotel with her safe deposit box key.

She now sat watching the local news as she waited for Shay to come and pick up her and Jayonne and take them to Rent-a-Center to pick out furniture. She would have gone and brought new furniture, but then again she didn't want to arouse an additional suspicion from Shay. She listened to the reporter go into detail about a brutal knifing that had occurred the day before. As they told the bloody tale Destiny wondered what would make someone do something so vicious as continually stab another human being. The news caster had said" a total of 79 stab wounds were found between the two victims." She couldn't imagine forcing a sharp object in to flesh once, let alone 79 times. There are some sick souls in this world, she thought to herself as she heard Shay's horn blowing outside her window. She checked herself in the mirror grabbed Jayonne and headed out the door.

Chapter 21

The past week had been hectic. Hova had finally gotten all the details of the killings and his worst fears had been confirmed. The infamous Death Squad was definitely behind the killing of his peoples. He relayed the info he received to Chulo and needles to say, the big man was murdering mad. He had an idea of where his cousin Des might be, but he didn't want to attempt to contact her because he wasn't sure what kind of surveillance he might be under. But that fact still didn't deter him from planning his next move. He could hear Salsa music coming from many apartment windows as he turned onto 143rd Street off of Amsterdam Ave in the early afternoon sunlight. Both sides of the street were heavy with Dominican hustlers, thugs, and murderers who eyed him suspiciously as he slowly made his way down the street in the rented Mustang. Hova knew the building number that he was looking for, but he was really looking for Chulo's truck.

When he made it just pas the middle of the block he was caught off guard by a vision of beauty. They connected eyes and she smiled. Her catlike eyes twinkled in the sunlight as she seductively took a sip of the bottle of spring water she was nursing. She was a medium build with a cinnamon complexion and a Jazzy short haircut that fit her facial features perfectly. She had blonde highlights and a lip gloss that Hova thought he could taste from the car. He knew the fact that she was standing on this block in Spanish Harlem probably meant that she was Dominican. He looked at the entryway for the building number she was standing in front of and his cell phone rang at the same time. She was standing in front of the building that he was suppose to meet Chulo in. He didn't even look at his phone before he answered. He knew he had been set-up. Hova didn't believe in coincidences.

"Who is she?" Hova asked Chulo who was on the other end of the phone.

"Her name is Nadia. She is my boy Pedro's neice. They use her to attract out of towners looking to cop some work. Pretty good traffic stopper huh?"

"She would've got my money," Hova said seriously. Hova looked over at Nadia who was still standing there smiling. "Come on up, I'm in 5A, "said Chulo looking out of the apartment window.

"On my way."

Hova double parked the mustang and walked towards the entrance of the building. As he approached Nadia he noticed that she was even more beautiful close up. She extended her hand in greeting.

"My name is Nadia. I've heard a lot about you."

"All good, I hope," Hova stated returning her smile.

When he pulled his hand back he had a piece of paper in it. It had a phone number on it.

"Call me...that is, if your interested in getting to know me better," stated Nadia, staring seductively at Hova.

"Will do," he said spinning off and going into the building.

As he entered the building and headed towards the elevator he noticed that it was considerably cleaner that a lot of the other buildings that he had been in around that are. He had done business with Chulo in this area on quite a few occasions. But then again this wasn't a "Business" call. He looked up above the elevator and noticed that it was on the third floor by the lighted floor indicator. He pushed the button that had the down arrow on it and heard the elevator come to life. As he watched the lighted three go blank and after a few seconds the 2 lit up, he thought about what Chulo was planning to do. Chulo was thirsty for revenge and in a big way. But Chulo didn't want Icon. He wanted the specific individuals responsible for his nieces' brutal murder. The idea he had was a long shot, but it could work. The elevator reached the ground floor and the doors slowly opened. An elderly black couple, easily in their 70's exited the elevator followed by a young light complexioned boy no older than four. The little boy who was looking curiously at Hova. Hova smiled at him and entered the elevator. When he exited on the fifth floor he saw that the hallways were empty and the floor strangely quiet. At the end of each hallway Hova saw that there were cameras that monitored the outer perimeters of the premises. As he approached the door that read 5A, he heard the locks from the doors being unlatched and it slowly opened. When he stepped inside he wasn't prepared for what he saw. The walls to the adjoining apartments on both sides had been knocked down to create one large open space. The floor was carpeted in a thick plush black and fire snow white butter-soft leather couches and in front of each couch was a glass coffee table. On two of the couches sat six men, three on each couch, separating and stacking face up and in order 20's, 50's, and hundred's. After the stacks were at a certain height they were fed into a money machine where they were counted labeled and put in rubber bands. On the other three couches sat nine men, three on each curiously eyeing Hova. On the remaining three coffee tables was enough weaponry to equip a small army. The sound of the door closing behind him caught him off guard, but when he saw the soundproofing on the backside of the door he understood why the hallway seemed so quiet. Chulo came out of a room to the far left of the apartment and approached Hova.

"I'm sorry about this," Chulo said motioning to the money and the machines on the tables," but my pick-up/drop off money man came through about an hour ago and I had to take care of business. Come on over here with me. I have something I want to show you. They should be done out here in about an hour or so."

"I know what you do. Handle your business" said Hova and followed Chulo to the room he had just come out of. Once again Hova was taken by surprise when he entered the adjoining room. What Hova thought was a room was actually another space the same size as the one he had just left. He realized that Chulo had the whole 5th floor of the building gutted and renovated. In this space was a large kitchen the size of an entire apartment. It was lined with brand new stat of the art appliances and shiny new stainless steel sinks and fixtures.

"Dam Chulo! This shit is laid out lovely," said observing the rest of the living space.

A large glass dining room table sat off to the side of the kitchen, under a small chandelier. There were six high backed chairs that surrounded the table. All the places where there should have been doors to exit the rooms into the hallway, had been covered and replaced by smooth wall. They proceeded through the kitchen and past the dining area to what Hova immediately recognized as the living space, or sleeping area.

"I brought the building last year. The owner got caught up in back taxes so I practically stole it. He knew what I was into and sold it to me under one condition. Most of the people that live here are elderly and have been here for 20 years or more. He told me as long as I didn't raise the rent, kept it safe, and didn't deal drugs out of it, he would sell it to me."

"Hold up," Hova said, "That's three conditions."
Chulo smiled.

"I know. Nevertheless I brought it. The guy who sold it to me lives on the third floor, Follow me."

They walked up two carpeted steps to where there was a king size bed and a maroon marble Jacuzzi. Hova noticed a row of monitors near the bed. He immediately recognized the hallway where he exited the elevator, but saw the he missed two more that he had to pass because they showed the front of the building where Nadia was still standing, and the entrance to the building.

"I brought it as a safe house to keep money and for my top guys to come and relax. But absolutely no drugs come in here."

"So what have you come up with to carry out this plan. You have got to understand exactly how dangerous these death squad motherfuckers are," said Hova.

"I feel you Hova. But what you have got to understand is how dangerous the men are that you just walked past out there." Chulo picked up the remote and pointed it at the large screen on the wall. "Check this out."

The woman stepping out of the new X-model powder blue Jaguar with soft leather dove gray interior was totally unaware that her movements were being surveyed. Even in her late 40's she was still a vision of class and beauty.

"My people have been on her for the past four days. She definitely stays active," said Chulo as Icon's wife Glenda entered the Bally's Fitness Center with her gymbag. Hova watched his once close friends' moms and felt mixed emotions. Since Chulo had told him of his plans to kidnap Icon's wife to draw out the death squad, he had moved his own mother out to his house in Jersey. He figured things were about to heat up and he wanted all of his family together and safe.

"You saw the arsenal of weapons that we have out front, but we have absolutely no intention on hurting this woman. I know she is totally innocent. But we know that when they have a location on were she is suppose to be and have a drop-off point for the ransom money, he's gonna send his goons. They my people kill them all," stated Chulo bitterly. Hova was listening to Chulo but his eyes were still on the screen which continued to show Icon's wife at various different locations. Then he saw something that caught his attention.

"Ho-Ho-Hold up Chulo. How do you rewind that thing?" said Hova.

"Ahhh, I thought that might catch your attention."

Chulo rewound the tape and pressed play as they watched Glenda pull up to the entrance of some ritzy hotel and go in the front entrance with a young Hispanic looking male. The scene changed as the valet got into the Jaguar and pulled off.

"It's some expensive hotel out in Long Island. My people left but Icon's wife and her friend didn't until the next morning," said Chulo.

"I'm really not surprised. It's just that she seemed kind of bold with it. Icon has eyes and ears everywhere," said Hova.

Chulo turned off the recording.

"We plan on making our move tomorrow. Did you take your moms out to your spot?" Chulo asked Hova.

"Yeah she's safe. You just make sure you don't leave any room for mistakes. And make sure you kill that Benzino motherfucka. Rumor has it he is a dangerous cat. I gotta slide outta town to check on something, but I will stay in touch."

They continued to converse about how the plan would be carried out and eventually made it to the subject of Hova's court case.

"So what is your lawyer talking about?" asked Chulo.

"Right now I'm looking at about 84 months, but I know they are waiting on me to fuck up. But I'm done. 7 years is already to long to be away from my family."

"Dam Hov, them alphabet boys is serious business. No way around doing that time huh?"

"I had thought about leaving the country, but I don't want my family to have to live on the run. They don't deserve that," said Hova seriously.

"You're a better man than me bro. I would be in the wind. Catch me if you can!"

"Believe me, I wanna bounce. But switching things up a bit, what did you tell shorty out front about me?" asked Hova in reference to Nadia.

"What do you mean? What did she say to you?" asked Chulo smiling innocently.

"She gave me this and told me to call her if I'm...um, interested."

Chulo looked at the piece of paper and threw his head back laughing.

"Ahh, I guess she digs you bro, which ain't really a bad thing. I may have spread it on a little thick when I told her you were a really good friend. But she obviously liked what she saw. I sure as hell wouldn't have told her to give you her cell phone number," added Chulo.

"Isn't it dangerous what she does? You don't know what type of time a lot of these guys that come through are on."

"I guess your right but we haven't had any incidents. And on top of that she has brought in some big spenders. She brings em in, but what keeps them is the price and quality of my product. Oh, and she is very selective," Chulo said.

Hova thought abut it and came to the conclusion that he may have just found a replacement for Veesha.

"A word to the wise Amigo. I would definitely give her a call. She's got a good head on her shoulders. Really smart chick with goals. Don't let what she does on the side fool you."

"On the side?" Hova asked curiously.

"Yeah. She's also part owner in a small daycare center and she owns two Lincoln town cars that she rents out by the week as taxi's. Like I said bro, a real smart chick," said Chulo. One of the men that were in front room on the couches entered and said something in Spanish that Hova didn't understand.

"Come and meet Angel's uncles on her father's side. They just arrived from Puerto Rico yesterday. Her father was killed in a car accident about 7 years ago and they come over to handle any serious business that I need taken cared of. They are not to happy about what happened," said Chulo walking towards the front room with Hova following.

The tables were now both covered with stacks of money. Even though it was easily over a hundred grand it didn't phase Hova in the least. To him it was a good couple of days work. Chulo made the introductions, but since they didn't speak much English the conversation was minimal. Hova told the big man he needed to make moves and Chulo walked him to the door. Chulo was undoing the locks when Hova spoke.

"Look Chulo, I trust you fully and I know you are pissed about what happened to your neice. But Icon is a clever, underhanded and heartless killer. A war with him will produce many more casualties. Please my friend, make sure your plan is foolproof," said Hova as the door labeled 5A slowly opened and Chulo absorbed his statement.

"One love," Hova stated as he gave Chulo a hug, and headed for the elevators. Chulo stood speechless. As massive presence focused on avenging his Angel's death.

* * *

Icon was at his home that he shared with his wife sipping his cup of coffee and catching up on world events as he read his morning paper. He was beginning to become frustrated with the search for Destiny and his latest bit of information had him downright furious. The front page of the NEW YORK TIMES had pictures of politicians debating and no doubt making promises that they really had no intentions on keeping. His cell phone sitting on the kitchen table rang. He looked at the number before he answered, but he already knew who the call was from. He answered on the second ring.

"Steve, my man, I've been waiting on your call all morning," said Icon.

"Sorry Mr. Wallace, but you know how traffic is on the Grand Central. I just turned into your driveway and I should be at your front door in about five minutes."

"Good, good. The door will be open and I'm in the kitchen. You know the way... Alright I'll be waiting," Icon said ending the conversation.

Five minutes later, Steve O'conner, head Homocide Detective and long time employee of Icon's casually strolled into his kitchen.

"Steve my favorite, most well paid crooked cop. How are ya?" Icon said in good humor.

"Well things could be better. You know you've taken care of me and my family for so many years, I hate when I can't come through for you and right now my hands are tied," said O'Connor.

He was talking about the latest developments in the double homicide case with Destiny. The reason for the anger that Icon was hiding. Over the Icon's trusted servant had served him well. He made critical evidence disappear from murder scenes. He sent homicide detectives under him and working with him on wild goose chases when they were on the right track. And he was paid well for his services.

"Please have a seat Steve. Coffee?"

"No thank you sir," O'Connor said respectfully, sitting down at the table.

"So tell me more about the FBI removing you from the case," said Icon taking a sip of his coffee.

"Well apparently there is something bigger going on than the picture we are seeing. Like I told you, I called in some favors and put some pressure on the streets to make sure your name was sage and flush out any new info. And I told you

I pulled in an old acquaintance that's working out in Long Island where they found Jake's body. They were actually working pretty close with me and Whitney through finding the truck in D.C. and tracking her last wearabouts to the Richmond Greyhound terminal. After sharing the bit of information about her buying a ticket to that town in Tennessee, they removed me and Whitney from the case and pretty much demanded that we not investigate any further. I don't know what it could be," said O'Connor sounding defeated.

"Well you know the FED's are handling Hova's case. Maybe that has something to do with whatevers going on," said Icon.

"Well I do have a couple of people in the Bureau that I made trade information with. I have them on it, but they are very cautious as not to arouse suspicion. They haven't let me down yet, but I have to be patient with them."

"I don't have time for patience!" Icon said slamming his fist down on the kitchen table and scaring the shit out of O'Connor.

"I want this bitch dead before the Feds catch up with her," Icon continued.

The tension was thick in the room. This was the Icon O'Connor had known and feared for the past 20 years. The cold and calculating monster that lay just beneath that cool surface. They heard a lite singing voice coming towards the kitchen before they saw her. Glenda entered the kitchen and was momentarily startled. She was wearing a pink sweatsuit bottom and a t-shirt with her straight black hair pulled back in a ponytail. The scent in the air of stale cigarette smoke that O'Connor had brought in with him, changed to a mild flowery but extremely pleasant fragrance. Glenda smiled and turned down the volume on her I-pod which was playing Beyonce's Flaws and All single. Icon had to admit that over the past few days there had been a dramatic change in her behavior. She had a glow that he hadn't seen in a long time and they actually had sex...no fucked, the past two nights in a row! She kissed Icon on the cheek.

"Hi Steve. Long time, no see," said Glenda.

"Ah, the beautiful Mrs. Wallace. You don't seem to age at all. What do you have a time machine back there somewhere?" asked O'Connor laying on the flattery.

"Your too kind Steve," then she turned to Icon," I'm heading out to the gym. Do you need anything before I leave?" She is being to nice, he thought to himself. Something is definitely going on. Or maybe that episode in the car after the funeral was just what the doctor ordered. Whatever it was, he wasn't trying to change it.

"No. I will be leaving soon to go run some errands. My day is pretty full, but you can call me later," stated Icon.

Glenda knew that since she hadn't seen Steve in a while, that this house call was probably in reference to that young bitch that killed her Jake. She wanted to ask questions but she knew that would be totally out of line. She said her good-byes and headed out to play. When she was gone finally Icon and O'Connor continued.

"Mr. Wallace, you know I am doing everything I can to track her down. And I can't put my finger on it, but there is definitely something else going on," said O'Connor.

"I know you're doing everything you can. Probably more than it's wise to. And that is why I am giving you this," Icon stated tossing a bank wrapped $10,000 stack on the kitchen table.

"Come on now. Don't look at me like that. I know I just gave you 20 grand last week. Look add this as an additional token of m appreciation as well as a reaffirmation of how important it is that I get this young lady before the FEDS do. Spread some of it around. Grease a few palms. Maybe you'll pry something loose. I haven't lost faith in what your capable of Steve."

O'Connor picked up the money. He would throw a couple grand at those two crazy Narc cops. He knew that they sometimes had access to other information because they worked closely with the Feds. He knew that Icon was counting on him and he would do everything in his power to produce.

Chapter 22

Benzino drove cautiously as he made his way east on the Long Island expressway. This drug dealing stuff, which was still new to him and the shit that came with it amused him. The benefits of the drug trade were obvious. He had already seen a cool quarter million in a very short period of time and he knew the profit potential was unlimited. Every one of his people that he lit with the headbanger green from the orient, couldn't keep enough. He saw the sign he was looking for. Exit 50, Wyandanch 1 mile. It had been a minute since he had come out this way. Even when he dealt with his boy 40, AKA "40oz Rich", one of the realest niggahz out "the Danch", he met him at the warehouse on the docks. But his was other business. He looked over at his good friend Chin who had recently come to the United States. They needed to talk about business, seeing as things were progressing much quicker that they had anticipated. Fortunately for Benzino, Chin's visit was unannounced and when he arrived at the warehouse on the docks his timing was perfect. It was just after 5a.m. when Chin's pearl white stretch chauffered Maybach pulled up quietly to the rear entrance and Chin with three of his most highly trained bodyguards exited the vehicle. Their instincts immediately put them on guard when they saw three shiny black Kawasaki 1100 street racing bikes parked by a door that was slightly opened. Chin immediately called Benzino's cell phone. After informing Benzino about his unscheduled arrival and telling him about the situation, Benzino smiled to himself and told Chin not to move in, but definitely don't let them leave. Benzino knew he had to play this one carefully, because a slaughter at the warehouse and for what reason would be difficult to explain to Icon. He would definitely sense foul play. Benzino arrived at the warehouse twenty minutes later in the

Navi and coasted to a stop with the engine off, parking in front of the warehouse. Chin was there waiting beside the Maybach. Chin saw the two mini-submachine pistols with silencers in Benzino's hands as he approached.

"No need for those. Me and my men have this under control," said Chin as he pointed to two of his bodyguards positioned on the roof.

The dawn of morning light was breaking in the distance, but dark skies were still dominant. Far off, the horn blast off a large cargo carrier ship could be heard headed out to sea. Chin's men had moved the motorcycles away from the rear entrance, so when the three stick-up kids stepped out of the building with duffel bags full of Chin's weed, they were shook to see that their means of escape were gone. Two of the men quickly removed firearms from the small of their backs as nervousness consumed them, but their weapons proved to be useless. The two men were spinning with their weapons pointing aimlessly when Chin's men both landed on their shoulders simultaneously severing spinal chord tissue and immediately paralyzing them both. The third man stood in shock as he watched his two accomplices laying on the ground shaking and screaming. Then he heard something quickly approaching from his left. Sounded like someone was running towards him. He tried to spin with his weapon but his duffel bag was in the way. He turned to see the small chinaman rapidly flipping like an Olympic gymnast headed towards him. Before he knew what was happening, Chin's bodyguard had his legs wrapped around his neck pulling him to the ground. The third man fell hard slamming his head on the pavement. The last sound that he heard was the chinaman scream and his neck snapping before he left this existence to meet his maker. Chin and Zino ran over to where the three men were all stretched out. Benzino checked the bags just to confirm that it was what they already knew.

"40 pounds. This would have brought them close to three hundred grand on the streets at retail," said Benzino.

"Was it worth it?!," asked Chin viciously kicking one of the two paralyzed stick-up kids in his back.

"I'll go get the truck. Have your men dispose of the dead body and get rid of those bikes. I got plans for these two clowns," Benzino said to Chin.

Benzino dialed a number on his cell phone. Marvin Toney A.K.A. "Pretty Toney" answered on the third ring.

"Who dis?" said Marvin in a groggy voice still half asleep.

"Yo Pretty Toney, this Benzino. Wake up fam," said Zino finally getting Marvin's attention.

Marvin and Benzino went back a few years. Marvin was an old acquaintance of Icon's, who was actually a hustler that retired from the game as well. Marvin was a dark brown skinned cat, stocky build, who was well known in his younger days for his knuckle game. Pretty Toney's hands were famous in the hood for knocking niggahs the fuck out! But now Marvin owned a few prosperous businesses. Of the business, one was a funeral parlor with a crematory on premises.

"Aight...aight. I'm up talk to me," said Marvin shaking off the effects of sleepiness.

"I need to see you. I'm leaving now and I'll be there in an hour-hour and a half at the most. Can you be ready for me?

"Yeah come on. I'm getting out the bed now and I'll be at the shop waiting for you," said Marvin.

They sometimes referred to the backroom of the funeral parlor as the shop A.K.A. the chop shop. Pretty Toney had disposed of quite a few corpses for Benzino and Icon over the years. Benzino and Chin arrived at the funeral home shortly after exiting the highway and pulled up to the rear of the building. Marvin was waiting in one of his many vehicles, a money green Metallic Chrysler 300 Dub edition, with two of his boys. Marvin hit the remote to open one of the three garage doors and Benzino pulled the truck inside. The muffled moans of the 2 men could be heard from them in the back of the Navigator. The two stickup kids knew that this was probably their last and final stop. They had seen what had happened to their other accomplice as well as the three chinamen takeoff popping on their borrowed bikes. When the back door of the truck swung open, the two men looked at the five men standing there. The fear in their eyes said all that the ductape that covered their mouths wouldn't allow them to.

"So what did these two do?" Marvin asked out of curiosity.

"Blatant disrespect, which you know I don't tolerate," said Benzino throwing one of the guys over his shoulder.

"Make that motherfucker walk. His feet ain't tied up. We got'em covered if he try some dumb shit," said Pretty Toney.

"Oh, they already tried some dumb shit. They're both paralyzed. Grab the other one and take him inside," said Chin.

They went inside and down some steps that led to the basement. They entered a brightly lit room that was extremely clean and seemingly made up of all cement and steel. There was a long conveyer belt that led to a sliding steel door that was connected to a huge metal object that took up an entire wall. There was an eerie rumbling sound that came from behind the sliding steel door and the room was extremely hot.

"Sit him over here against the wall in a sitting position.

The sound of the roaring flames of the crematory could clearly be heard in the stuffy room. The walls were lined with wooden boxes in the shape of caskets that were used to send bodies to be burned down the conveyer belt and into the oven. A door that led to the main funeral parlor opened and a small man appeared. To everyone who had seen Pops, his first impression was something that would always remain with you. Pops was 5 foot 2 inched tall. He had a pinkish colored albino skin color and a large dark brown birth mark on his face that covered his left eye and half of his nose. He wore a NY Yankee hat that many had figured by now was probably attached to his head since he was never seen without it. He had a dead eye that wandered and his face was contorted, twisted into a perpetual snarl, from one too many strokes. This snarl made his mouth resemble a pig's snout. To say his features were grotesque would be an understatement. He lived in the attic of the funeral parlor which Marvin had redecorated to suit him. Pops was fucked-off in the looks department and scared the living shit out of children, but he was undoubtedly the best man for the position.

The two paralyzed attempted robbers didn't notice Pops had entered the room until he spoke.

"You ready for me boss?" Pops asked Marvin in an unusually deep and scratchy voice.

"Holy-fuckin-shit! What is that?"Chin whispered tapping Benzino and pointing at Pops.

"Not just yet. What's up Pops?" Benzino asked the old man.

Pops face broke into on what a normal persons face would have equated to a smile noticing Benzino for the first time. This look was considerably more horrifying than his face at rest.

"Zino! How you been? Where is Icon?" said Pops looking around for his old friend. In the past Icon had taken care of Pops financially after he had taken care of a problem. The mention of Icon's name brought immediate recognition from the stick-up kids. It wasn't until now that they realized how bad they had fucked themselves. Benzino ignored Pops question.

"All right you two. I got a proposition for you," Benzino stated to the robbers. The robbers' hearts began to race in excitement and hope. Maybe they thought, there could possibly be some chance of survival. Of course they would be paralyzed, but they would still be alive. They both looked at the disturbing vision that was Pops as he approached them. They figured he was the guy who ran the roaster and one of them quickly spoke up.

"What?! What is it.....This proposition?" asked one robber. They both remembered the long reflection they had on the ride out from the city in the back of Benzino's truck. They had both grown up together in the PJ's. They had been the tightest of homeboys for over 15 years. The third guy who had gotten killed at the warehouse was down with them but these two were tight. They were thinking about these things when Benzino spoke.

"A fight. Between you two. The winner lives. The looser dies in the cooker," Benzino lied.

"Bap! Bap!" the smaller of the two hooked off on his boy.

That homeboy shit went straight out the window.

"Yo son? What da fu-" the man who had been hit first started. He was considerably larger than the other man and probably the reason why he had got stole on. Little man wanted to get his shit off quick, because he knew that he didn't have a chance if the bigger man hit him first. But the punches barely fazed him. He knew that this was strictly about survival. His instincts soon kicked in when he saw the look in his friends eyes made the statement that he wasn't trying to die. He tried to grab his friend who had now begun to swing wildly. This didn't work because he didn't have the use of his legs as leverage and he caught numerous glancing blows to his head and shoulders.

"You better fight back, or you're headed for the fryer," one of Marvin's men said.

The smaller man didn't even see the overhand right coming. It landed on the bridge of his nose and pain exploded through his sinuses causing his eyes to water. He stopped swinging. The right hook that followed made a loud cracking sound and made the smaller guys eyes roll back in his head.

Everyone in the room knew the fight was over. Except for the larger man who had rolled over onto his friend and began to relentlessly pound on his face. Blood began to splatter on the ground and walls before it was ended.

"OK, OK enough," said Benzino.

One of Marvin's men and Pops had already removed one of the cheap coffin boxes off the wall and left it open on the conveyer belt. The bigger man sat against the wall breathing heavily trying to catch his breath after the brutal punishing he put on his once close friend. He watched his old friend now unconscious, being lifted off the floor and carried over and put in the wood box. He watched Pops walk over to a round dial on the wall and turn it towards the right. The sound of the flames behind the wall immediately got louder. Pops then went and retrieved a nail gun and sealed the wood box wit the smaller robber inside. The room was quiet except for the sounds of the crematory as instructions were waited for.

"I want you to pay close attention to this," Zino said to the other robber," go ahead Pops. Start the belt. As directed Pops pushed a button which started the conveyor belt. As the box started moving slowly towards the sliding steel door the larger robber looked on in horror. The steel door slid open upwards revealing the angry mouth of fire waiting to consume it's victim. Suddenly there was sound from inside the box. But it was muffled. Then the knocking began. It soon turned into pounding. He was no longer unconscious and would be burned alive. Just as Benzino had expected. The screaming began as the front of the box came into contact with the blue flames. Benzino gave the signal for Pops to close the steel door. He pushed the button for the door to close, but nothing happened. The screams became louder as the box went further into the flames. Flesh could now be smelled burning.

"Close the fucking door Pops!" screamed Marvin.

"I'm trying. Something is wrong. It seems like the door is stuck."

"Fuckin shit stinks," said Marvin's men leaving the room. Benzino tried to keep a straight facr and not laugh as he watched the other robber look on in fear. The nerve of these bastards trying to rob him. AS the conveyer belt pulled the rest of the box into the fire, Zino winked at Pops and gave him the signal to close the door. They had done this a few times before. Benzino wanted the remaining robber to see his friend die. Viciously, fighting for life.

"So. Who put you up to this," Benzino asked the remaining robber. The robber was still in shock from what he had witnessed and couldn't speak. Benzino leaned down in front of him and waved his hand in front of his face to get his attention.

"Hey Yo. What's your name money?" asked Benzino.

"Curtis. They call me Curt in the hood."

"Who's bright idea was it to commit suicide and try to take something from me?"

"I told that niggah Lamar that we should have checked this shit out some more.But him and that greedy Darnell was in such a rush to hit a lick. If I would have known this had anything to do with Icon I wouldn't have touched this shit."

Benzino couldn't let this cat live now even if he wanted to. He remembered the look of recognition on their faces when Icon's mane was mentioned by Pops.

"So which one of the other two is Lamar?" asked Chin speaking up.

Curt pointed at the crematory.

"Good. An appropriate sendoff for such a wise man. But something about all this troubles me. It just doesn't add up. This Lamar character would have had to get his information from someone I deal with directly. They are the only ones that know about the warehouse," said Benzino.

Curt saw that if there was really any chance of him surviving, the information that he knew just might be it. He never for one second believed that Benzino and the Chinese man had nay intention on letting him live. Not for one second.

"You know a chick named Veesha?" Curt asked Benzino.

"Yeah," He said with a confused look on his face, "what does she have to do with this?"

"Well this chick Veesha also be fuckin wit this bi-sexual chick named Tiffany. Lamar use to freak with Tiffany and she give us info on cats that's getting paper and we go get em. Veesha came to that warehouse with you last week to meet somebody. You told her to wait in the car but she said she had to use the bathroom because you were inside for so long. After she entered the building and used the bathroom she got nosey. She peeked in your office and saw you and the guys you were with counting out a lot of paper. She came back, told Tiff and Tiff called us. But like I said dude, if I knew Icon was connected to this I wouldn't have touched it," said Curt.

Benzino stood there silently raging. That trifling bitch. He looked at Chin who was shaking his head in disappointment. Not only did Benzino's carelessness almost cost them enormously, but he let a chick almost blow his cover. Unfortunately for Curt this information had the reverse effect on Benzino. His negligence had been exposed in front of Chin and now on top of being furious he was embarrassed. The removal on the tech .22 with the silencer from the inside of his jacket was so lightening quick that it caught everyone by surprise. The three quick shots left tiny holes and almost no blood as they entered Curt's forehead. Benzino reached in his pocket and pulled out a wad of bills. He threw the money to Pops.

"Take care of the rest of this for me Pops. Pretty Tony, I'll holla at you soon. Me and my friend here have business to tend to back in the city," he said referring to Chin. He should have known better than to take Veesha to the warehouse. In the past it hadn't been a big deal because he wasn't doing any dirt at the place of legitimate business. Now he had to worry about a leak from this Tiffany chick getting back to Icon and things were going to good for that right now.

Chapter 23

Destiny had awakened this morning to that feeling again. She looked around the room at her furnishings and smiled to herself shaking off the feeling. She listened to the sounds about the apartment and realized it was quiet. Just as she begun to get nervous because she didn't here Jayonne stirring,she remembered that Shay had stayed over the night before and was suppose to take him to church with her. Destiny still couldn't understand how Shay could do and say some of the stuff she did and still go to church every Sunday. Destiny didn't feel God would accept her as she was, especially after killing two people. After all, one of the commandments was Thou Shalt Not Kill, right? But she wanted her son to have a chance if this place everyone wanted to go to called HEAVEN really existed. Shay had told her that she had to many blessings in her life for their not to be a merciful God. Shay told her she was still learning about building a relationship with Christ and she couldn't learn about it anywhere else but in church. She told Destiny that God could use all his children that he created, and used Moses a murderer and The Apostle Paul who was a killer of Christians to do amazing works through. Destiny lit the half a blunt that she left in the ashtray the night before. She sat on the side of the bed and blew the smoke out slowly after a long deep pull. She looked at the phone. She really wanted to call Veesha and get word to Hova she was o.k., but her sixth sense told her that it wasn't a good idea. Just then the phone rang.

"Hello?" she answered after two rings.

"Oh, so you are up. Me and Oney just finished eating breakfast at IHOP," said Shay.

"Did he eat all of his food?"

"Yeah. I got him strawberry pancakes. All that didn't go in his mouth was on his face," Shay said jokingly.

"So I guess you're on your way to the Lord's house, huh?"

"Yes we are. And that's why I called, to see if maybe you had changed your mind and might come with us." Destiny thought about it for a second. There was a voice in her head. It was far off but it was there. The voice said Come my child. My everlasting love is waiting for you.

"Nah cuz, not today. Maybe next time."

"Alright, alright. Well we gonna hang out together until about five. I'm gonna show off my little cutie to a few of my friends and give you a little time to yourself," said Shay.

"Alright. That sounds cool. I had a few things that I wanted to do. This will give me the opportunity. But Shay?"

"What's up cuz?"

"You know I trust you, but take care of my little boo-boo."

"I hear you loud and clear. If you need me call my cell," said Shay before ending the call.

When Destiny hung up the phone she went and retrieved a phone number from her purse. She would call the number and set up a meeting. She was going through a period of transition and had also been considering pursuing a dream that she had. She wasn't sure what her future held, but she had nothing to lose trying to fulfill it. She made the call and set up the appointment for 12:30. She was hoping that the people she was calling would be willing to handle business on a Sunday and she was grateful to see that they were. Destiny showered and picked out something nice to wear from her recently acquired wardrobe. Once she was dressed she admired herself in the powder blue, long skirt and jacket set with her black sling-back shoes made by Enzo. The mirror reflected a woman ready for business, all except for her red eyes. After a couple drops of visene she was ready to roll. She had to admit that they did have some good weed down this way. Shay said her peoples dealt with some Mexicans from a town called Morristown not far away. Destiny had rented a caravan in Shay's name to get around in and planned in turning it in once she brought a vehicle of her own. She had noticed Shay giving her suspicious looks over the money she was spending. But if she had been suspicious up to this point, her next move would definitely lead to questions and some sort of explanation. She went into her sons room where she kept the money she had left over, that she hadn't put in the safe deposit box. She counted out $2,500 and put the rest back in her stash. After setting the security system she left the apartment and headed for Office Max. She needed to go on-line and unfortunately she had procrastinated on getting a computer, which would soon become somewhat of a necessity. Had it been during the week she would have went to the local library.

After she got the information she needed she went to her appointment. She smiled to herself on the ride over. After her research at office max she realized that it was much easier to get the ball rolling on her dream than she ever imagined. When she pulled into the parking lot she was even more pleased to see an older black woman sitting in a new pepsi blue Cadillac CTS. Destiny pulled up beside her and parked. The woman looked over, smiled and motioned for her to get out of the car. Destiny got out of the caravan into the sunlight looking ready for business.

"Good afternoon Ms. Archer. My named is Lydia. Lydia Moore. We spoke earlier I believe," said the woman approaching and firmly shaking Destiny's hand.

Lydia Moore appeared to be in her late forties. She was also in great physical shape and appeared to have a significant amount of Indian of Latino in her lineage. She had a sort of Pam Greer likeness that emanated power in her presence.

"Nice to meet you Lydia. Thank you for coming out on such short notice."

"Well, you know business is business. Come on let's go inside," said Lydia.

Lydia produced a ring of keys. She tried a couple unsuccessfully until she found the one that unlocked the door to the empty storefront. When the door swung open and Destiny smelled the fresh paint and new carpets her heart quickened. She stepped inside slowly and looked around. She began to visualize her dream and what she would put where. The storefront sat at the end of a row of stores located in a newly built shopping center. Destiny had noticed the sign that read RETAIL SPACE FOR RENT the day Shay had brought her car to the shop across the street to get her alarm fixed. She had been thinking about calling the number since that day.

"Take your time and look around. I'm gonna go over and talk to one of my other renters. I'll be back in about five minutes," said Lydia.

Once Lydia was gone Destiny stood in the middle of the empty space. It was a bit smaller that the place that she use to work in. She turned to her left and closed her eyes. When she opened them she could visualize what would be the Beauty Parlor side of her store. She cold see the wall lined with elegant booths, shampoo sinks, and mirrors lined with lights. Four stations she thought. Yes, four stations would be sufficient. She wanted it classy and not cluttered. She knew her clientele would be unique. She visualized the waiting area with a large flat screen, all the latest magazines, and of course a section where the hottest black authors on the markets books could be purchased. She had heard from Shay that these exclusive literary works were also a good source of income. Destiny visualized the decorative floors that she would put down on the Beauty Salon side and the Maroon leather chairs and wash bowls that she had seen and priced on-line at office Max. Even though the Beauty Salon aspect of her venture would be a new experience, she was sure that she could find chicks and maybe even guys with the skills needed to build a reputation as one of the best spots in town to get that headpiece done up right! But the other half of her business was where her expertise lay.

Before this whole mess occurred, Destiny worked in one of the most exclusive lingerie' shops in Nassau County. As she stood and turned towards the other side of the store, she envisioned what would be her own personal baby and the main reason for wanting this space. She pictured in her mind racks and racks of erotic and seductive lingerie' that she would personally pick and arrange herself. She had seen the income potential of this industry and enjoyed helping chicks and couples make decisions on intimate items that would enhance their homelives. But the sad part was that she enjoyed it so much because she could somewhat live through the people she helped. Since Jayonne's conception she had put a padlock on her heart and her pussy. She shook that recollection from her thoughts and imagined the wall of shoes and intimate accessories she would sell. She thought that the idea of a sexy lingerie' store and Beauty Salon combined would be a sure winner with the women. She had even came up with a name for it. THE PRETTY KITTY. She was still standing in the middle of the store smiling like a kid on Christmas morning when Lydia returned.

"So, I take it that you like it?" said Lydia startling Destiny.

"Oh yes," she responded not wanting to seem overly excited. "How much is it a month?"

"Do you mind if I ask you a question Ms. Archer?"

Destiny immediately became uneasy. What could she possible want to know except if she could afford the payments.

"Sure. What do you want to know?" asked Destiny faking confidence.

"What exactly do you plan on doing with this space?"

Destiny wasn't really sure why she was asking. Then she thought about the area she was in and how receptive her idea would be taken. People had a tendency to act shady, especially the elderly when it came to a business that promoted sex. Destiny told Lydia of the idea and concept.

"Young lady, that is absolutely brilliant! The reason why I asked is because from the moment I saw you, I liked you. This can be a tough town for black businesses. I've seen quite a few fail because there's not a big black business market. But I believe that you could possibly pull in business from all the surrounding small black communities as well as the white chicks that spend," said Lydia.

This inspiration gave Destiny the confidence she needed to seal the deal once she was told the payments and terms of the lease. Destiny gave Lydia a cash deposit and first months rent and told her thank you. Thank you for helping her with her dream.

* * *

Columbia sat up in her king size bed with her arms wrapped around her knees and tears rolling down her face. She was starting to begin to think that she was losing her fucking mind, Since that first creepy phone message, she had received at least one a day, similar to each other, but none of them were the same. The last one had just come through about three minutes ago. She wanted to call Icon or Benzino, but she was sure that when she told them what she thought the calls were, they would both be ready to admit her for a psychological evaluation. She slowly climbed out of the bed and walked over to the caller ID again to make sure her mind wasn't playing tricks on her. The light was blinking signaling an incoming call, but the screen was totally blank. In fact every time one of those calls came in from God knows where, the screen always remained blank. But that didn't make an sense at all. She even called the phone company as wee as used *69 in an attempt to trace the orgin of the call. But as far as the phone company's records, no call ad registered coming through the line. This last call had made the hairs on the back of her neck stand on end.

"Uhhhn-issss-uhhh.   Reeee-pennnnt.   Yurrrrr Sinnnnsssszz!" said the eerie voice on the other end of the line.

The voice was always the same, somewhat familiar, and the most recent calls seemed to have other voices in the distance, screaming, moaning, or a mixture of both. There was no doubt that these calls were meant specifically for her. It had been many years since she had heard her name given to her at birth. Since returning from overseas Benzino had even stopped using it. Uhniss-uh, she assumed, equated to Anissa, which was the name her mother had told her when she was younger, that her grandmother gave her at birth. Columbia walked over to the mirror in her bedroom and stared at her reflection. She looked like a stressed out mess. She wondered if that was why Icon hadn't called her in a few days, which was definitely not normal. Repent your sins was the message. Columbia reflected back to her earlier years. The arguments between her parents would forever echo in those dark recesses of her memory that she chose suppress for good reason.

"Where did you hide the money?" her father would scream at her mother.

"Baby please. That money is for food and clothes for the kids," her mother would respond with fear in her small voice.

"I'm gonna put it right back. I just need to flip it a couple of times until I get on my feet. I'll put it right back," he lied, repeating the lie her mother had heard more times that she cared to count.

"No! not this time. I'm taking them shopping in the morning," her mother had said fed up with the routine.

She knew that if she gave Killer the money he would be somewhere nodding with a needle in his arm in less than a half-hour. Little Anissa would sit in fear and anticipation of what she knew was coming.

"SMACK!" was the sound that seemed to echo in her mind throughout the tiny apartment. "Give me the fucking money bitch! I'm the man of this house!"

"OK! OK! Please-please don't hurt me, I'll get it," her mother would scream fearing further abuse.

Columbia would turn up the television and cover her ears. She rocked back and forth sitting in front of the TV with hot tears of fear and helplessness. The helpless feeling came from the time she heard a similar situation playing out. She had run into the bedroom to help her mother. But the look on her father's face, a look that she had never seen before, had so thoroughly scared the shit out of her that she never attempted to intervene again. She would wait for the front door of the apartment to slam shut signaling that her father had left. Little Anissa would quietly get up and slowly walk to her mother's bedroom door where she would stand watching her mother. Benzino always seemed would be sitting on the bed with her large Bible, quietly reading passages from various books. Anissa would patiently stand waiting for her mother to acknowledge her presence which she knew she would. Her mother would look up, most of the time with her eye swollen shut and pat a space on the bed next to her signaling for Columbia to come sit next to her. She never concealed the blatant signs of physical abuse. She wanted her daughter to see, in hopes that she would never let herself be subjected to such a life. Columbia would listen intently and sometimes lay on her mother's lap until she drifted off into a peaceful sleep. To this very day she could recite many verses of scripture, but saw no need to. Repent your sins, she thought to herself again and then considered all of the sins she had committed. The voice on the phone was strange, yet the more she heard it, the more familiar it sounded. She had heard it scream in hate. But the last time she had heard it, Columbia and Benzino were hiding in a dark closet.

"Remember, daddy will always love you," her father had said.

But she was sure that both of her parents had been killed that night. So how was it possible that he could be calling her? That was just it, it wasn't possible. And why would the phone company tell her that no call came through the line when there was clearly a voice on the other end. Columbia didn't believe in ghosts or that communicating with dead people was possible. Or did she?

* * *

Benzino and Chin made it back into the city just in time to meet lunch hour traffic. They had rode most of the way in complete silence. He knew Chin was disappointed to see Benzino had shown such carelessness, but he was about to make amends. Or so he thought.

"Yo, check it out Chin. I'm really sorry about this shit and I promise nothing like this will ever happen again," said Zino.

"Look we have known each other for a while now. I also know that dealing drugs is something that is still new to you. But we can't have mishaps like this. Just understand that this is a dirty game and no one plays fair. The cops and the hustlers are all on the take. What you saw today was a clear example of cats out for blood money. You just have to be more careful," stated Chin.

"Yeah I hear you. This will never happen again."

Traffic eased up when they finally made it back to Brooklyn. Benzino pretty much knew that Veesha was just a pawn in this game. He wanted the queen who truly believed she was a king. Of course he knew the chick Tiffany, who had turned out so many chicks that her name rang bells all through the hood. He had even run across a few certified dime pieces, that had a tattoo of her name either across the top of the pussies or on one of their asscheeks. He had also seen Tiffany up in the club, ballin just as hard if not harder than a lotta niggahs. He remembered one night he was at Jay-Z's 40/40 club and she was up in the spot...bubbling bananas! See this Tiffany chick was an amazon beauty, standing 6ft tall. But honey was definitely killin it in the looks department. She had an olive-honey light-skinned complexion of the smoothest skin, full sexy lips and a midway down her back blonde weave that fit her so perfectly it was like she had been born with it. And with measurements of 40-22-40 she was built like a 3-story brick house. But now she had crossed the line, Benzino thought as he turned the corner and saw her pink Escalade sitting in front of her usual hang out spot.

"That's her truck right there," Benzino said to Chin as he pulled into the parking lot of the strip club.

Benzino knew that this was her hang out spot, but had no idea of the vested interested that she had in CHEEKS. Tiffany was also a shrewd business woman who was on top of her game. The Italian cat who ran the club was really just the face in front of the business. Tiffany was the paper behind it. Everybody knew she was a hustler, but very few knew how heavy she was in the game. A few years earlier she was down in Miami with three of her baddest bitches up in club RAIN. She was up in the VIP with a few professional ball players that were sweating her and her crew, when she met one of the biggest extasy pill connects in the United States. He was a short older Columbian cat that looked totally out of place. He gave her 10 E-pills and a phone number in a small clear glass bottle along with a phone number. She knew what they were of course because Tiffany and her crew had been buying them since they hit the MIA. And not to mention they were the best pills she had ever tried.

"I can tell you are from out of town beautiful. I can also see that your paper is long. If you like and you want to do business, I will make you an offer that you can't refuse," he had said to her before he spinned off into the crowd.

And that he did. She made the call and a couple hundred grand not long after, she became one of the largest E-pill suppliers in the N.Y., N.J., and Connecticut area. But she was smart and kept her anonymity in tact. She only did business with one person with the agreement that her name and face were kept out of all transactions.

Benzino and Chin fell up into the strip club to see that it was pretty active for this time of day. They were immediately confronted with heavy cigarette smoke and the overwhelming stench of feminine douches and various perfumes clashing. Not wanting to look suspicious Benzino and Chin located and headed towards a table off to the side of center stage.

As Benzino sat down, he parted his coat and felt the weight of his twin mini submachine guns. When he got ready or saw the opportunity to make his move, he wanted easy access. But their efforts to remain low key were quickly diminished when the girls located the two men whose presence had the aura of money and power. They were soon approached by two of the club's biggest money makers. And they looked like they had just walked off the pages of the latest issue of smooth magazine. The high heeled stallions approached the table with confidence.

"Now what do we have here? Would you fellas like to order us a couple of drinks?" asked the well tanned Canadian hottie known as NAYA.

Chin didn't drink alcohol which Benzino knew, but in order to get at his target without looking questionable, he knew it was best that they play by the rules. He looked over at Chin.

"I'll have an orange juice," said Chin.

"Let me get a Corona with lime and you ladies can get whatever you like," said Benzino.

The ladies took their orders and headed off to the bar. Benzino didn't know it, but Chin was already beginning to feel a strong attraction to NAYA. The DJ was doing his thing as the slow jam FALSETTO filled the club and the chicks working the club danced seductively and collected their dough. The power of the pussy was truly amazing! Benzino carefully scanned the dimly lit room looking for his target. Not to his surprise he spotted Tiffany sitting over in the purple and white leather couches. Surrounding her was four of the approximately twenty chicks that were working the club. He would keep a close eye on her and wait for the right moment. Then he would make his move.

Chapter 24

Tiffany saw them as soon as they entered the club. She was getting her shoulders massaged and feeling the intense euphoria of the triple-stacked E-pill that she was rolling off of. She tensed up.

"What's the matter boo-boo? You see something you don't like?" asked Princess, the cutie giving her the massage.

"A little trouble just walked in the door. Nothing we can't handle though," Tiffany said fearlessly.

Survival and betrayal had long ago instilled in her a deep seeded and festering hate for men. When she did fuck a man there was always an ulterior motive behind her actions. Her natural father which she had been greatly attached to since birth, abandoned her and her mother.

"When is my daddy coming home?" she would ask her mother.

After several failed relationships with men and women, her mother met and moved in with the man who she thought was the answer to all of her prayers. But this man, along with his two sons, would turn out to be Tiffany's worst nightmare. In the beginning Tiffany immediately formed a bond with her mother's boyfriend who had treated her like his own. The family would take outings like picnics, trips to the zoo, and once even a week-long vacation to Disneyworld in California. Her step brothers were five and seven years older than she was and were very protective of her. But when Tiffany turned ten years old two significant events took place that would forever changing her life. The first was her mother being diagnosed with breast cancer. The second was the recognition of the physical changes in her body. She would wear big shirts and pants in the beginning in an attempt to conceal her spreading hips and sprouting tits. But she began to develop so quickly that her big clothes became useless.

She was already beautiful and got a lot of attention in school, but now the guys a couple years older than her with raging hormones began to give her extra attention. Her mother began to get more and more sick and eventually had to go into the hospital for chemotherapy. The chemo made her mother begin to lose her hair, as well as the interest of her boyfriend. Tiffany began to notice how the interactions between her and her father had changed. The occasional landing and lingering of a hand on her breast. Or how he began to coincidentally have to use the bathroom while she was taking a shower behind the see through glass doors. She was naïve at first and just brushed it off. By the time she turned twelve years old, she stood 5 foot seven and had curves that would make the average woman envious. By the time her mother had finally lost the battle with cancer and passed away her stepfather had begun forcibly raping Tiffany. One day her step brothers had come home and caught their father in her room in the act. Tiffany had thought that she had finally been rescued. Now somebody else knew what was going on. But they, being cut from the same cloth as their father, had other plans.

"If you don't let us get some, we are going to the police," they had told him. And that was what had happened over the next two years. On one of these occasions was when Tiffany had been thrown into a whirl of confusion. She had almost become accustomed to them shoving themselves up in her and grunting a few times until it was over. She had even found out that if she twisted her hips a certain way or contracted her pussy muscles that she could make them finish the whole ordeal much quicker. But one day they had come into her bedroom and stripped her naked. Her stepfather then had his sons stand on either side of her and hold her legs open, high and wide. She watched in confusion as her stepfather lowered his face towards her pussy with his tongue sticking out.

When he began licking her pussy she gasped for air and bit her bottom lip. She tried to fight the feeling, as what felt like bolts of electricity began shooting through her whole body. Soon her hips started to sway and her eyes rolled back in her head...and they all noticed her reaction.

"Oh? So, this little slut likes this huh?" her stepfather asked and started licking faster. She was shaking her head no, but her breathing was becoming heavier and heavier. When her stepbrothers began to suck on her now rock hard nipples and her stepfather began to rhythmically slide two fingers in and out of her wetness, she felt a new feeling that she had never felt before. It seemed to start in the bottom of her feet and build in intensity as it slowly traveled up through her thighs. When she came she screamed like a wild animal, as she felt sensations that she had never felt before. The experience and the fact that she had enjoyed the feeling so much, disgusted her enough to make up her mind to put an end to it. So at fourteen years old she packed a bag and ran away. Tiffany took an Amtrak train from Georgia to New York to find her grandmother that she'd never met before, who lived in Brooklyn. Tiffany knocked nervously on her grandmother Grace Williamson's apartment door in the projects with a stomach full of butterflies. She knew that if this woman didn't acknowledge and accept her, that she would be doomed to survive in the cold and unforgiving streets of NYC. Fortunately her grandmother accepted her with open arms and no questions asked. Tiffany quickly became a main attraction in the PJ's due to the group of girls that she gravitated towards. She remembered the interactions that she had witnessed her mother have with other women before the relationship with her stepfather, and having developed such a passionate hate for men, she began to experience sexual relations with chicks. She grew to love her grandmother dearly who was sort of like the Big Momma of her project building. But Tiffany would never forget the day that she returned to the apartment after being out all night with the crew of girls that she hung out with. When she swung open the apartment door and saw her grandmother hanging from the ceiling with her tongue cut out, she vowed that she would never love anyone again. She also vowed to get the people responsible for her death. She smiled as she watched NAYA set down the Corona and orange juice in front of Chin and Benzino. It was funny how things played themselves out. She couldn't believe her luck when Veesha came blabbing about the infamous Benzino, the man under Icon who was rumored to be responsible for her grandmother's brutal murder. But the fact that Curt and Lamar were supposed to hit some warehouse and he was sitting in a place where she was known to hang out at was no coincidence. That was the reason she had sent over two of the most seductive women in the club. Tiffany knew the power of the pussy of course... she had one! Tiffany figured that things probably went sour at the warehouse and now he was here with this Chinese dude for her. Well, she thought, I have other plans.

* * *

It had been a hectic morning, Benzino was thinking. His nerves were in knots and he could feel the tension building from these recent events in his muscles. Or at least that was what he rationalized in his mind as he took another sip of the ice cold Corona. He knew that he shouldn't be drinking alcohol, but he figured one beer couldn't hurt. Maybe it would relax him a little. He looked over at Chin, who Naya had persuaded to buy a lapdance. Chin was smiling ear to ear as Naya straddled him and was slowly grinding her ass into his crotch. He nervously sucked down his orange juice as he enjoyed the show. Tina, the other dancer that had originally approached them reappeared in front of Benzino.

"Your friend seems to be having a good time. Are you gonna let me dance for you baby?" she asked Zino.

Benzino opened his mouth to respond only to find himself slurring his words. He looked up into Tina's smiling face and saw that she appeared blurred in his vision. He not only saw one Tina, he saw two.

"What the fu-?" He started as he looked over at Chin whose head was rolling to one side.

Benzino saw that something had gone terribly wrong and attempted to get up out of his seat. He realized that he had no control over his motor functions as he flipped backwards in his chair and crashed heavily to the floor banging his head. Chin also attempted to make a move but with the amount of drugs that Tiffany had put in their drinks, all it took was for Naya to wrap her arms around him to subdue the Chinaman. Benzino remembered the guns in his coat and made a weak attempt to reach for them. Had he not been so heavily drugged, the spiked heel that came stomping down on the back of his hand would have caused him to scream out in agony. But it was only dull pain and when he looked up into the barrel of a shiny chrome sawed off 12-gauge shotgun he knew he was in a fucked up situation.

"So," Tiffany said walking up next to the chick holding the shotty.

"It seems like our guests had cruel intentions," she said removing the submachine guns from Benzino's coat.

Benzino looked around and saw about twelve red dots all pointing directly at his face. The strip club had cleared out and topless cuties in thongs stood with an arsenal of various weapon pointed at Benzino and Chin waiting for Tiffany's instructions.

"Tie em' up," was the last thing Benzino heard before his world faded into darkness.

Chapter 25

When Buck had first seen the headline in the newspaper about Lucy's brutal slaying, his first and only concern was how it was going to affect his brother. Buck had also known about Lucy's battle with her drug addiction, but he had seen it firsthand from a whole other more personal level. About six months earlier one of the local young hustlers had come to the shop in a burnt orange drop suburban because one of his twelve television screens had burned out when he was down in Daytona. He had known the dude for a long time and he was a respected customer, so when he brought his truck in Buck handled the problem personally.

"Yo Buck," Tone had said," I only got one DVD wit me and it's of me and my crew freakin this bitch. If you got another one you might wanna put that in."

"What the fuck folk? You think I ain't seen pussy before?" asked Buck as he pushed the play button on the remote to test the new screen.

Tone had known the chick Lucy use to mess with Bucks brother and that was why he had tried to stop him. But it was too late.

"Oh shit! What is this, some rape shit?" asked Buck.

"Nah bruh, we just gave shorty an eight-ball and she touched-up the whole team."

But now as Buck watched Donovan out of the back door of their house, it looked like his brother was taking it pretty good. Donovan was working up a good sweat shooting baskets on their NBA regulation height half court basketball goal. Buck was really concerned about all the time that Donovan was spending at home. Donovan had never really had a social life, because he had pretty much spent all of his time with Lucy. But now that they weren't together, Buck had noticed that every time he came home Donovan was there. But now he was working on doing something about that.

"What's up big bro?" Buck asked headed towards where he was shooting around.

Donovan heard the voice of his little brother and turned around right after releasing a long three-pointer. Swish. Nothing but net.

"Hey youngun. I'm just trying to get a good sweat in. Getting a little exercise. That's all."

"How you been holding up? We haven't really kicked it too tough since you been home," said Buck trying to ease into where he was going with the conversation.

Donovan walked over towards his brother slowly bouncing the basketball.

"I ain't gonna front youngon, this has been a rough homecoming. I'm still trying to work myself out of the war zone mentality. You know it's hard after having it mentally programmed into you everyday that you're a killing machine. That your sole purpose is to seek out the enemy and kill. The platoon sergeant I was under wouldn't tolerate any form or sign of weakness. So now I'm home, and the expectation is that I just have this smooth transition back into society and live happily ever after. Well I'm here to tell ya, it ain't that easy."

Buck took in his brothers words thoughtfully, but there was no way he could truly understand what he was going through.

"I had no idea what you were dealing with Don. But I want you to understand that I am here for you and willing to help out any way I can."

"Well you could start by hooking me up with one of them cuties you know. Some female companionship would be nice. You know Lucy was really the only woman that I-," Donovan started but his sentence trailed off.

Buck couldn't believe that it was going to be this easy. He didn't want to lead on that he and Shay had already been playing matchmaker on the low. Buck had never seen Shay's cousin, or so he thought, but E had said the chick that came to the shop with Shay was all that.

"I don't know Don. You know how some of the chicks are that I come across. But let me see what I can do."

"Yeah, because when I went to church with ma last week them women wanted to attack me," said Donovan with a nervous smile.

Buck thought about Shay and where she said she was going with her cousins son and couldn't help but laugh himself.

"Yeah man, them church cuties will eat a good man alive!"

Buck hadn't realized that he had left the door open until he heard the barking. Any body else that would have heard the well trained monsters coming towards them would have been scared shitless. But, he turned around just in time to catch all 180 pounds of playful Rottweiler full in his chest.

"Oh shit!"said Donovan as Corrupt tackled Buck and started playfully licking him in his face.

But he had laughed two seconds to soon as Sheeba blindsided him doing the same.

"Aw come on girl," Donovan said falling to the ground laughing but still playfully wrestling with his dog."Ya'll mafuckas too big for this shit."

They'd had the dogs since pups and this was the first time that the dogs had caught them together since Don had been home. They wrestled with the dogs for a few minutes and then the dogs ran back into the house. They laid their huffing and sweating and tired just like they had when they were younger, and the dogs were much smaller.

"Yo let's go inside and clean up. I want you to take a ride with me somewhere?" said Buck.

Donovan got up and brushed himself off.

"Where we headed?"

"Just come on and don't ask so many questions. You trust your little brother, don't you?"

Of course he trusted his younger brother. As a matter of fact he realized that besides his mother, there was no one else walking the planet that he trusted. A half hour later they were cleaned up and headed to Knoxville in the Caddy. Three-six Mafia pounded from the backseat as Buck cruised down I-81 doing 85 mph in the afternoon sun. Donovan had to admit, getting away from the town for the first time since he'd come home did relax him a little. Buck looked over at Donovan who was deep in thought and decided to fuck with him. He reached up over his sun visor and pulled out a sandwich bag with some exotic green and a natural leaf blunt wrap paper.

"Grab the wheel and steer the car," Buck said letting go of the steering wheel.

"Oh shit! Come on bro. We doing over 80 miles an hour and you know I don't like doing this shit," said Donovan grabbing the wheel and easily maneuvering the Caddy.

This wasn't the first time they had done this. As a matter of fact every time Buck use to go to stereo shows in Atlanta or Texas to meet face to face with vendors, Donovan would at some point grab the wheel so he could twist-up a fatty. It had been a few years, but Donovan hadn't lost his touch. When Buck was almost done rolling his blunt Donovan saw the opportunity to get a little payback. They were in the slow lane on the four lane interstate and quickly approaching the rear of an 18 wheeler. Buck looked up and saw the truck and hit the blinker to signal they were changing lanes. He noticed that Donovan hadn't moved the wheel to change lanes and looked over at him to see him with an evil grin.

"You like playing games, huh?" said Donovan holding steady in the lane.

"Come on Don! Switch lanes before we hit the-"Buck started saying as Donovan swerved the Caddy missing the rear truck bumper by inches.

"Yo, you trippin bro. That shit wasn't funny. You almost made me fuck up the blunt," Buck said smiling but scared to death.

"Aw, relax bruh and light that thing," said Donovan.

Buck looked at him like he was nuts. Donovan had always hated weed smoke.

"Since when did this smoke stop bothering you?"

"Since them Iraqi prostitutes turned me on to some real green. Now light that shit and pass it, unless you too cool to smoke with your big bro."

Now Buck was confused as well as a little worried. Donovan had always been the goody-goody. He would drink a beer every now and then but any drug was definitely out of the question. Buck looked at Donovan curiously.

"Like I said lil-bro, there's a lot about me that has changed. But don't worry I can handle myself."

Not knowing what else to say, Buck fired up. The stress level over in the middle- east was high to say the least. Donovan hadn't smoked as many times as his talk game led Buck to believe, only three times in fact, but he had enjoyed the relaxing feeling he got from the high. But now as he waited for Buck to pass him the blunt, he felt a sort of nervous anticipation. After a few pulls Buck passed the blunt and Donovan hit it. This was actually the first time Don smoked a blunt. He had smoked out of weed pipes and joints, but never nothing that hit like this. He choked.

"Damn bruh. You alright?" asked Buck as Don sounded like he was coughing up his lungs.

Don wiped the tears from his eyes and took another hit. This time he held it in, laid his head back on the headrest and blew the smoke out of his nose. No Donovan thought to himself, this blunt shit was definitely different.

"Here you go bruh, I'm good," he said passing the blunt back to Buck. "It don't take much for me to feel a buzz."

The atmosphere became laid back as both brothers zoned out and slowly nodded in unison with the music. They entered Knoxville and cruised through a couple of the neighborhoods they were familiar with. The honeys and hustlers were out in the projects and everybody turned heads, as the showcar caught their attention. After putting his floss game down, Buck headed to the hottest clothes spot in the city. He pulled into the parking lot to see that it was fairly empty. Donovan looked at Buck curiously.

"What are we doing here?"

"Let's just say this. Them sweats and fatigues ain't gonna do you no justice in your social life. So this is my homecoming gift to you," Buck said turning off the stereo and getting out of the car.

"Come on."

Donovan reluctantly got out of the car and followed Buck into the store. He had never really cared much about his wardrobe. As long as it was clean and it fit right, he was good. Donovan knew that he was far from a bad looking man. But he really had never considered what significance his wardrobe played. As soon as they entered the store they were met by a curvy white chick, with micro-braids that ran down her back to her ass. She was ghetto but jazzy in her low rider jeans and Manolo blahniks. She had seductive hazel eyes, but a little too much eyeliner.

"How yall fellas doing today?" asked the salesgirl making conversation. Her eyes lit up when she saw Buck's watch and he figured she was probably working on commission. She smiled at Donovan.

"What's up shawty? We bout' to make you a grip. Let me see ten of your newest and hottest outfits. Shirts and jeans. Let's see what you think we would look good in and then we'll go from there," Buck said.

"O.K., I gotchu. My name is Amanda and I am here to uh....serve you," she said with a flirtatious smile, "what sizes will you fellas need?"

"Let's start out with 38's and 40's."

"I've been a solid 36 in the waist for years," said Donovan.

"Yeah and you need to loosen up a little...literally," said Buck seriously, but joking.

"Aight, give me a few minutes and meet me by the dressing room," said Amanda and disappeared off into the large store.

Two other sistahs who were also salesgirls looked at Buck disapproving. You snooze, you loose, Donovan thought as he shrugged his shoulders and headed over to the sneaker wall.

"You still wear size 11's?" Buck asked Donovan looking at some Bathing Apes and all white Air Force ones.

"Yeah, but you really don't have to do this."

Buck ignored his statement and grabbed another pair of sneakers and two pair of boots. He was gonna let the other chicks get the sale for the shoes, but changed his mind when he remembered the look they gave him.

"Here we go fellas. Let's start with these," she said laying down 5 outfits. She disappeared again.

"She was moving so fast, I couldn't give her the shoes," joked Buck.

Buck had to admit, the chick had good taste. She had fly outfits from Gino Green, Red Monkey, Moneyville, which was a hot new line on the rise, and Imperial Junkie. Donovan began by looking at price tags.

"Oh hell no bruh! $460 for a pair of jeans? Do you know what I could buy with that money?"

"Just try em on," Buck insisted.

Realizing that he had no wins he tried the clothes on in the dressing room. By the time Donovan came out, Amanda had came back with the other outfits as well as the shoes. He had on a studded Gino Green Global hoodie, a new pattern flavor Red Monkey jeans and white air force ones, when two lovely ladies strolled in the front entrance. Klock Wurk wasn't only a hot spot for mens fashions, but womens as well. The two honeys were both jaw droppers, but the deep chocolate complexioned seductress, with legs that seemed to go on forever, locked eyes with Donovan as she passed the dressing room area.

"Damn bruh, you see shawty sizen you up?"

Donovan locked eyes with her and smiled as she passed in her Roberto Cavalli dress that was color coordinated with her Louis Vitton purse. She smiled and kept it moving. A large man appeared from the back of the store.

"Long time, no see Buck. What's it been two weeks big spender?" said Tex the owner of Kloc Wurk.

"My man Tex. What's good playa? I brought my big bro through to spend some money witcha. Ya peoples been taking care of us real good," said Buck referring to Amanda. Kloc Wurk was still a fairly new store, but it was the hottest spot between there and Memphis to go shopping and Buck had given Tex a lot of business.

"I'm gonna take all of these, including those shoes over there and the outfit that he's got on," Buck told Amanda and handed her his black card.

"Hold up. I just got the first shipment of my new clothing line I started. It's called En Vivo and the shit is hot. I'll be right back," said Tex and went into the store stockroom.

While they were waiting, legs approached Donovan and put a phone number in his hoodie's pocket.

"Call me," she whispered in his ear with an African accent.

He was stunned as he watched her pay for her merchandise and left the store with her friend. Buck watched it all, smiling the whole time.

"Check these out," Tex said returning with his hot new En Vivo designs.

"Oh yeah Tex. This is what it is right here playa. Let me get one in each of them flavors," he said to Tex." Ring this up too, "Buck told Amanda.

"So are ya'll going to that concert day after tomorrow at the arena?" asked Amanda.

Buck was trying to keep it on the low, but figured now was as good of a time as any to let the cat out the bag...a little.

"Yeah we gonna swing through and check it out. If Trey Songs and J-Holiday are performing the hot new joints they got out, it's gonna be flooded with cuties," said Buck.

Donovan put two and two together and figured out what his brother was up to. He didn't protest as Buck thought he might have. Donovan was really ready to move forward with his life and he figured if his successful younger brother was willing to help, it was only a blessing. Lord knows he needed one. They left Kloc Wurk and went to Fridays to eat, where once again Donovan caught the attention of quite a few ladies. They hit the interstate an hour later and headed back to town. Maybe things are changing for the better he thought as he watched the reddish orange sun descend on the mountainous horizon. He certainly hoped so.

Chapter 26

Shay watched Jayonne sleeping in the car seat. She knew he was tired. Today was probably the first time in a while that he had any interaction with other children. He also seemed to enjoy her friends and people at church making such a fuss over him. She was really becoming concerned about the reality of her cousin's uncertain future. She could tell by the look in her eyes that her situation was taking a toll on her. Destiny had always been outgoing and self motivated. But her short relationship, if that was what you wanted to call it, with Jayonne's sperm donor, had taken its toll on Destiny's life. This character Lucky had blew in and out of her life and the only good that came from it was Jayonne. Shay wasn't sure how Destiny would react to her playing matchmaker with Buck's brother Donovan, but she would soon find out. Shay had never met Donovan, but she had heard enough about him to believe that he and Destiny may be a good match. She had heard the story from Buck about Donovan's ex-girlfriend and it broke her heart. She was from the projects and had witnessed firsthand the turmoil and devastation that drug addiction can have on families and relationships. Shay pulled into one of the marked parking stalls in front of Destiny's townhouse.

"Come on baby, we're home," Shay said over her shoulder waking Jayonne out of his sleep. When she got to Destiny's door she saw a crown Victoria with blacked-out windows pull out of a parking spot headed towards the exit. She didn't pay it much attention as she knocked on the door carrying Jayonne. Destiny was on the couch wearing sweats and a cutoff shirt, crunching numbers for her business venture on a pad. She jumped up off the couch barefoot and pushed her reading glasses up so they sat on top of her head. She opened the door excitedly wanting to tell Shay about her day and saw that her son was asleep in Shay's arms.

"Take him and lay him down on his bed," she whispered. "I have something important I want to tell you," said Destiny.

"Good, I need to holla atchu too," Shay whispered back and took Jayonne to his room.

Destiny wondered what that could be about. Well, she figured, I'll find out soon enough, as she heard Shay coming back down the stairs.

"So, you first. Shoot," said Destiny.

"Oh no. I saw the look in your eyes when you opened the door. What's on your mind?"

Destiny tried to find the right words to start.

"Let's sit on the couch" said Dez.

Now Shay was getting nervous. Most of the time when people had bad news they, wanted you to sit down. They sat on the sofa.

"You remember the place I use to work for where they were about to make me a manager?"

"The place that sold thongs and freaky stuff? Hell yeah how could I forget. You remember all the stuff I brought from there," said Shay. Of course she did. She helped her pick out most of it.

"So, you remember how much I liked my job. Well I found a place for a lingerie store that was perfect. I went out and looked at it today and priced the equipment and inventory and gave the lady a deposit and month's rent and-"

"Whoa, whoa, whoa! Deposit-store-inventory. What are you talking about Destiny?"

Destiny caught her breath and calmly told Shay what she had done and her innovative idea of combining it with a beauty parlor. Pretty Kitty.

"Well it doesn't really sound like a bad idea, but hello?! The figures you have here in fixing the place up and inventory alone come to over 30 grand. Where do you plan on getting that kind of money?"

"Well...um...that was kinda the other thing I wanted to tell you about," said Dez nervously.

"OK, I'm waiting," said Shay eyeing her suspiciously.

Destiny proceeded to tell her about the money that she had stashed away in the safe deposit box and how much was there. She told her that she could have it set up and a GRAND OPENING in two weeks. Shay couldn't front. She admired her cousin's determination and motivation in the face of adversity. And that reminded her.

"But honey," Shay started, "You're on the run for two suspected homocides."

"Oh. And there was something else," Destiny started and Shay stared expectantly.

"I put it in your name."

Shay ran everything her cousin had told her through her mind and began to become irritated, until she caught the look in Destiny's eyes. She knew the look and hadn't seen it since before her pregnancy. She also knew that in the back of Destiny's mind, that she felt this may be her last chance to live out her dream. Everything melted away except the love that she had for her cousin. Shay broke into a bright smile.

"Looks like we're going into business together," said Shay hugging Destiny.

Tears flowed freely from Destiny's eyes at the thought of the love Shay was showing her. Destiny remembered Shay had something to tell her too.

"So what'd you want to talk to me about?"

"Well it was about getting you out of the house and maybe finding a friend," said Shay.

"And what, you had some plan to help me find this friend?"

"Well that was…kinda what I wanted to talk to you about," said Shay hitting her cousin with her own newsbreaking line.

Destiny without much effort thought back to the last time she'd gotten some dick. Dam she thought, the right kind of pussy pounding right about now was just what she needed. But she was not the one for meaningless sex. She wanted her pipes cleaned lord knows, but the plumber had to be somebody special.

"OK, what have you been up to Shay?"

"Well you know about the guy I've been seeing, the one that owns the audio shop?"

"How could I not know who Buck is by now? The mystery man of your dreams that somehow I've never met."

"That's not fair. He's really busy and the little bit of time we do get to spend together well you know-"

"Anyway."

"Anyway, he's got tickets to a J. Holiday and Trey Songs concert out in Knoxville. He's got a brother who sounds like a really nice guy-"

"Sounds like? You haven't seen him? Haven't met him?"

"Well no. But he's only a couple years older than Buck and Bucks a cutie," she said.

Destiny thought about it. What was the worse case scenario? Bucks brother could look like Shabba Ranks, Destiny thought as she reflected on some of the guys Shay had dated in the past. But it was only for one night and she owed her cousin that much. Plus she would get to hear two of her favorite artists sing songs that she could dream had some meaning in her life.

"I'm in Shay, but this is only for you. You know me well and if this niggah look like whodunit, I'm gonna get yo ass back."

But Shay had high hopes for the blind date. Buck had told her more info about Donovan, but she figured that she would let Destiny and Donovan get to know each other on their own. They talked some more and then Shay headed home. Destiny lay in bed and tried to fight the feeling again that was slowly rising. The feeling that she was being watched.

* * *

Hova had just crossed the Mason Dixon line, from Pennsylvania into Maryland. He had been on the road for four hours and had at least another six to go. He was kicking himself in the ass for not thinking to make this trip earlier. He wasn't one-hundred percent sure that he would find Destiny and Jayonne by visiting his sister Shay, but it was as good a possibility as any. And he was running out of options. As he drove, there were two main questions that were flowing through his head. One was what the outcome would be with his good friend Chulo's scheme to retaliate against the DEATH SQUAD. And secondly and most important, the whereabouts and safety of Destiny and Jayonne.

Chapter 27

They had been watching her. She had left earlier than they had anticipated this morning. And she had actually almost spotted Chulo and his henchmen in the Maroon chevy mini-van. Had it not been for the heavy rain falling this dreary Monday morning, the distinctly out of place vehicle would have stood out like a sore thumb. Glenda had made various stops since earlier this morning and now they thought, this will be the opportune moment for the abduction. Earlier Chulo had considered calling the whole thing off. He really only wanted the people responsible for his nieces murder to be held accountable and punished for their actions by means of street justice. After Icon's wife had entered the gift shop, the mini-van pulled into the parking lot and parked next to her Jaguar. The three men then proceeded to pass around the hundred dollar bill, filled with high grade uncut powder cocaine mixed with crystal meth. The combination had them ready to go up against an army. So in extra go mode, they waited on their victim.

* * *

"Would you like to have this gift wrapped," asked the elderly cashier in the gift shop.

"Yes ma'am, I would appreciate that," said Icon's wife. It had been a hectic morning for Glenda, running around making preparations for the small surprise gets together for her husband's birthday. She had left extra early in an attempt to get everything done, so she could go meet up with her….friend. She was actually making plans to bring the affair to an end. Guilt had begun to get the best of her and what had started out as an act of retribution had actually turned into a hindrance that could turn into big trouble. She had turned her boy toy's world so far upside down that he begun to ask when she was leaving her husband, which of course she had absolutely no intention of doing. She had become accustomed to her lavish lifestyle and the finer things. See before Glenda met Icon, she was extremely good friends with them twins broke and hard times. Glenda had no intentions on hanging out with those lowlifes again. So today she decided to terminate her little escapade on the side.

Glenda exited the store glad to see that the rain had let up significantly. She opened her umbrella to shield her from the drizzle and took out her cell phone. She pushed the autodial on her phone to call home. Icon was sleeping soundly when she had left this morning and she moved quietly in an attempt not to wake him. As she started out into the parking lot Icon answered the home phone.

"What's up baby?" he answered looking at the caller ID.

"Hi," said Glenda said in a sing song voice," I was just calling to see if you were up. Maybe wanted to do something today."

They had been getting along pretty good, so it wasn't totally unexpected that she wanted to spend time with him. He knew she was still going through the healing process of losing Jake.

"Sure, I don't mind. My slate is clean for the day," said Icon. She was approaching her car and reached in her purse removing her car keys.

"OK, baby. I only have a couple more stops and I should be there in say, an hour or so. Do you need anything?"

She stuck her key in the lock paying no attention to the mini-van with the dark tinted windows. Glenda's back was to the van when she heard the side door slide open. She saw the reflection of a man in a black ski-mask in her window and her heart jumped in her throat.

"IIICOON!!" she screamed into the phone before dropping it. He tried to grab her but her reflexes were quick. She dropped and slipped out of the first kidnappers hold, but when she tried to getaway she was savagely tackled by a second attacker. She hit the ground hard.

"Get the fuck off me! Help! Somebody please help me," Icon heard his wife scream on the other end of the phone. Furious that she had put up a fight and was making this difficult, the first attacker kicked her hard in the stomach. That took any fight that she may have had left in her, as she balled up into a fetal position. They quickly picked her up and tossed her in the van. Chulo had heard her call out Icon's name into the phone and couldn't believe his luck as he picked the phone up. Hopefully he had heard it all and would know that shit was real.

"Yo," Chulo said into Glenda's cell phone.

"I don't know who this is, but you have no clue what you're getting yourself into."

"Oh yes, Mr. Icon," Chulo said mockingly," I do. We'll be in touch."

Chulo ended the call and hopped in the van. A few people had come out of the gift shop. As they sped away, people memorized the license plate. But once police ran them they would see that they were stolen. Now, Chulo thought, it's time to put the next phase of his plan into effect.

* * *

Icon put the phone down slowly into its charger. We'll be in touch, the voice on the other end had said. Someone had kidnapped Glenda. They hurt her. He could hear her struggling in the background. Icon could feel his blood starting to boil. Relax, he told himself. He knew that he could outthink most men and something told him that there was a bigger picture here that would soon reveal itself. Something was definitely going terribly wrong. He had been trying to get in touch with Columbia and Benzino since the night before with no luck. Since they had known him, he had never not been able to contact either of them.

He had begun to ponder the most recent events. Could this be tied into Hova and the girl he had been trying to locate. He knew that the statement he made about Hova's sick mother had definitely struck a nerve. Or was the taking of his wife some type of leverage; a bargaining chip so Icon would call off his goons. Then he thought the worst. Could these people have snatched Columbia and Benzino as well? Impossible. He considered all the recent murders connected to Jakes death and all the bodies burned and dumped in rivers tied to 45 pound plates over the years. It soon became overwhelming and he needed a drink. He was starting to feel alone and vulnerable and weakness had never been one of his character defects.

He didn't like the feeling that he felt. His whole life he had only learned how to deal with things that he didn't like in one way. He eliminated them. They said they would be in touch. He considered calling O'Connor, but figured only as a very last resort. He went to the liquor cabinet and poured himself a glass of $600 a bottle cognac. He took a slug and felt the welcome relaxing burn of the alcohol as it went down. He looked at the phone. Yes, he would wait.

* * *

By nightfall last night Chin's men knew something was wrong. When he left with Benzino, Chin had told them that he would contact them once they had wrapped things up. After numerous attempts to contact him by his cell phone, they contacted his father. Master Wong asked for details of the events that had taken place. Master Wong had been a MADE MAN so to speak in the Chinese Mafia for years and had learned from experience that, in this life, especially when it came to certain family members, reassuring precautionary measures were best if taken. So, two years prior on Chin's twenty-first birthday he gave him a watch. A watch that he made Chin promise to wear at all times. But this was no ordinary watch. Master Wong had had a tracking device put in not only Chin's watch, but all of his immediate family members. The company that sold these watches could track the individual down by satellite anywhere on earth. Master Wong made the call and they found Chin in a matter of seconds. The strange location only added to their fears.

The five men in wet suits and scuba gear surfaced 10 feet away from the Mahogany and gold colored 80 foot luxury yacht. Tiff's Bitch was the name on the back panel of the machine that bobbed gracefully at the Marina on Long Island sound. Master Wong had said the place was called Cold Spring Harbor. Their reinforcements should be parked in the marina parking lot on standby by now. They saw the ladder that led on board. It seemed to be quiet, but it was a large boat. They didn't know what they were up against, but they knew they had to save their boss if he was on this boat. The lead man checked his wetsuit and withdrew his weapon. After he motioned to the others and they did the same, they started up the ladder.

* * *

Columbia couldn't believe she was here. She had considered other options, but due to the nature of the events that were happening to her, this just seemed to be the most logical. After what she had witnessed last night, she was about to lose it. She had been dreaming that she heard her father's voice again.

Only this time it wasn't that creepy voice. It was in the same beautiful voice that he used to sing her to sleep in when she was a very little girl.

My Princess-Princess You truly are my world And my Lord has sent to me, A gorgeous baby girl.

Her eyes had popped open when she heard her daughters familiar giggle. She gasped for air when she saw the silhouette of a man's body that distinctly resembled her father standing over her daughters crib. She grabbed one of the knives off her nightstand and threw it. It went through the vision and lodged in the wall above her daughter's crib. The silhouette turned and appeared to be looking at her and then vanished into the wall behind the crib.

That was the final straw. This morning she called her babysitter and set out to try and find some answers. Now as she looked at the address in her hand and the number on the rundown brownstone she was standing in front of and saw that they matched, she had second thoughts. It was something about the building that made her feel uneasy. Wait. No, it wasn't the building, but the strangely mysterious atmosphere that surrounded the building.

"Can I help you?" said a short fat man in a too tight knockoff Coogi t-shirt. He seemed to appear from nowhere on the nearly deserted city street.

"I-I'm looking for-"

"Did you call earlier?"

"Yes."

"Inside. She's been waiting on you."

Columbia apprehensively fell in step behind the man as he led her into the building. As soon as she entered the building the presence of uneasiness that she felt outside multiplied times ten. She stopped. The fat man turned around.

"Come on. It'll be OK," he said. She didn't believe him-at all. They came to an apartment in the back of the building where he entered with his own key.

"Maritza is the best in her field," he said looking over his shoulder. Both sides of the dark hallway were lined with tall candles and with pictures of the Virgin Mary holding baby Jesus. But Columbia didn't feel like Jesus would have anything to do with this place. They were met by an older woman in all black. Columbia couldn't tell if she was Asian or Latino by her facial features, but her head full of long thick black curls led her to believe she was the latter.

"Thank you Milo. That's all for now," she said dismissing him.

Columbia followed Maritza deeper into the apartment. She was thinking, dam even with the candles It's dark as fuck in this bitch.

"Ah yes. Dark as fuck it is. But it is necessary to communicate beyond." Columbia stopped cold.

"How did you know-what-what, I was thinking," asked Columbia trembling.

"I am Maritza. Come," she said and continued walking. They entered a large room that seemed to have what appeared to be hundreds of candles lined on the surrounding shelves. There was a table in the middle of the room with a chair on each side.

"Please sit," Maritza said motioning to the chair opposite her. Columbia slowly sat down looking around the room.

"Try to relax and start from the beginning," said Maritza. Columbia ran down the sequence of events, from the first phone call at the record label, up to the bizarre occurrence that happened last night. When Maritza asked her how her father had died Columbia froze.

"You have to be completely honest with me if you want my help. It's the only way I can help you," Maritza declared. So Columbia told her the story of how her parents were murdered and they were left orphaned.

Maritza eyed her curiously waiting for her to continue. Columbia thought, shit you read my mind before, figure out the rest. Maritza smiled and Columbia swore she saw some hint of recognition.

"Wait I'll be right back?" Maritza said before leaving the room. She returned three minutes later with a cup and sat it on the table between them.

"There seems to be a strong attempt from your father's spirit to tell you something. Exactly what is what we need to find out," said Maritza taping a piece of plain white paper to the table.

"What's in the cup?" asked Columbia. "The blood of a virgin." Columbia wanted to bolt. She dared not ask where she got it from.

"What is your father's name?"

"His first name was Carlito." Maritza dipped her index finger into the cup and began to write his name in blood on the paper.

"What are you-?"

"Shhh! Silence," demanded Maritza.

Maritza carefully and meticulously wrote her father's name on the paper. When she was done she wiped her finger clean and reached across the table and joined hands with Columbia. As soon as they were holding hands Maritza began to chant, in some inaudible language that was foreign to Columbia. A gust of wind blew across the room causing the candles to flicker. Suddenly the paper with the blood on it burst into flames. But for some reason a calmness…a familiarity, came over Columbia. And she wasn't scared. When she looked in Maritza's eyes, all she saw was fire. Columbia could tell that she was looking directly into the pits of hell.

"My princess-princess," Maritza began to sing in her father's voice.

"Daddy?" questioned Columbia as a tear rolled down her cheek.

"Yes, my gorgeous baby girl," his voice continued from Maritza. "Anissa. I never meant to frighten you but I had to get your attention. My sins have doomed me for eternity. I have been watching you and you must change your ways or your fate will be the same. The end is nearer than you think. Repent and have everlasting life in heaven with streets of gold. With your mother. I couldn't let you go on without telling you the truth. My granddaughter is beautiful. Repent-Repent-Repent-"the voice faded away.

"No daddy wait! Please don't leave me-pleaasse," she sobbed. But her father's spirit had disappeared. She knew somehow that she would never hear from him again with his message delivered and understood. She looked at Maritza who was now drenched with sweat and out of breath. Columbia rose from the table.

"Thank you," she said to Maritza and left the apartment. The experience was surreal. She knew she had just come as close to hell as she ever wanted to.

Chapter 28

Benzino's head was throbbing. The affects of the drugs were wearing off. He tried to get his eyes to focus. The light was too bright. He tried to move his arms and legs but they were both bound. The last thing he remembered were-guns. Lots of guns! He shook his head trying to clear the fogginess. Where the fuck am I? He thought. He felt like his whole body was slowly rocking. No floating. What the hell did they drug us with?

And Chin. Where was he?

"Hisssss-hissssss."

Benzino felt a chill run up his spine at the sound. Now he was intensely alert. He slowly turned his head to where the sound was coming from only to have his worst fear confirmed. Not one, but two 17 foot and at least 10 inch in diameter thick snakes. Boa Constrictors.

"Move very slowly. Sudden movements make them nervous," he heard a voice come through a speaker in the ceiling. A woman's voice. He did move slowly as he propped himself against the glass wall. That was when he saw Chin.

"Your friend wasn't so lucky."

He saw a third snake. It was wrapped around the top portion of Chin's body. It was the tightest around his neck, where it had literally choked the life out of him. Chin was dead. His head was swollen and his eyes bulged, nearly hanging out of their sockets. When his instincts kicked in and he began to look for a way to escape, he realized that he wasn't in a room, but in a large glass tank.

Tiffany used the glass room as well as the yacht to entertain high dollar and private patrons, such as politicians and corporate executives, with private freak shows by girls from the club. It was located on the lower level, totally secluded from the main deck. Benzino scanned the area trying to find a clue that would tell him where he was.

"Your friend got his hands loose and tried that martial arts shit. Unfortunately any rapid movements make my babies nervous," said Tiffany approaching the outside of the glass making herself visible.

She was wearing a chordless headset microphone. Two other females appeared closely behind her. They were both holding AR-15 assault rifles.

"Do you have any idea why you are here Benzino?"

"Yeah, because you sent those clowns to rob me", he said.

"Yes. That's part of it. And I assume they met the same fate as your friend there," she said motioning to Chin. He looked at Chin again and then at the two snakes opposite him.

"You said that's part of it. What's the other part? If you are going to kill me you might as well do what you gotta do."

"You do work under Icon don't you?" she inquired.

"Yes, I oversee a few of his business operations. But what does he-"

"Oh cut the bullshit!" Tiffany screamed, "you know that cripple bastard is a cold blooded murderer-he killed my grandmother!"

She told him the story of how her grandmother had talked to the news people about the people in the black van. She finished by telling Benzino how she came home and found her grandmother hanging from the ceiling with her tongue cut out. He wondered if she knew that it was he who had personally committed the handiwork. No, that was impossible. There was no one else in the apartment. He was thorough when he checked it out afterwards.

He could see the resentment and determination for revenge in her eyes. But he also thought he saw something else. A sliver of daylight coming from the door at the top of the steps behind Tiffany and the chicks with the guns. It was quick, but he was sure that was what he saw.

"I want you to bring him to me. Icon. I need him secluded and I know that you are the one who can do it," she said. And that's when it happened. The glass exploded.

* * *

Five of the Chinese Mafia's top hit men had boarded the yacht. With their silencer attached weapons drawn, they covertly navigated the surface level of the vessel. They had split off in two groups and took separate sides of the yacht. It appeared to be vacant, but they knew by the size of it that there had to be another level. After they were sure that the surface was secure and they hadn't been detected, they maneuvered towards the door that led to the lower cabin.

As they approached it they heard a voice. One of them tried the knob and found that it was unlocked. The voice coming from inside was that of a woman.

"Cover me while I see what I can see," said the lead man.

He slowly opened the door. He saw the backs of the women and the weapons they were holding at their sides. Seeing that they had the upper hand because they had their backs to them, he motioned for the rest of the assassins to enter.

The one girl was so emotionally engaged in her tirade, that they were all able to enter undetected. And the girl's sloppiness would cost them their lives. Then they spotted Chin. All five raised their weapons simultaneously aimed at different targets. Three were aimed at the back of the women's heads. Two were aimed at the large snakes in the glass room. The leader nodded and they all fired. The glass exploded into a million pieces as did the young ladies heads.

"Pfft-ffft-Pffft-" was the sound of the silenced weapons. The smooth action of the Heckler and Koch 10 mm cannons ejected spent casings from the extended clips. Blood, hair and glass matted together in clumps on the ground. A large shard of glass from the room collapsing lodged in Benzino's shoulder. The snakes laid motionless with large chunks torn from their flesh.

"Be careful. The one wrapped around Chin is still alive," Benzino warned one of the men that was headed towards him.

"Untie him," the leader motioned to Benzino. He then walked over to where the large snake was wrapped around Chin. He grabbed it just below its head and put a bullet through its neck. Once all the commotion had been brought under control, one of the men pulled the glass out of Benzino's shoulder.

"We have to get him to a hospital," he said, "and someone has to inform Master Wong of what's happened to Chin. Let's get both of them out of here."

* * *

The anonymous phone call had dropped the missing pieces of the puzzle into place. It was late afternoon and finally the rain had come to a halt. Overall, it had been a nasty day to say the least. The caller had said that the whole thing was over some little hot in the ass young Puerto Rican girl, who had obviously been the niece of the kidnapper, this Chulo character.

The caller had said that the kidnappers would demand $400,000 from Icon for the safe return of his wife Glenda. They just wanted the people that had killed Chulo's niece. The people in the black van. But for $100,000 this anonymous caller would give him the location of his wife. He had to admit fair exchange wasn't robbery, and of course a half-million dollars for the safe return of his lifelong companion was a sum that he would pay without blinking. He knew too well, the rules and art of war. Even though they had their problems, he really deep down inside would be lost without the familiarity of her presence. In the early evening the call that he'd been waiting for came. It came from Glenda's cell phone. Everything the anonymous caller had stated has been confirmed. The caller asked for $400,000 to be delivered to a location in Far Rockaway Queens. They would then release Glenda unharmed and without a scratch. But they had already harmed her. He had intentions on making them pay. A smile came to his lips as he considered what they really wanted. They wanted the killers in the black van.

Icon was beginning to get really worried about Benzino and Columbia. He had finally contacted Columbia about an hour ago, but she was short with him. The tone in her voice, one that she never used with him, caught him off guard. She had the nerve to have and attitude after she had seemingly dropped off the face of the earth for a couple of days. Just like a woman he thought. He didn't have the time or the patience to try and figure out what her problem was. And with her carrying an attitude like that, the last thing he wanted to get her involved in was the kidnapping of his wife. That would only complicate matters more.

But Benzino was a totally different story. Knowing how important his position was, being the second in charge over Icon's business affairs, he would never ignore calls from Icon-unless something was wrong. Hundreds of thousands of dollars in Icon's funds were under the control of Benzino on a daily basis.

After setting up the drop-off of the funds to the anonymous phone caller, he began to set the plan in motion to get Glenda back and teach Chulo a lesson that he would never forget. Icon summoned the remaining members of the death squad for an emergency meeting at 'Butta Cutz'. An hour later P, AJ, and Sonny came in the rear entrance of the shop, just as Icon was ending a phone call. AJ was dark skinned, muscular, and had fetish for inflicting pain. He was recruited by Icon from Norfolk Virginia due to his reputation subjecting victims to punishment with a baseball bat. Sonny was brown skinned, from Miami and had hands to rival Sugar Ray in his day. Sonny was recruited after rumors of him punishing Zab Judah in the bathroom of the 40/40 club after Judah stepped on his Gators. P was a medium build light skinned brother from Harlem, that had originally run with a crew from Kingston Jamaica known for their murder game. P was a monster with anything that spit slugs and could hit a man between the eyes, with any handgun, from 50 yds away...with one eye closed. He was the closest of the crew to Zino, and he also hadn't heard from him in the past two days.

Icon informed them of the situation at hand. After hearing what Icon had planned to do, it was only reaffirmed that they were employed by a devious mastermind. The whole thing was to go down at ten o'clock tonight and timing Icon had told them, was of the utmost importance. Icon dismissed them with their orders and began putting the wheels of his plan in motion.

This was something that had to be done, Columbia thought as she crept across the damp grass leading up to the large house. She saw a light on in the bedroom and knew that he was home. She moved catlike and with a purpose. She picked the lock after disabling the alarm and slipped inside the back door. Columbia clutched her weapon tightly, feeling the weight of it in her hand. It was a cannon. Benzino gave her the snub nose .44 caliber revolver with the silencer as a Christmas present last year. He had jokingly told her, you can't bring a knife to a gunfight.

Yes this was necessary, she continued to tell herself. As she approached, she realized that he wasn't alone. He was on the couch and there was a woman with him. She saw the champagne bottle and the two glasses. This had all started with him. When a strobe light began to flash in a corner above the plasma TV, she realized that she had tripped a motion sensor that she wasn't aware of. Shit.

"Columbia?" asked Simpson startled. She had come to kill the man who carried out the hit on her parents.

"Yes," she said making herself completely visible.

"What's going on? What is this about?"

"It's about something I should have done a long time ago. This is retribution for the death of my parents that you killed," she said through clenched teeth.

"Columbia, what are you doing? Have you lost your mind?" asked the girl with Simpson, who she just realizes is the receptionist from 'ELITE'.

"No wait," Simpson started, "Let Columbia finish her talk about retribution for the death of the parents I killed.

Simpson began to laugh. "This bitch has lost her mind if she believes I am responsible for the death of her parents. I saved your fuckin life. Saved you from death or an existence of living in an orphanage!" Like I did, he wanted to add.

"Shut the fuck up, you piece of shit. You should have let me die. You had us broke and trained like fuckin dogs! We were too young to know the lives that you manipulated us into living. What kind of human being does what you did to two children? You sick fuck!"

Mona looked back and forth between Simpson and Columbia.

"What the hell are you two talking about? And why do you have that gun?" asked Mona.

Columbia pointed the .44 at Mona's head and fired. BOOM!

The huge slug made Mona's head explode like a grapefruit. The smell of her bowels loosening and blood filled the atmosphere. Simpson looked on in shock. Columbia got a little satisfaction from his expression. Blood, brains and Auburn weave slid down the wall behind the couch.

"Oh, does the visual disturb you? It was nothing to me. See, you have been out of the killing fields too long. But this is still my life. My double life. I've had a certain lets say revelation as of recent. And you Simpson, you must die," said Columbia leveling the cannon at Simpson's chest.

"No wait. I have money in a safe in the master bedroom. It's over 2 million dollars. You can have it all. I know it won't replace your parents or in any way be payment for the psychological torment you've been subjected to. But it will secure your daughter's future," said Simpson in a final plea for his life.

"Just please don't kill me. We can clean this up." He said referring to Mona, "and act like this never happened."

Columbia thought about it. But not for long. It was the perfect opportunity for her to take her daughter and start over somewhere fresh. They went up the carpeted steps and entered the luxurious master bedroom. Simpson removed the picture from the wall and began spinning the dial to open the safe.

"Slowly. Any sudden moves and-"

Simpson yanked the safe open, grabbed the 9 millimeter and tried to spin and get off a shot, but he was too slow. Columbia hit him once in the shoulder causing him to spin and drop his weapon.

"I was hoping that you gave me a reason. I was going to kill you anyway," she said before she hit him twice in the heart killing him instantly.

She cleaned out the safe and once she got home would find out that it was closer to three million. Yes, she thought, it was definitely time to repent and start over somewhere new with her daughter.

* * *

"You do know that my husband is going to kill you," said a tear stained face and angry Glenda.

She was sitting in a dimly lit room with her hands and feet bound. There were only two people guarding her. Two vanloads of Chulo's men had gone out to handle the money pickup and deal with the black van killers. The nerve of these people, Glenda thought. She was putting up a good front, but the truth was she'd never been this scared before in her life. Icon had sheltered her well, keeping her away from the violence and negativity she knew he was involved in over the years. And now as she looked at the guns that the men that were guarding her held, she trembled in fear, knowing that if they had to, they would use them on her.

She was attempting to scare them with her threat which they seemed to totally ignore as they continued to shovel more cocaine up their noses. When the huge Latino man had left he said that they were going to take care of something. It's time to make it happen was what he had said. She was still oblivious as to what this was all about, but she figured it was the inevitable, and what her husband had plenty of-money.

Something outside the window caught her attention. It was dark outside the darkness obscured the vision of whatever it was. But she had a feeling. A bad feeling.

* * *

Chulo and his men saw the black van slowly approaching. "Here it comes. Get ready," he said into a walkie talkie.

They were in two mini-vans ready to ambush the people who had killed Chulo's niece. The van stopped in front of the drop-off spot for the money, but nobody got out.

What's the fucking hold-up? The engine of the black van began revving. The tires began to spin burning rubber and the van took off racing down the dark street.

"I think they spotted us! Go, go after them! Don't lose that fuckin van!" screamed Chulo at the driver.

Chulo figured that this may be the only chance to get the people responsible for his niece's murder. He refused to put all this time, effort, and manpower into finding these people only to let them slip through his fingers. The black van turned a corner up ahead.

"Come on! Hit the gas, they're getting away!"

"I don't know what they have under the hood, but that thing is moving!" said the driver. They turned the corner and spotted the van up ahead. The street was still damp and the tires on the mini-van spinned when the driver hit the gas. The second mini-van slid around the corner just missing the first. They both sped off back to back in pursuit of the black van. The black van dipped in and out of traffic when it hit a main strip. There was an intersection up ahead. The light was red as all three vehicles quickly approached at 70 miles per hour through the streets of Queens.

The black van shot through the intersection.

"Stay on him! Don't loose them!" screamed Chulo anxiously. The first mini-van sped through, hot on the Death Squad's tail. Just as the second mini-van was entering the intersection it met full force wit a speeding ambulance headed to a shooting in the projects. Two men shot and a young girl had supposedly caught a stray. The impact caused the mini-van to roll and flip into a telephone pole. The twisted metal caught on fire and the full tank of gas caused it to burst in flames. But the occupants had already been killed from the double impact of the ambulance and the telephone pole.

Chulo watched it unfold through the back window. But he had no intention on stopping. They continued the chase. Chulo felt his anger rising. Now more deaths had been senselessly caused by these bastards. It was mandatory that they die. The black van began to pull away from them again as it picked up speed. It was headed towards the highway. Aw shit. But the mini-van was on them. Chulo saw them get onto the on ramp of the Belt Parkway headed back to Brooklyn.

The traffic on the parkway was light at this time of night.

"Pull up beside them. Maybe I can get a shot off or we can run them off the road," Chulo stated in desperation.

80 miles per hour.

90 miles per hour.

They pulled beside it. The windows were tinted black. Chulo rolled down the window and let off a shot disregarding the other cars on the road.

"BLOCKA! BOCK-BOCK!" sounded off the shots.

FUCK! The bullet proof driver's side window deflected the slugs effortlessly.

"The windows are bulletproof! Ram those bastards!" As if they heard Chulo the black van leaped forward and began to put distance between them. The black van had put about a quarter-mile between them. What the fuck is under that hood?!

The black van exited at Alantic Avenue. They hit the streets of Brooklyn at 70 miles an hour.Chulo's frustration rising.

They turned off Atlantic into an area of streets lined with warehouses. The black van skidded into a parking lot and disappeared behind one of the warehouses.

"Follow them!" When they turned into the parking lot, the van was nowhere in sight. They sped to the rear of the warehouse, only to see the black van sitting there. It was idling under the full moon and star lit sky in the middle of the rear parking lot.

"Get out and surround them!" Chulo barked. They grabbed assault rifles and filed out of the mini-van, taking up positions around the black van. It sat there idling. All five men stood with their weapons aimed. Ready to kill. Tired of waiting, Chulo gave the order.

"Fire!"

Balls of fire erupted from the barrels of the rifles as slugs tore into the black van. Almost simultaneously as the slugs ripped into the dummy van Icon had loaded with explosives, it exploded shooting hot steel everywhere. Chulo and his men were shredded instantly, killing them all. The remains of the van that had been lifted 20 feet in the air when it exploded, sat in the middle of the parking lot, a fiery ball of wreckage. The carnage would be a mess to clean up, as body parts lay scattered about the area.

* * *

Icon watched the screen go blank and turn into snow. He sat down the remote that he had used to control the black van from the back of 'Butta Cutz'. He knew the camera he had mounted to display the drivers view has been destroyed in the explosion. He figured as much. When he had been convinced by Benzino to purchase this equipment of technological genius from the developer in China, he never felt that he would have any use for it. What fools they were to fuck with him. Well they got what they were looking for.

* * *

Sonny pulled up the camera that was attached to the rope. He was standing on the roof with AJ and P, and had just confirmed that Glenda was in the building. She was in an apartment on the second floor and two men were guarding her. He saw that they were both doing some drug in powder form, but couldn't be sure of what it was. Coke or Meth would have their nervous system ready to react to the slightest sound, and that could prove to be most dangerous.

On the screen attached to his phone he'd seen Glenda squint in recognition of something she noticed outside the window. Their mission was to safely get her out of there and back home to Icon.

"Can you hit em' from the window?" asked P.

"Yeah I got this. They looked like bulls eyes sitting there shoveling that shit up they nose. Plus I'm ready to wrap this up and find out what's up with my niggah Zino," said P.

"Aight, strap up and let's boogie. The rope is at just the right length to line you up with the window. Me and AJ are going in and waiting by the entrance to the apartment for your signal," said Sonny.

As P knotted the rope, AJ and Sonny headed down to the second floor. Once they had left the roof P removed a half a blunt of some exotic from his pocket and fired up. He always got his mind right before he set it off.

* * *

Glenda watched as one of the men got up from the table.

"Gotta piss. I'll be right back," said Juan clutching his weapon and going down the hall to the bathroom.

"Take your time. Chulo and the rest of them should be coming in any minute," said Felipe getting up from the table. Fellipe walked over towards Glenda with his eyes wide and mouth twitching from the effects of the cocaine he'd been sniffing.

"You know I owe you for that shot you gave me earlier. You're in pretty good shape. I wasn't expecting you to react like that," he said as he rubbed his crotch and started to reach for her tit.

P had jumped off the roof and came swinging through the window on a rope clappin twin 10 mm Remington's, with extended clips. The window shattered and Felipe literally ate the first eight slugs taking them all in his face. He landed in like a bag of rocks as Sonny and AJ came crashing through the front door.

"I only got one. I don't see the other one," said P using one arm to untie Icon's wife and the other extended ready to fire.

Just then bullets began ripping through the wall.

"Get down! He's in one of the other rooms!" said Sonny.

"He's in the bathroom! It's down the hall!" Said Glenda remembering earlier when Chulo had taken her to use it.

The two bedroom apartment had one long hallway and the bathroom was at the end of it. P told Icon's wife to stay down as he crawled across the floor on his stomach headed towards the hallway.

A straight line of bullets ripped through the wall again just above P's head. AJ jumped over P and ran down the hallway blasting at the bathroom door. Juan let out a scream of agony letting AJ know he hit his target. AJ kicked down the bullet ridden bathroom door just in time to see Juan take his last breath.

"I got him! Let's get up out dis bitch!"

P grabbed Glenda and they hit the street running.

Chapter 29

Agents Haugen and Moran had been watching Destiny for close to two weeks. They had gotten a break in their hunt for Destiny when they realized that her cousin Shaylin Archer was at student at ETSU, which was located in Johnson City Tennessee. Once they put a trace on her activity they saw that her credit report had been pulled as an applicant for a three bedroom townhouse in a gated community. Bingo. They had immediately put a tail on her with specific instructions to not apprehend the suspect, Ms. Destiny Love, if spotted. Due to the fact that their star witness and confidential informant on the case was now deceased, they had to handle the case a little differently.

It was an absolute necessity that she feel safe. They wanted Destiny to believe that she was out of harm's way and would continue to live her life as normal as possible. The glue that held the Feds case together was the buy money. Every time Jake would take Destiny money that he was supposedly getting from Hova's workers, it was actually marked bills that came directly from the agents. Jake had refused to wear a wire and based his reason on a lie that Destiny searched him every time he went to her house to cop. But Jake being the scum that he was, was playing both Destiny and the agents.

He was spending less than he told the agents that he was with Destiny and keeping the extra work for himself which he quickly resold in the street. But Jake was also unknowingly pocketing marked money, which went back into circulation in society. Due to the fact that he never wore a wire, the feds had no clue what actually went down in Destiny's crib. They were so desperate to nail Hova, that they had compromised the whole investigation. So now even though they had the drugs that Jake had come out of her house with they needed the marked money to make the case.

Fortunately for Destiny they didn't pick up her trail until after her trip to the bank and safe deposit box. And as of now they had seen no indication that she had that kind of cash on hand. They had already been inside and searched the townhouse thoroughly one day while Destiny, Shay, and Jayonne had been out and about. But now there had been two new major developments in the case that just might blow the whole thing wide open.

They had followed her yesterday as she made her solo rounds. It was actually the first time she was able to move freely without her son. They were definitely surprised when she went into Office Max and used the computer and as soon as she left they were on it. They had a salesperson go back and pull up every site that she visited. Wholesale lingerie' and beauty salon equipment? What the hell was she doing? But they had been so caught up on the computer activity that they totally missed her meeting at the vacant store front.

They had caught back up with her when she returned home, but they had shut down their surveillance for the day when her cousin returned yesterday evening with her son. They had got a call last night from the local agents that had been helping them on the case by keeping an eye on Shay's activity. Sometime, real late last night, a new mustang with N.Y. tags had cruised through her parking lot. The guy, a young black male got out and was looking in Ms. Archer's house and car windows. They didn't know if it was anything, but they just wanted to let them know. Shay had left with Buck so no one had answered when Hova had gone to her apartment door. Agents Haugen and Moran already knew that Hova's fiancé had rented him a mustang from the airport, but didn't think he had the balls to leave the state being as that was a condition of his release. They would soon realize they were wrong.

As they sat now in the crowded parking lot of the office building next to the bank watching Destiny exit, they wondered jut how much of their marked money she carried in the large Louis Vitton bag tossed over her shoulder. They weren't too sure about that, but one thing was becoming clear. Things were starting to look good for their case.

* * *

Hova saw the green Cadillac pull into Shay's parking lot, but didn't pay it much attention until it pulled up next to the mustang. Shay was in the passenger seat with her attention totally focused on her new love as she sat behind the dark tinted windows. She had to admit to herself that she had let her guard down and Buck has swept her off her feet and up into the clouds.

"Boy what am I going to do with you?" she asked smiling devilishly.

"First of all," Buck responded, "you gon let me taste them sweet lips again before you get out my whip."

They headed to meet each other's lips and Buck noticed the cat in the mustang next to them.

"So you ready for the concert tomorrow?" Buck asked when they separated.

"Hell yeah! I been looking forward to it, but I'm really excited to see if your brother and my cousin hit it off."

"Well, from what you told me last night about her business venture, she seems to have a head on her shoulders. I think that's just what Donovan needs in his life right now."

Buck noticed that the guy in the car next to them still hadn't gotten out yet and was watching all the cars that came in and out of the parking lot.

"Do you know this dude in the car next to us?" asked Buck.

Shay was smiling as she turned to look over her shoulders. Her face froze. Her eyes went wide in shock and confusion.

"Oh shit," she whispered.

"What's wrong shawty? Is dude gone be a probl-" Buck was reaching under his seat.

"No! No, it's o.k."

But was it really ok? Hova was supposed to be locked up according to Destiny. Man she wasn't prepared for this.

"Look baby, that's my cousin from New York. His name is Hova," she leaned over and gave Buck a quick kiss. "I'm good. I'll call you later. I promise".

She didn't give Buck time to respond as she quickly exited the Caddy. Hova saw Shay get out of the car and smiled at her which she wasn't expecting. They'd had their problems in the past, but she remembered how proud that he'd been the day she left for school.

"So, one of us made it," he had said to her. She was packing her last bag getting ready to go to the Port Authority to catch the bus to Tennessee.

"Yeah," she had said weakly, "no more big cuzzin Hova to keep the mean boys away." He had been her and Destiny's keeper for many years.

"I think I taught you enough to take care of yourself. You'll be aight. You got Archer blood running through those veins," he started," but I really am proud of you for being smart enough to get away from here. Make the family proud." He gave her 5 G's and told her if she needed anything just call. Now as she slid into the passenger seat of the mustang, she vividly recalled that conversation.

"What's up college girl? I see why you ain't called. Looks like your friend there is getting money. I ain't mad atcha," said Hova looking for a reaction.

"Yeah he aight. Owns his own business. And he treats me right," she paused," so when did you get out of jail?"

"How did you know that I was locked up?"

"The same way that I know you wouldn't just pop up in Tennessee. You know Destiny and Jayonne are here, and she's scared to death." Hova dropped his head and let out a sigh of relief.

"Thank god. Is she safe? I mean-"

"Yeah she's safe. But are you sure you weren't followed. I don't know much about criminal stuff, but I know the Feds go all out investigating shit."

"I'm sure I wasn't followed. I took a few detours and alternate routes on that long ass drive down here," said Hova. They went into Shay's apartment and Hova sat on the couch. He looked around the nicely furnished apartment and had to admit that Shay had done ok for herself.

"So where is Destiny and Jayonne? I want to see my little man," he said looking around.

Shay walked into the kitchen and took out a spring water from the refrigerator.

"Oh, they don't live with me if that's what you thought. She's got a really nice place across town. I'll call her in a minute, but we need to talk first," Shay said sitting down next to Hova.

"About what?"

"Don't take this the wrong way, but I've been with her over the past couple of weeks and she is just beginning to get her life on track. I'm not gonna hide them from you or anything like that, but I would like to know what your intentions are?"

"What do you mean, what my intentions are? I want to see her and make sure she's aight, being her situation was caused by me?" Hova said becoming defensive.

"She had a significant amount of money with her when she got here. Your money. But she just took a big piece of it to start a business and-"

"Hold the fuck up! You think after all that shit that I know she been through, that I drove all the way down here over some money!? Shay, what kind of niggah do you think-," he had to stop himself.

Calm down Hova, he told himself. He had to remember that Shay really didn't understand the relationship that he and Destiny had. She was just looking out for her best interest considering that Shay had actually been there with her through this whole ordeal. He saw the look on Shay's face and realized that he had scared her.

"I'm sorry for yelling at you. I know you don't want her to go through anymore than she's been through already. That money that she has was actually hers. I was only a couple of months from shutting everything down. When I was done, I wanted her to buy a house so that Jayonne and her has some security."

Shay looked at him skeptically, but it didn't take long for her to come to the conclusion that he was telling the truth. All their lives he'd been their protector. She had no reason to think that things were any different now.

"Aight, but I'm not just gonna take you over there. I'll call and let you talk to her and let her make the decision on what she wants to do," said Shay.

"I can respect that." Shay called Destiny and told her someone was there that wanted to speak to her.

"Who?"

Before Shay could respond she handed Hova the phone.

"What's up Dez? Before you say anything just listen. You of all people know how I feel about phones. I just want to see you and oney and make sure you're aight and if you want me to get on the highway and bounce right after I'm gone. My lawyer finally came thru and-"

"Shut up boy," she said through tears," why are you saying all this crazy stuff? Of course I want to see you. Where are you?"

"I'm over Shay's crib. Are you coming here?"

"Yes-I mean yeah, I'm only a few minutes away. Want you to get back on the highway? What the hell?"

"I'll let your overprotective cousin Shay explain when you get here," he said looking at Shay smiling. Destiny and Jayonne arrived at Shay's front door ten minutes later. When Shay opened the door Destiny was holding Jayonne and still had tears streaming down her face. Destiny handed her son to Shay and ran straight into Hova's arms who as soon as he saw her and that she was safe let a few tears of his own escape. Destiny hugged him tighter than she ever had before. Finally after all the shaky ground she had some familiar sense of security. Her big brother. Her protector.

"Uncle Hova!" Jayonne screamed out reaching for him.

"Little man!" Hova said excitedly and extended one of his arms for a group hug.

"Oh, this is too much for me. I'm gonna roll a blunt," she said after she gave Jayonne to Hova.

Three Heinekens and two blunts later they had cleared the air and had a better understanding where everybody stood.

"Well them peoples that I was telling you about over the phone from jail can get you all set up with a new identity. License, birth certificate, and credit cards. All I need is a passport photo and you'll be straight," said Hova.

"I don't have many choices. I hate being a fugitive and living on the run because I was protecting myself, but it beats going to jail for so called murder."

"Muhdah mommy?" said Jayonne smiling catching everybody off guard.

They then realized that they had to be very conscious of what they were saying. Hova later told Destiny about the scheme his boy Chulo was suppose to pull off because of what the people that were looking for her had done to his niece. If everything went as planned they should all be dead by now. Destiny wanted Hova to come to her new place so she could cook him something to eat and tell him about the plans for her store and this crazy blind date that Shay had set her up on. But she wanted to go, she told Hova looking at Shay. It would give her a chance to break out of the cocoon she'd been living in for the past couple of years. A chance to take a chance.

* * *

Just like old times, Destiny thought as she sat on her couch with Jayonne and Hova later that evening. They had just finished eating a dinner that Destiny has been preparing all afternoon. Shay had stayed at her apartment claiming that she was tired from the night before and had a test early the next morning. But she really knew that Hova and Destiny needed to talk. They were watching A RAISIN IN THE SUN on DVD as their food digested.

"So do you want to talk about it?" Hova asked.

"What do you mean? Oh-"she stopped realizing that he was talking about the shooting.

"I understand if you don't want to?"

"Nah, it might do me some good. You know you've always been my shrink?" she said smiling nervously.

"I remember the first niggah I shot. Seeing what a bullet does to flesh is something that sticks with you. Especially if you the one pulling the trigger."

"I don't know. It's like as soon as I heard them outside my window, I knew who and what it was. You know I never trusted that fake bastard Jake, and I swear I have no regrets about killing him."

Hova dropped his head in guilt and Destiny knew her statement had the effect that she wanted. She wanted him to feel guilty to some extent.

She continued, "But he deserved to die like that. I mean by that big ass gun you left at the house. He knew it was just me and my baby in that house. You should have seen him and that other niggah standing there after they kicked my bedroom door open," she said with resentment.

Hova had heard that she killed them with the AK-47 and wondered why she didn't use the .380 that he brought for her to keep on her.

"I still got the little gun you gave me," Destiny said pulling it from between her tits. "This is like my American Express Card. I never leave home without it."

Hova listened and could hear just how much this all had changed her. He knew it would, he just didn't know how much. But, he knew now that it was time that he laid all his cards on the table. He knew that she would probably be pissed, but he knew that he owed her honesty. The course of her whole life had been changed because of him and no matter what; she would probably be on the run for the rest of her life.

"I already told you that the paper you got, I was planning on giving you anyway, but there are still some things I need to tell you that I didn't want to say in front of Shay," Hova said shifting uncomfortably on her couch.

Destiny just looked at him waiting for him to continue.

"Well for starters if you really don't want to be here I have a house in Jersey. A big house. And I would love to have you and Jayonne close to me."

"I always knew you probably had another crib somewhere else. Most niggahs that get money do. That ain't no big deal. But I'm starting to like it here and I wanna see if I can make this business thing work."

"But that's not it, there's more," he paused, "I got a fiancé and two daughters at my house in Jersey as well as a couple million in the cut. I think Jake probably thought you ha my stash money hid at your place too and that was what he was after."

Destiny's head was racing with thoughts. She didn't say a word as she looked at him in disbelief. Hova had two daughters, probably little adorable girls, that he had kept a secret from her. And a fiancé?

"I don't understand Hova. Why would you hide of all things, your family from me?"

Now he had to decide whether to answer this question truthfully or by saving her feelings with a lie. The truth was he didn't think that Destiny was on the same level as Lisa and to a certain extent he was embarrassed about his prior life in the projects. Destiny represented a part of that life. Hova hadn't even told his mother about his other family until he was forced to take her there.

"Foolish insecurities and not trusting Lisa to love me for who I am," he said half truthfully.

"That's really a lame excuse Hova," said Destiny clearly hurt.

They continued to talk and he told her all about his daughters and son on the way. Even if she did feel more comfortable down here he would bring the whole family after the baby was born. She was upset at first, but as usual she couldn't stay mad at him for long.

Chapter 30

Hova was waiting at Shay's crib when she got home from taking her test.

"We've got to stop meeting like this. My neighbors are going to think you're a stalker." "Ha-ha. You got jokes,"said Hova. But Hova wasn't really in a joking spirit. He had called Chulo's phone last night and all day today and had gotten no response. This was definitely not a good sign. He had even called Nadia, the cutey from in front of the building and she'd said that she couldn't get in contact with any of them. Whatever it was going on, he would have to deal with that once he got back to New York. He couldn't let himself be distracted by the possibilities of what could have gone wrong with Chulo's plan.

Once they were in Shay's apartment Hova got right to the point.

"Look I need you to take a ride with me somewhere. I sent Destiny to Wal-Mart to take them passport photo's so I could send em out and get her ID straight. She had to go to home depot to get some stuff for her new spot too. That will give us plenty time to do what I'm trying to do," said Hova.

"And you're talking in riddles right now. What exactly are you trying to do?" asked Shay.

"Just come with me. I told these people that I would be back in less than two hours, and that was about an hour ago."

Shay figured that she wouldn't get far at this rate.

"Aight, let's go," she said.

They left the complex and fifteen minutes later they pulled into the RANGE ROVER dealership. Shay gave him a look that said, you can't be serious, as he put the mustang in park and they got out. Hova saw that the shiny black Range that he had talked to the salesman about was sitting out front and reasoned everything had went through. The night that he got to town and couldn't locate Shay, he got bored and did some cruising.

When he rode past the Range Rover dealership and saw the black truck on matching black blaque diamond 26 inch rims with the 'special price' sign across the front window, he pulled in to get a closer look. He took down the phone number. And now that he had found Destiny and saw that she was driving a rental he figured it would be a perfect gift to go along with her new life and new identity. When he called his fiancé Lisa and told her to put the truck in her name, she began to protest. He calmed her down and said that he would explain later.

"Everythings done and she's all set to go. Ms. Lisa Johnson faxed me back the paperwork I sent her. It's all yours," the salesman said handing him the keys.

"You brought a truck Hova? Are you serious? How are you gonna get it back to New York?" asked Shay.

"It's not for me. It's for Destiny so she can get out that rental."

"Damn!" she said jealously, "Don't take this the wrong way-but-are ya'll fuckin?!"

"Nah, you silly mufucka," he said playfully," I just know how much she wanted one of these. I know ya'll going to that show tonight and I'm just trying to do my part to make her life as happy and comfortable as possible. It's also helping me deal with the guilt of all this being my fault."

They walked over to the truck and opened the driver's side and passenger doors.

"I took it for a test drive earlier. This shit is sweet."

"She's gonna go crazy over this thing. It has a DVD player....and how many TV screens?" asked Shay counting them.

"Six. They say it was a special order, but the dude got killed in Texas. Supposedly a drug deal gone bad. At least that was the story that the salesman volunteered."

Shay rubbed her hand across the white leather seats that were covered with black and grey Louis Vitton LV emblems. Then she looked over the back seat and saw the see through custom made speaker box lined with four Rockford fosgate high performance sub woofers. The box had two 600 watt hifonics amplifiers attached to it.

"Start it up. I want you to park it at your spot until ya'll get ready to go to the show. Then you can drive it over there when ya'll dates come by to pick you up," Hova said to Shay who was sitting in the driver's seat.

Before Hova had moved Destiny out of the projects, there was a cat in the hood that had a snow white Range, and every time she saw it, she went crazy. Hova use to joke with her by saying," I'll get you one. You just gotta pay me back." But now he felt like he was in debt to her and was doing everything he could to make things right. He followed Shay out of the dealership. He couldn't wait to see the look on Destiny's face when she saw her new toy.

* * *

The feeling that she was being watched was too strong. But her mind wouldn't let her give in to the feeling. There was no way she could absorb the thought of going to jail and away from her son, for what she knew would be a very long period of time. She wasn't a criminal, she thought. How could she survive in jail? She had read those gripping street tales that had been penned by the incarcerated female novelists. But she couldn't understand the reality of a day to day existence in a prison system. She pushed the thought to the back of her mind and began to get ready for the concert.

Jayonne had been a ball of excitement every since he laid eyes on Hova. Hova had agreed to watch Jayonne so that Destiny could go out and spread her wings a little. But he also told her that he had to be on the highway first thing tomorrow morning headed back to New York. She smiled to herself as she looked at the Roberto Cavalli dress laid out on the bed. No matter what, this evening she would thoroughly enjoy herself.

She allowed herself to dream a little as she envisioned the possibility having a man in her life that would make her world complete. Destiny remembered the fairytale her mother had fed her young, hopeful, and influential mind. She had told her that every princess had a prince charming somewhere in the world, ready to sweep her off her feet and live happily ever after. That this prince would be handsome and rich and they would have beautiful children. But just as quickly as she allowed herself to fantasize, the freeze frame in her minds-eye shattered like a hammer smashing mirrored glass.

The night that the psychotic homeless woman pushed Destiny's mother in front of an express subway train while she was on her way home from work, her dreams had died on those cold steel tracks along with her mother. Her mother hadn't died a literal but a spiritual death. She was able to scramble back under the platform of the station, but not before the steel monster traveling at 50 miles per hour severed her left arm and foot. The incident had changed her mother from a sweet, caring, and supportive parent, to a bitter, hateful woman mad at the world.

Destiny's part-time biological father who would make occasional holiday visits to see his trophy baby's mother, one of four, had seemingly fallen off the face of the earth. Being it that his beautiful baby's mother was less than acceptable to him as an accomplishment or notch is his belt, he abandoned them both totally to move on to his next unsuspecting victim.

Unfortunately Destiny's life had followed a somewhat similar pattern. No she hadn't been physically maimed, but the pain in her heart was close to the emotional equivalent. Even though Destiny had not been attached to her baby's father Lucky, who happened to be a one night stand, the damage had been done.

She slipped into her dress and looked at her reflection in the mirror. God had truly blessed her with breathtaking beauty. There had to be a God, she reasoned. For some things on this earth, there was just no doubting the creator. The beauty of her son's smile. The magnificence and color scheme of a rainbow, or the setting of a perfectly round orange sun, in a magenta background, behind a skyline.

After applying the finishing touches to her make-up, she strutted with pride into the living room like a runway model. Hova was just ending a call on his cell phone as Jayonne sat closely up under him with his attention trained on Sponge Bob on DVD. She stood in the middle of the living room and spun in a circle with her arms in the air.

"What do you think? Will I knock em' dead and bring em' back to life?"

"That dress is bangin," said Hova genuinely impressed.

"Pretty mommy! Pretty mommy!" said Jayonne diverting his attention from Bob.

Destiny looked at her watch. "Well, they should be here soon," she said.

"Shay just called my phone. She said they were on their way to her house and as soon as they got there, they were all on the way here," said Hova.

Destiny thought it a bit strange that Shay called Hova's phone instead of hers, but quickly brushed it off as nothing. Her mind was focused on the night ahead.

Buck pulled the caddy into the parking lot next to the Range Rover parked in front of Shay's apartment. He had to do a double-take when he saw the truck with the new 30-day tag in the back windshield.

"Yo that's this dude named Jazzy's truck We put the rims and stereo system together for that, and installed it two weeks ago. He had paid for it in full through the dealership, but I heard he got bodied down in Texas," Buck said to Donovan.

"That shit is sweet. What do you think it's doing here?" asked Donovan.

Shay had been waiting for them to arrive and was coming down the sidewalk leading to the parking lot. She approached the car and leaned down to give Buck a kiss.

"Hey baby," she started. And then to Donovan she said "Hi-i," in a singsong voice. Oh hell yeah! She silently thought to herself checking Donovan out. He smiled at her and she had to catch herself.

"Dam Buck. He is a cutey. Destiny might not be ready for big Bro."

Destiny? Donovan thought. Where had he heard that name before? Buck had told him about Shay's cousin but now he had a name to go with the mystery girl.

"I have to drive this truck over to my cousin's spot. It's a long story, but it will make sense when we get there. My cousin, the dude that was sitting out here yesterday when we pulled up, he brought it for her," said Shay cutting off Donovan's train of thought.

Buck thought about what they had charged the dealership just for the work they had done. Not to mention what the price of the truck was. Whoever this cousin was, he was holding heavy to be spreading love like that.

"Aight we right behind you, but we gotta get on the road soon. It's gonna take us an hour and a half to get there."

* * *

Destiny saw the Range Rover when it turned into her parking lot.

"Oooh! Oooh! Ooooh! Hova look!" Destiny screamed as it slowly crept towards her house with the customized grill shining.

He tried to hold back his smile imagining how she was going to react when she found out that it was hers. When it parked and Shay got out Destiny was thinking, no this bitches' man don't got my dream truck? But when she saw the green Cadillac pull in beside Shay, the same green Cadillac that had took her and Jayonne to the hotel when she arrived in town, she was completely confused.

"So I take it you like your new truck?" asked Hova smiling.

"My wha-who-niggah whatchu talking bout?"

"I said-"

"Boy I heard what you said, but what I'm asking is-"

Hova pulled the papers to the Range Rover out of his pocket and handed them to her. She read them and looked up from the papers to meet his gaze, but she was still confused.

"Look babygirl. I know you're starting a brand new life on a bunch of different levels. A new business, meeting new people in a new area. I saw the truck at the dealership and remembered how you use to act when that white one use to come through the hood. I knew how happy it would make you so I snatched it up. That's all you, brought and paid for. Go check it out."

She was stuck. Tried to talk, but the lump in her throat wouldn't let her. She threw her arms around his neck.

"Thank you Hova and I know what you're trying to do. This isn't your entire fault. I knew the danger involved in being a part of your business. It was just at the time, I didn't care about the consequences. So with that being said, once my business takes off, which I know it will, I have every intention on paying you back for this-no matter how long it takes."

"I hear you loud and clear, but you got some people waiting on you." She smiled then turned around and ran out her front door screaming towards her new truck.

* * *

Donovan and Buck saw her come running out of the townhouse at the same time. "Oh shit!" They both said in unison. "Yo that's shawty from the bus station wit da lil youngun," said Buck. "That's her cousin? That's why the name rang a bell. She told me at the bus station in Richmond." "Looks like you might have you a winner if you act right."

No, Donovan would never forget the beautiful woman that caught his attention in the crowded terminal. Had even given him the nerve to approach her and ask if she needed help. He watched her beautiful smile beam as she inspected her new toy. Donovan saw Hova walk out of the townhouse with the cute little boy who he quickly remembered was her son. Now Donovan was smiling to himself as he recalled how the little guy had taken a liking to him. He had always had a soft spot for kids. He and Lucy had planned on having four. Two girls and two boys.

His heart rate increased as he realized she was done checking out the truck and it was time for their second introduction. He pulled down the passenger side sun visor and checked himself out in the mirror.

"You good playboy. You remember what Shay said when she saw you-cutie," said Buck poking fun at his big brother." Come on let's go say hello."

* * *

Recognition registered on Jayonne's face when he saw Donovan headed over with Buck.

"Hi Donovan. So you're my blind date, huh?" said Destiny smiling.

"Wait a minute. You two know each other?" asked Shay.

"Yep. We met at the bus station in Richmond on my way down. Donovan and Buck were nice enough to give me and Oney a ride to the hotel."

Donovan smiled and Destiny melted. She would never forget that Denzel smile.

"This is too much of a coincidence," said Shay.

"Destiny," said Donovan.

"Yes?" said Destiny.

"Oh. No," he said. "I was just thinking out loud."

Hova introduced himself to the two brothers and asked what they did for a living. He was stern faced like a father on a girls first date. A soldier and a business owner. As a matter of fact, the guy had said, his shop customized the Range Rover. Hova was wearing a Yacht Master Rolex and Buck immediately noticed it.

"Ughhk, nice watch," said Buck impressed.

"You like it. I won it in a beauty contest." Everybody burst out laughing.

"I'm just fuckin wit ya'll. On the real these two chicken heads are my heart. I've been lookin out for them for a long time. All I ask is that you treat em' like you would want your mother or sister to be treated," Hova said to Donovan and Buck. "Now ya'll get up outta here so me and oney can go cutie watchin at the mall. I'm trying to get a couple numbers before I leave up out Ten-a-ki."

"Don't be using my son for no ho-magnet, "Destiny said jokingly.

"You a little late for that Dez. Me and oney been running that game on honeys for a minute. He gotta learn from the best. Why do you think he's such a flirt? R-Kelly and T-Pain ain't got nothing on me and oney."

"Well we need to make moves if we gonna catch the opening act. How ya'll wanna roll?" asked Buck.

"Me and Donovan can roll in my new truck. We can follow ya'll, if that's cool," Destiny said quickly surprising everyone. "That is if you don't mind Donovan."

"Well shit Naw, I don't mind, a comedic voice said in Donovan's head. He smiled.

"I take that as a yes," said Destiny hopping into the driver's seat. Her head was in the clouds. She couldn't remember ever being this happy before. She watched Donovan walk around the front of the truck looking like a Sean John model and thought, yes cousin Shay I owe you for this one big time.

* * *

Agents Haugen and Moran were watching through the venetian blinds in the townhouse adjacent to Destiny's. The local authorities that had been assisting them with their surveillance on Destiny were there as well. Their observations of Shay's movements had led them to and individual whose activity had always been questionable. Every since that huge drug bust and the fall of the infamous Donovan Anderson Sr., Dexter Anderson AKA "Buck" had become a person of interest to the DEA. As they watched the Caddy and the Range Rover exit, local Agent Opie of the DEA spoke.

"I think there may be more to this puzzle than we're seeing. Agent Haugen, when were you planning on moving in?" asked the fat bald annoying black man.

Agent Moran wanted to answer, but he felt like his personal feelings towards this character may slip out and that was unprofessional. Outside of his clown-like demeanor two things puzzled Moran. For one there was no place in America that he could think of where law enforcement officials were fat and dumpy like this guy. And secondly which was comedic on a whole other level, he had never heard of a Blackman named-Opie?

"We had planned on apprehending the suspect tomorrow in the early morning hours.Why do you ask?" stated Haugen.

Opie told them about Buck's father and the biggest drug bust that the area had seen. He said Buck was suspected of still carrying on some part of is father's enterprise but no evidence had ever been uncovered. Maybe with the appearance of this Mr. Darron Archer, a known NY drug dealer, they could tie them together and build a case. He asked for a two week extension before moving in. Opie didn't hesitate to state how much help came from his people on the investigation.

"Well I can't promise you anything," started Haugen, "But I don't see how that would be a problem. It looks like she doesn't have any intentions of going anywhere. And if we can snag another fish in the net, all the more better. I just have to contact my superiors and I'll let you know for sure."

Agent Opie had already known Buck was clean as a whistle from the last investigation that led to a dead end. But now that he saw the opportunity to manipulate this situation to his advantage, he would find some link, even if he had to create one, to lock Buck up for suspicion. Opie had a few informants at his disposal and he pondered on which one he would throw into the equation.

* * *

They arrived at the sold-out show with plenty time to spare. Buck had thought that he would have to drive the speed limit because Destiny was concerned about safety. He had been cruising at 70, which was the speed limit, when Destiny shot past him doing 90 miles per hour. He quickly got the message and they burnt up the highway.

"I see you got some driving skills," said Buck as they walked through the parking lot.

"NYC baby. Drive or get ran over," said Shay responding for Destiny. The parking lot was packed with some of the hottest whips from Tennessee and North Carolina. Destiny and Buck's vehicles had attracted quite a few fans and recognition as they had cruised through the parking lot.

The inside of the arena was more crowded than the outside. Holy shit, Destiny thought as she saw all the different crews of girls and dudes buying snacks and souvenirs as well as exchanging phone numbers. It wasn't until then that she had realized how much she had really shut herself off from the world. Even though they weren't disrespectful, Destiny could feel the stares of the dudes that were checking her out. She saw that Shay and Buck were holding hands. Donovan looked at her and saw that she seemed a little nervous.

"Are you ok?" he asked taking hold of her hand.

The warmth, contact, and slight intimacy of the gesture sent a feeling that she couldn't describe through her whole body.

She smiled gratefully.

"Much better now," she said squeezing his hand. They had talked non-stop n the trip to Knoxville. She informed him that it had been over two years, since before her son was born, that she'd been on a date. He reluctantly told her that this dating thing was new to him as well. He had also told her that he recently lost someone who had been very close to him at one time. They laughed a lot, almost cried once, and overall knew each other a good bit more than they did at first.

Three hours later they were heading to the after party still running off of energy from the Trey Songs and J-Holiday serenades. Buck had given her a couple of CD's to listen to out of his car and one of them was J-Holiday. Destiny was ecstatic as they followed Buck, with the single can't breathe playing at a low volume. The clarity of the customized system sounded like J. Holiday was in the back seat singing.

"I'm having a wonderful time Don," stated Destiny. "I had actually forgotten how much fun a night out could be with the right person." The wall of nervousness and unfamiliarity had slowly melted sway to almost nothing.

"So you think I'm the right person," he asked from the passenger seat.

"You're doing real good so far." Donovan had to really think about how to word what he was about to say.

"Well," he paused "There's still so much you don't know about me. My life has made me a kind of-complicated person. I mean I'm still adjusting to living a quote, unquote normal life post war. I get the sense your life may be a little complicated right now as well and I would hate to bring any more turmoil into the life of you and that wonderful son of yours."

Even his honesty and truthfulness were intoxicating.

"Yeah," she said with a nervous smile. "I do have my mess that I'm working through. But hey, this is only day one and look at the progress we're making. I like to believe that I'm a pretty good judge of character, a trait that I feel I passed on to my son. So already you're batting 2 for 2. And I gotta confess. The gear you rockin now is tight, but when I first saw you in that uniform. Oh-my-God,"she said biting her lower lip.

"Thank you for the compliment. I'm truly flattered. It means a lot coming from someone as beautiful as you."

They ended up having a great time dancing the night away. But Destiny didn't forget that Hova had told her that he had to roll out early in the morning. They made it back to Johnson City at around two thirty that morning and respectfully went their separate ways. They exchanged an intimate kiss to end the date and as Destiny drifted off to sleep she reflected on the moment.

Chapter 31

Benzino woke up in a strange bedroom. As he drifted into consciousness he could hear voices vaguely off in the distance. He saw Icon and Chin's father Master Wong and recent events slowly began to come to his memory. The men that had rescued Benzino from the Yacht had gotten him to safety. Master Wong had then contacted Icon and told him the series of events and an account of what happened as he had heard from Chin's men that had been at the warehouse.

AJ, Sonny and P had gotten Glenda safely home and as soon as Icon saw that she wasn't physically harmed, he had his driver take him to Master Wong's safe house, one of many in Chinatown. Kidnappers and home invaders were notorious for doing unthinkable things to women, especially attractive women, when they were helpless. He immediately tried to contact Columbia after he found out what happened. But once again she was unreachable. But this time he left her a message that was sure to grab her attention.

Benzino saw the look on Icon's face. Even though Benzino was on heavy doses of morphine for pain, he could see the expression of anger and disappointment. There was no doubt that Icon had found out about Benzino's betrayal of his trust by dealing drugs. He also knew the love that Icon had for him, and hoped that he would allow this one bad choice be a lesson learned. After all, none of them knew the real reason behind how they ended up out on that yacht.

"How do you feel? Wong's doctor said you got cut pretty bad," said Icon refusing to call another man Master.

"I can't feel much of anything now," he looked around," where is my sister?"

"I don't know son. The past few days have been complete turmoil."

"Look, I can explain-"

"I'm sure you can and you most certainly will. But now is not the time. I'm just waiting for the doc's ok to get you out of here. I'm taking you to my house where I can have you looked after properly," he paused." Simpson was found dead in his home with that receptionist Mona from the record label. Neighbors claim there was a white Porsche seen leaving the area last night."

Icon let the statement sink in to have its desired effect. But now when he looked at Icon again, he looked 20 years older than his usual self. While he had been off dealing with consequences that his selfish actions had caused, his mentor, his father had been dealing with other major issues. And Benzino couldn't read what, but he saw something else in his eyes that was terribly disturbing. The doctor was finishing up with his inspection of the wound and checking Benzino's vital signs.

"I have a few questions that I'd like to ask," interjected Master Wong.

"With all due respect Wong, I request that you hold off with your inquiries until he is fully recovered. I will even send my driver to escort you to my home," Icon stated with an undeniable finality.

There was a tension clearly in the room.

"As you wish. At this point nothing will bring my son back to life. But I definitely need some clarity to have closure to all this," stated Mater Wong.

"Well as long as you have competent care givers to deal with this kind of injury, he is free to go," said the doctor.

Icon immediately made the call to his limo. Five minutes later AJ, Sonny and P, along with Icon's personal physician entered with an extra wheelchair to accommodate Benzino.

"Be careful moving him. He's pretty bad off. But with the right treatment he should be healed up pretty good in a month or so," added the doctor.

Icon was being lenient because he did really care about Zino. But one of the things that he had a low tolerance for was betrayal. Once you lost his trust, the relationship would never be the same. Dealing drugs behind Icon's back, which is what Benzino had been doing according to Master Wong, was something that was unforgivable.

* * *

It had been three days since the concert. Destiny and Donovan had spent a significant part of each of those three days together. Destiny was beginning to believe that Donovan might be the man that she had dreamed about. So far as she could tell he was honest, truthful and a gentleman. Not to mention the all important fact that her son had found himself a new best friend. Two days ago she had finally taken the time out to go and buy that computer that she knew she needed. Last night after dinner she'd gone on-line to place a few orders for the salon and lost track of time. When she had come out of the room after using the computer, she was stopped cold in her tracks by what she saw on the couch. Donovan and Jayonne were sleeping peacefully and looked just as natural as any other baby boy sleeping on his father's chest.

Donovan as well was starting to believe his life was making a turn for the better. When Destiny and Jayonne had come to Donovan's house to pick him up yesterday, Mrs. Anderson had requested to meet this new young lady that had been recently occupying her eldest son's time. Her suspicions about Destiny initially rose from the extravagant vehicle that she drove. But as soon as the beautiful girl and her son entered her dining room where Mrs. Anderson was drinking coffee at the dining room table, her feelings changed.

"Mom this is Destiny and her son Jayonne."

"What a beautiful young lady and darling little boy."
Jayonne was smiling brightly at the elderly woman. Mrs.
Anderson had planned on giving her a thorough interrogation,
but something about the young lady told her that this one
might be just what her son needed. When Destiny and
Jayonne went outside to the truck to wait on Donovan, his
mother called him over to her.

"I think you've got you a good one son. In these days
and times you don't see many young ladies with that look in
their eyes over a man. She is definitely, how would you young
people say, feeling you," Mrs. Anderson said winking at her
son.

"And just how do you know that mom?"

"Because I use to greet that same look in the mirror
every morning when me and your father first started seeing
each other."

This morning though, was the first day for Jayonne at
daycare. Destiny had a lot of work to do in preparation for her
Grand Opening and she wouldn't be able to do them and keep
an eye on her son at the same time. Not to her surprise she
soon found out that Donovan was multi-talented and more
than willing to do whatever she needed him to do. She'd had
intentions on hiring a contractor to construct a wall to
separate the two sides of the business and install the
necessary fixtures.

But Donovan had made her promise to just get the
materials and tools and he and a few of his old buddies would
handle the labor. So she brought the materials and Donovan
brought three of his buddies and two cases of beer. Now it
was nearing four o'clock in the evening and they had been
there all day hammering, sawing and drilling. She was putting
up curtains and Donovan was securing a shampoo sink when
they both looked up and locked eyes.

She kissed the inside of her hand and blew him a kiss. Donovan smiled and silently mouthed, who me? She nodded yes and gestured with her index finger for him to come to her. She watched him walk the distance between them. His hard muscles in his wife beater glistened with sweat and she felt her crotch moisten.

"What's up beautiful?" he asked when he approached her.

"Come closer," she said." It's a secret."

He kneeled down so she could whisper in his ear.

"Shay is keeping Jayonne tonight. I planned something special," she said and put a finger over her lips indicating a "shh".

He felt his heart rate quicken. Even though he had spent the night at Destiny's place and they had extremely strong physical urges and attractions, they had never engaged in intercourse. He knew that it was coming and he wasn't sure when, but he was more than willing to wait until she was ready. He hoped that she wasn't feeling pressured or indebted to him because of his generosity. But he also didn't want to offend her with the wrong response. He decided to play it safe as possible.

He kissed her lips. "If you planned it, it has to be special."

Destiny wanted him. At that moment she couldn't think of anything she wanted more. She had the urge to drag his ass to the back, into the bathroom and give him a quickie. Nah, she thought. She figured there would be many opportunities to engage in spontaneous sex in the near future. But the first time had to be an experience that neither one of them would forget. After she took him home to shower and get some clothes, she had intentions on going to Victoria's Secret and buying an outfit especially for the occasion.

Lord knows she was long overdue. She had burned out more batteries on her little battery operated buddies than she cared to think about. They had definitely fulfilled the need at the time, but it was the feeling afterward, laying in that lonely bed longing to be held that she really wanted to be filled. And now she had that opportunity and she had every intention of taking advantage of it.

* * *

"Girl watchu cooking up in here? It smell like Red Lobster in this bitch," said Shay coming in the front door.

"I got some shrimp scampi, crab legs, cheesy potatoes, wild rice and a few other things going down. Does it really smell good? I want tonight to be extra special for Donovan."

"I guess he told you about-his ex, huh."

"Yeah, that's so sad about her. I remember seeing the story on the news when I first got into town."

"And they still don't know who did it." Destiny acted like she didn't hear that last statement. And she would always act that way anytime there was mention of the subject. She would never forget how deep they had went last night when they exchanged confessions. At first she was unsure how to react. She listened to his story as he reenacted the event slowly through light sobs and tears and concluded on a deeper level, which probably only she cold understand that there were many factors that led to that climax, and Donovan really couldn't be held responsible for the outcome.

She believed that she could read his heart and knew that it was bleeding. He'd shared his experience and tactical training in intense combat situations and she couldn't imagine what that reality was like. She'd fired that assault rifle only once and it was similar in the sense that her and her son's life was at stake. But she was still unable to shake that horrifying nightmare. In her dreams she could hear the earsplitting blasts and see the bloody mess that the weapon had made. That and much, much worst had been Donovan's harsh reality for the past two years.

And she believed that the two deeply wounded souls were exactly what each other needed to heal. It was unexplainable, but also undeniable, the unique connection that had formed in such a short period of time. She'd laid her head on his chest and listened to his heartbeat. She felt safe and at home, finding a peace that she never thought she could have, as he stroked her hair.

"That is strange, isn't it," she replied nonchalantly.

"Well, is my baby ready? We are gonna have a ball tonight."

"He's in the room sleep. The nursery said he had a difficult time adjusting to the other kids at first. But by the time afternoon kicked in he was the life of the party. I wonder where he got that from?" she asked Shay smiling.

"Ha-Ha. So you got jokes. Well I got one for you. You betta not hurt this boy up in here tonight. I know you ain't had no dick in a minute."

"Yeah it's been a minute. Shit, hurt him? I'm nervous as shit," she lied. Nervous she wasn't. She knew exactly what she planned to do with Donovan and she was eager with anticipation.

* * *

Buck was dropped off Donovan at Destiny's about twenty minutes after Shay and Jayonne had left. When she'd opened the front door to let him in he was awestruck. There had been too many candles to count as the front door had swung open and the low playing sounds of Anthony Hamilton mixed with pleasant aroma of the dinner that she'd prepared set the mood. Donovan was so captivated by the setting that it wasn't until she had closed the door that he noticed her.

She was absolutely stunning. As she slowly walked toward him he tried to form words in his mouth but he couldn't. Destiny was wearing a see through lace nightie that left very little to the imagination. She also had on silk slip-on shoes with just enough heel to flex her calf muscles, accenting her hips. He looked at the perfectly shaped breasts that he had dreamed about and was amazed at how firm they were for their size. The large erect nipples gave him an immediate erection. Destiny slowly approached him and her perfume, a light flowery fragrance hypnotized him.

"I see your excited to see me," she said grabbing his dick and giving him a slow passionate kiss.

"Damn gurrl. You gonna start something that-"

"That's exactly what I planned to do," she said undoing his pants and slowly dropping to her knees.

She released his swollenness and gasped in shock as she stroked it in her hand.

"This is just an appetizer," she said. "The main course is after-well-the main course." She took him into her mouth with the skill of a seasoned pro. For a brief second Donovan had wondered when and how she had acquired her skill. But her technique and expertise made that a short lived moment when he realized how much she enjoyed giving him pleasure.

Destiny had watched those videos and practiced on those toys until she was sure she had it right. According to Donovan's moans of pleasure, she was sure she was right on point. She had vowed that the next man that she got, she was going to keep him and she took every step in preparation. Destiny tried to accommodate Donovan's entire 10 ½ inches in her mouth, but found that she could only take just over half. She had not yet mastered the art of the deep throat but she figured she would get plenty practice on this one. After all, she had a lot of catching up to do.

She felt him getting harder in her mouth and used her hand to stroke him faster. She took him from her mouth momentarily.

"Don't hold back baby. I want it," she said and put him back in her mouth. That was all he had to hear as he released himself and watched in amazement as she swallowed every drop.

"Wait right here," she said standing up. "I'll be right back." She returned a minute later with a warm washcloth and carefully cleaned him up. She remembered that she'd read somewhere that the percentage for keeping your man happy was much higher when you did three things in a specific order.

Suck em'.

Feed em'.

Fuck em'.

The women that were in the survey admitted there was no formula for all men, but this was the method that got the best results.

She was so horny she thought that she was going to go crazy. Her entire crotch was soaking wet and she could feel her juices running down her inner thigh. She needed to relax a little. She walked Donovan over to the couch and lit one of the pre-rolled blunts that sat in the ashtray.

An hour later, fueled by a couple of mixed drinks and a meal loaded with aphrodisiacs she led him slowly by the hand to her bedroom. More candles. OK, Donovan thought, you think you gonna turn me out? Hell yeah! But this was gonna be a two way street. He walked up behind her and softly moved her hair to the side. He kissed her and she threw her head back.

"Oooh, that's my spot," she purred.

"Oh yeah? For some strange reason I thought this might be your spot," he said reaching around and massaging her clit with his middle finger.

216

"Mmmmm, shit boy! What you know about that spot?"

"Lay down on your back and let me introduce you to my little friend," said Donovan rapidly flicking his tongue over her earlobe.

She slowly turned around and seductively removed her negligee'. She lowered herself to the bed she and Donovan engaged in a passionate kissing frenzy. Donovan left her lips and took a good tour of Destiny's body with his tongue. Her neck, her shoulders. He got to her tits and began to gently nibble on her large erect nipples.

"Mmmmmm, that's it." He slipped a finger inside her and massaged her clit with his thumb. "Ooooh, shiittt," Destiny moaned in ecstasy.

He continued down, kissing her stomach. He stopped and kissed the scar from her c-section and she relished in the intimacy of the gesture. He removed his fingers and began to tease her by licking her inner thigh.

"Please don't' tease me," she whispers. He slowly spread her open, keeping an eye on her face. He wanted to see her facial expression. When he slid his tongue through her heat, she closed her eyes and bit her bottom lip, lifting her pelvis trying not to lose contact with his tongue. He wrapped his arms around her thighs and pulled her towards him. Twenty minutes later she had bucked and came hard twice and he thought there was a chance she may have whiplash.

"I want you inside me," she said as she pulled him down on the bed and removed his pants.

Donovan was on his back as she straddled him. She lowered herself slowly and tried to take him all in, but saw that she had to pump her brakes about three-quarters of the way down. He cupped her hips and they slowly rocked until he was all the way in.

"I've....never....felt....anything....like..-ooohh   goddd Donovan! I'm going to fuckin cummm again!" said Destiny as he jackhammered that pussy. They both released at the same time and collapsed it sweat and sex juices. They were both exhausted and spent, but they managed to sexually assault each other for another two hours before it was all over. Now that they had consummated their relationship they both vowed to be there for each other as Alicia Keys sang-I won't tell your secrets....

Chapter 32

O'Connor got a break. He found out that he had to spread almost the whole ten grand, but now as he sat waiting for his contact to arrive at the situation he realized that it was money that was well invested. Even though he was a gangsta, Icon was always a man that it was good to have in his corner.

There was a quick knock on the office door and Agent Julia Bittinger slipped in the office door. She was a chubby, nerdy looking white woman with glasses and Spikey hair. Here we go again, he thought as she came in smiling. O'Connor remembered the cost of his last bit of information. His recollection of the task was that it was similar to screwing a little boy.

"Hi Steve,"she said in a poor attempt at sounding sexy.

"How are you Jules? Looking good, "he lied wanting to be nice as possible to get the info he needed.

"I've been on a special assignment undercover for the agency. I've built quite a few cases on some guys in the Bartolli family. They're new breed of the Bonanno family doing things that the old school guys never did. Like dealing drugs."

"That's interesting, but I really need that info that you have for me. Finding the location of this girl is of the utmost importance."

"OK Steve," she said removing a slip of paper from her bra."This is the name and location of where she is, and the address of some business that she is supposed to be opening."

"Wait a minute. Opening a business? She's wanted for a murder. Why do they know exactly where she is and haven't locked her up yet?"

"Well, what you paid for was her location, and that is exactly what I gave you. There are some other things going on with this young lady and in a big way. That bit of information is going to cost you extra-bigtime.

* * *

Icon was busy trying to stay on top of his business affairs, but the task was close to impossible. The three closest people to him in his circle were out of commission, dead, or missing in action. Benzino was still in recovery and under heavy medication, but he was still able to answer a few questions about business affairs. Very few.

Columbia and their daughter were still missing in action after a week and he was beginning to assume that the worst had happened to them. The doorman at her building told Icon that he hadn't seen her since early the morning after Simpson was killed. He said that she had their daughter and a large bag when she left, but that was it. Icon was wrecking his brain trying to figure out a reason for her recent activity. But the sad reality was, he was oblivious to the obvious.

They had given his long time friend Simpson a soldier's sendoff yesterday morning. Icon was still having a difficult time accepting the fact that he was gone. Icon for the most part was his family, outside of the old school G's that associated with Simpson and Icon over the past 30 years.

But now as he sat looking at the piece of paper that O'Connor had sent a messenger to deliver, he was ready to bring to an end this business of the elusive young girl that had killed Jake. That would definitely make Glenda feel better about the ordeal that she had recently gone through. The anonymous caller had said that some guy named Hova helped Chulo put the pieces of the puzzle together. Mr. Archer seemed genuinely concerned for this cousin and her son's welfare. Yes he too should feel the loss that Glenda was feeling.

But what further aroused concern in Icon, was the statement O'Connor had made in reference to Destiny. He said that his source confirmed his suspicions about there being more going on than they were seeing. It was complicated but he was working on finding out exactly what was going on. Whatever was going on was major for her not be locked up and them have a location on her. If he was gonna act, he needed to act fast! He put in the call to AJ, Sonny, and P.

Chapter 33

Fat Dave had known Buck for 15 years. They didn't have a tight relationship but Buck knew him well enough that he would smoke a blunt with him and talk about what was coming out new in audio equipment. So when he saw Fat Dave pull up in his black Volkswagen Bug, he assumed that Dave was probably looking to upgrade his boom-boom. He remembered that Dave was originally from Bristol Tennessee and he ran with some cats that dabbled in the music biz and they occasionally came across some bomb ass weed from Cali.

Buck watched fat Dave through the front showroom window as he got out of his car and slowly walked towards the entrance. Buck looked past fat Dave and saw the "PRETTY KITTY" neon sign that had been mounted yesterday by him and Donovan and had to smile at the ambition of both Destiny and Shay. Fat Dave came in with two rolled blunts behind his ears.

"Sup Buck?"

"Working hard. Trying to stay ahead of the pack."

"Aw come on Buck. Everybody knows you the man."

"Nah playa. I'm just the man next to the man with the plan." Dave walked over to the amplifiers on the wall. He looked at a couple and their price tags and then turned to Buck.

"I need to holla atchu about some big business Buck."

"What's good?" "It's kind of heavy. You want to go out to my ride and smoke? I got some of that official Cali funk."

"That's cool. Let me go in the garage and let E know I'm going out front."

Buck spun off and headed to the garage. He came back a minute later and they went out to Dave's car. But as soon as they got in the car, Buck felt an uncomfortable vibe.

Fat Dave lit a blunt and passed it to Buck, then he lit the other one.

"This shit is pretty good. I got it from this cat name Jiggy out in Bristol. This is the best shit to hit the town in a minute."

"Yeah this shit is pretty good. But what is it that you wanted to rap about?"

"Well, I know you don't get down, but a lot of cats that come through your spot be moving weight. I got a lil something I've been doing on the side around my old way. I'm trying to cop some work and I thought that you might be able to help me out."

Buck tried not to show an outward reaction, but he was boiling inside. This motherfucker actually had the audacity to disrespect me by coming to my place of business trying to buy drugs, he thought. He was midway through the blunt and he reached over and put it out in the ashtray.

"Nah playa. I can't help you out on that one," said Buck. Fat Dave saw his attempted victim was slipping away.

"Aw, come on Buck! You gotta know som-"

"I'm getting out of your car, right now. I don't ever want you to come to my place of business again. If you do, I'm not responsible for what happens to you. Oh, and tell whoever sent you," he leaned over and lifted up fat Dave's shirt exposing his wire and microphone. "Nice try. Wrong guy."

Buck got out and scanned the area to see if he could spot any suspicious vehicles. He didn't see anything out of the ordinary. But he knew they were out there somewhere.

* * *

"Shit!" said Agent Opie slamming down the headphones that he was listening to Buck and fat Dave's conversation on. "He didn't bite did he?" asked Agent Moran. 230

"Nah, but we'll get him."

"Not on my time you won't. Look, it's clear that this kid is clean. We have to wrap up this investigation. Your two weeks are up," stated Agent Haugen. This was Opie's third attempt and failure and they were all becoming frustrated with his personal vendetta. They had already been to the bank and switched out the marked money with clean money, with a signed affidavit from the bank and it had been marked as evidence. It was illegal and could burn their entire case, but the Feds did pretty much what they wanted to do. They had a 98% conviction rate.

"Call home base and let them know that we are moving in soon. It's time to rearrest Mr. Archer and book him with the additional indictments," said Haugen.

They were frustrated and tired of Opie and Tennessee. Now they had to figure out the best way to move in without much resistance.

* * *

The remaining active members of the death squad stood around Benzino's bed as Icon spoke. Benzino's arm was still bandaged pretty heavily and he really wished that he could make this trip. Every since Icon had shown him and Columbia that picture of Destiny and her son, his feelings towards this whole operation had changed. As soon as it became personal he'd kinda fell back and let Icon's inside people handle it. But now the ball was back in their court. A federal agent had said that she was in Johnson City Tennessee. There was no way he could run interference on this one. Oh, how he would if he could.

They said that they were leaving this afternoon and would arrive sometime tomorrow morning. They were suppose to get it done and get back.

Icon had been grilling and probing Benzino with questions to try to find out the where abouts of Columbia.

Had she ever talked about leaving? Was she acting strange in anyway when he last saw her?

Benzino was frustrated and scared for his sister and her daughter. Of course it didn't take him long to come up with ten reasons for her to kill Simpson. But what he couldn't find a logical reason for was-why now? As far as her disappearance, he considered another one of their victims' people seeking revenge, but that theory kinda flew out the window with Simpson's safe being empty and the doorman at her building telling Icon he saw her and his niece leave willingly.

"We're leaving right after we leave here and we should get there sometime early tomorrow," said AJ.

"We just have to check out the area and map out an escape route before we move in. It shouldn't take long though. If all the information is accurate we shouldn't be longer than 2 days," added Sonny.

"Well let's get this show on the road. I'm ready for all this to be over with," said an agitated Icon.

It was apparent the toll this all was taking on him.

"Have you considered any other resolution pop? I mean this is pretty dangerous. We are out of N.Y. and don't know what to expect down there?" questioned Benzino.

Icon jumped as if he'd been slapped. How dare Benzino question his judgment?

"This bitch killed my son! He was a fuck-up, but he was my blood." And with that, there was no more conversation. The room was thick with tension as Icon's glare held on Benzino.

"Now move out!" Icon said without looking at his hitmen.

Chapter 34

The GRAND OPENING was turning out to be a huge success. Every chair on the Salon side of 'Pretty Kitty' was filled with women getting their hair done as well as waiting customers. The radio, television, word of mouth advertising, and flyers with discount coupons printed on them had all been great marketing tools. Shay had spread the word to all the black girls on campus and Buck had told the hustlers that came through his store about some of the nightwear on the lingerie' side and that it was worth checking out.

Destiny had hired five sistah's and one shim, that were known to be the best in the area. But she and a middle aged white woman named Susan ran the other side. Susan had never worked in a lingerie' novelty store, but during the interview with Destiny something about this blonde haired blue eyed Amazon told Destiny that she would be perfect for the job. The only thing white about Susan was her skin.

By one o'clock in the afternoon, Destiny had already blown her projected sales quota out of the water. What had really taken her by surprise were the sales of the street literature book section. It seemed like everybody who was waiting was either reading one or talking to somebody who had read the book they were reading. Destiny and Susan were just finishing up a sale when they heard something that sounded like low thunder rumbling. Everybody looked up at the same time as the car turned into the parking lot.

The bowling ball paint job of the convertible seemed to change colors in the bright sunlight as the Bentley flying spur coasted to a stop behind the car parked in front of the salon. Purple. Green. Black. It kept changing colors as the sound system vibrated the front window of the 'Pretty Kitty'.

The three chicks in the car looked like contestants from America's Top

Model. The 24 inch chrome Ashanti rims spun one way and then back in the other direction. The black on the tires looked shiny wet.

"Aw shit, not these bitches," said one of the girls waiting to get their hair done. The driver got out looking like Halle' Berry with a short-short skirt and half-shirt taunting the customers with her flat stomach and thick thighs. Her burgundy hair with blonde highlights shined in the sun along with her exclusive diamonds. The other two, Brazilan and German neither speaking or understanding much English, sat in the car with shades on looking like movie stars.

"Who are they?" somebody asked.

"That's that niggah Nut's bitches. You know, the N.Y. niggah that went to the Fed's then came home and started buying up all that property and shit. He owns all kinds of businesses from here to Knoxville. Those are his show pieces," one of the other customers said as Keisha headed towards the front door.

When Keisha opened the door, the sounds of Lupe' Fiasco's Superstar, could be heard clearly bumping from the Bentley. Keisha waved and said "Hi ladies," flaunting $50,000 worth of tennis bracelets paid for with good pussy. She went to the lingerie' side and began to scan through the racks of clothing.

"I guess she's too fly to find a parking space like the other paying customers," one of the jealous patrons stated loud enough so she could hear them.

She did, but she ignored them. She was so past the petty shit of hating bitches. She was loving life, her man, his mansions, and their two toys that sat out in the car waiting for her. Of course she had flown out to Cali and shopped on Rodeo Drive, as well as burnt up Fifth avenue on shopping sprees. But Nut had given her 5 G's and told her to spend as least two at this new store. His good friend Buck had told him about this place opening when he had put the new system in the QX56 Infinity truck a few days ago.

"Gotta support the black businesses," Nut had told her. Whatever, she thought. She just hoped that they had some fly shit-and she wasn't disappointed.

"You have got some really nice stuff here," said Keisha.

"Thank you. I hand picked most of the merchandise myself," said Destiny walking over to where Keisha was looking through a floor display. "My name is Destiny. I'm the store owner.

"Well, hello Destiny. I'm gonna go get my-um-girlfriends and park this car. We are about to spend some money with you."

Destiny knew a good customer when she saw one from experience. Cater to the customer, she thought.

"Look, there's more parking in the back lot. You can park next to my truck, the black Range Rover," she said with pride. "I'll open the back door and let ya'll in."

"OK. I'll be right back. Have some of your nicest pieces out for us," said Keisha going out to the car to get Sofia and Silvia.

Destiny immediately went into the back to get her high dollar exclusive shit that she had chose not to put on the sales floor until she saw what type of crowd she had coming through. She knew from experience the effect shoplifters could have on a small business.

* * *

"Damn! Honey bad as a Mahfucka!" said P as he watched Keisha come out of Destiny's store. "Shit, you see what dem hoes is pushin? I'm ready to try my hand," said Sonny.

"Nah, Playa. I ain't even feeling this spot. I'm ready to do what we gotta do, and get up out dis bitch," said AJ.

They had been scoping out the area for the past few hours. It was real laid back compared to N.Y., and that was all the more reason that they were playing it cool. They had already gotten some suspicious stares in the black rented Suburban with the New York tags. They didn't really give a fuck about the crowd. After all they had run up in NYC projects and killed in broad daylight.

"I'm witchu AJ. Let's do this shit and blow up outta here" said P. They were sitting in the parking lot next to Buck's shop. They all cocked their weapons and then AJ started the suburban.

* * *

Destiny was spreading out outfits on the glass display counter top excitedly. Susan came from the back of the store with another armful.

"Do you think that they might buy all of these?" Sue asked setting them down.

"Did you see what they were riding in?" answered Destiny.

"I only seen shit like that in movies and videos," Susan paused and looked out the front window. "What the fuck is going on!"

Destiny turned and was about to say something, but couldn't make the words form in her mouth. She grabbed her head as it had started to spin making her nauseous with fear. She watched in disbelief as six crown Victoria's skidded to a halt in front of her store and what seemed like 30 men and women in FBI shirts and bulletproof vests poured from them.

"No! Please! Not now!" her thoughts screamed out in her head. She wanted to run but she was stuck.

The front glass shattered as two Federal Agents came crashing through, rolling and landing on their feet with their weapons drawn.

"Nobody move! Everybody down with your hands behind your heads," they shouted as the other agents came flooding in the door.

Out the back door, the thought popped into her head, and on impulse her legs started moving.

"You! Stop!" An agent yelled. "That's her!"

Destiny was through the storage area and burst out of the back door. She immediately stopped when she saw the two undercover cars with officers leaning over the hoods with their weapons aimed at her. Oh god, no! she thought as she threw her hands in the air.

"Please-don't-shoot-me," she managed to get out through sobs. "My baby-My baby My baby," she cried dropping to the ground thinking about her son.

Who would raise him? Who would love him? Who would take him to school on his first day? How could she live without touching, holding, or kissing him?

"Get on the fucking ground and don't move!"

Shay came running out of the back door with a curling iron in her hand, tears streaming down her face.

"Noooo! You can't lock her up! You can-"

The first slug ripped through her left tit and through her heart. She didn't even feel the next two because she was dead before she hit the ground. The cops saw the curling iron fall, knew it wasn't a gun and knew they fucked up.

Destiny freaked.

"Oh no-no-no-no!" she screamed running over to Shay's bloody lifeless body.

The agents had let down their weapons. Destiny stood up spinning and pulling the .380 from between her tits. She squeezed off five wilds shots that miraculously hit both agents before she was tackled from behind by Agent Haugen. Her gun went flying.

"I got her! I got her! Don't shoot," he yelled.

Everything had gone terribly wrong and he had witnessed it all. He pulled her arms behind her back and cuffed her. She felt the cold steel click on her wrists and began to kick wildly.

"Don't make this more difficult than it already is Destiny. I don't want to hurt you. I already have to make sure these other Agents don't beat you to death for shooting two of ours," said Haugen restraining her on the ground.

He had her face pressed to the ground and she was facing Shay's body not ten feet away. She could also see the three girls that were in the Bentley standing in shock watching the events that unfolded in front of them. Destiny was crushed and mentally tormented as she continued to absorb the reality of what was going on. But there was a glimmer of hope. A small and distant one, but it was there. The chance that a jury would see that her killing Jake and BG was an act of self-defense. After all they did come into her home and the detectives investigating the crime had to find their weapons which had to be suspicious.

Three agents lifted her up off the ground and stood her up on her feet. She vaguely heard one of the Agents reading her her rights. But everything seemed surreal. Shay was dead. Hova her protector had left town, Jayonne was with Donovan and Buck.

Fuck. Donovan, she thought, might not be able to handle this. And she feared the worst.

* * *

"Shit that was close! Icon is not going to like this at all," said AJ. They had been just about to turn into the parking lot when the line of crown vic's cut them off. They thought it was a set-up until they saw, where who they knew were Federal Agents were headed. The suburban had run up on the curb trying to avoid them before they made a bee-line towards the interstate.

"Well there was nothing we could do. We couldn't move in without peepin out the scene. We didn't know the Feds were gonna move in," said P. Sonny was quiet as he got on interstate 81 North. All he knew was that they needed to get the fuck outta that town. They would deal with Icon back in New York.

Chapter 35

Donovan, Jayonne, and Buck entered the Federal Courthouse in NYC. It had been five days since the raid on the store and Destiny had been arrested. The FBI had been short and not very helpful at all with their attempts to find out what was going on with Destiny and what she was being charged with. Buck had taken Shay's death hard. Her family had transported her body back to NY and was set to bury her tomorrow.

Donovan had been doing his best with Jayonne, but it was extremely difficult to say the least. He could cry for hours on end asking for his mommy. But Donovan and Buck's mother had been very instrumental in soothing Jayonne at difficult times. She was able to bring the natural element of mothering instincts, but it was still tough watching him deal with the loss.

They walked into the large courtroom and the first thing they saw was the "UNITED STATES OF AMERICA" government seal standing twenty feet tall from top to bottom, on the wall behind the Judge. They walked down the isle and found seats on the second row. Donovan was holding it together, but just barely. He had been having the same recurring nightmare since the day of the arrest. He had arrived at the scene about a half hour later with Buck, after Buck received the disturbing phone call.

The FEDS were pulling out as they were pulling in, and Destiny was handcuffed in the backseat. They had locked eyes for maybe three seconds, before Destiny mouthed a clear "I LOVE YOU", and the car pulled off. The look on her face would haunt him forever, but he vowed not to let her go through this alone. He too had fallen deep in love with her as well. He felt the need to protect her, but what could he really do but make sure her son was safe and had love. That, he was sure, was what she would want him to do.

The judge entered the courtroom, was sworn in and called for his next case.

* * *

Destiny was still absorbing the shock of everything that had transpired over the past week. Not only had she lost her cousin to a tragic death, but she had shot two Federal Agents and been charged with conspiracy to distribute crack cocaine. That fucking bastard Jake! It wasn't enough that his trifling ass betrayed Hova once by trying to rob her, he had also been working for the Feds as a confidential informant. The court appointed lawyer that had come to see her and explained the nature of her charges, had told her that Hova had been rearrested and implicated as one of her other seven co-defendants. Of course the lawyer hadn't said anything about Jake, but Destiny automatically knew who it was.

"Destiny Love," the court officer called out to the bullpen that held offenders waiting to see the judge.

She didn't respond vocally. She rose slowly from the steel bench in her orange jumpsuit and boat shoes and walked over to the holding cell door. She stuck her hands through the hole in the middle of the door where they put the cuffs on her wrists. By now she was already infamously well known for her itchy trigger finger. She was past the point of trying to figure out how things had turned into what they were.

That was until she was led into the crowded courtroom and saw the love of her life and her son sitting in the crowd among the cameras and reporters. She probably would have cried if she'd had any more tears. But she'd cried herself out. The first two days she cried and puked so much that they had to keep her under constant medical watch. After she arrived at the Washington County Detention Center, they had made her wait for 2 hours before they dealt with her at all. But when they finally did process her she had declined her phone call because she wasn't in the right frame of mind to talk to anyone.

When the female Correctional officer called her out of the dreary, all cement holding cell for her strip search, two other female guards had to literally lift, carry, strip, and re-dress her. The image of Shay lying in a pool of blood had sunken in sending her into shock. They had given her medication, but that just put her mind in a cloudy fog until she was extradited back to New York.

The first night in jail in NY was the worst. From her cell she could hear and see the familiar sounds of the city. They had put her in a cell with a cute brown skinned African girl named Iman. Iman was incarcerated for her involvement in a huge bank fraud and counterfeit operation. She had already been there in the cell for six months. Iman saw that Destiny was in bad shape and did what she could to try to lift her spirits. She fed her, talked some sense into her and braided her hair which had become a mess by the time she came to New York.

"At least you look much better than you did when you got here," Iman had said this morning before Destiny had left the cell to go to court. "You didn't want Donovan or your son to have seen you like that."

Once Destiny had gotten comfortable with Iman they'd had long talks getting to know each other. Of course Destiny had never gone in depth about her case, but she'd told Iman all about Donovan, Jayonne, and her cousin Shay.

As she was walked in front of the judge, she couldn't take her eyes off of her son and Donovan. Even as the United States Attorney read off her charges, she drifted off into what could have been, but what she knew now could never be. The day the store opened and business was going well, she thought to herself about a future with Donovan and her son having a father figure in his life. She saw the house with the swimming pool and the vacations to Disneyworld in her minds eye. Holidays and family gatherings. But now she saw Donovan restraining Jayonne who was crying and reaching. As the drug charges and the shooting of two officers charges were read off, she saw Donovan's tears start to fall. Her tears soon followed. One of the officers had died. No, there would definitely be no bail the judge said. But she never took her eyes off her son and Donovan.

Destiny wanted to suck and hold-in the visual as much as she could, no matter how much it hurt. She knew that happiness in any shape form or fashion was no where in her near future. They'd called her a vicious killer, a key player in a major crack cocaine conspiracy.

Then she was being shuffled back towards the holding cell. A trial date had been set, but she didn't hear it. She was in a long dark tunnel in her mind with no light on the other end. When she was returned to her holding cell one of the court officers came back and handed her a sheet of paper with a name and number. The name at the top of the paper above the number said Donovan.

* * *

"I did the best I could Icon," said O'Connor entering Icon's office.

"I know you did O'Connor. But what was it that was so important that you needed to talk to me about?"

AJ, Sonny and P had returned and informed Icon of their close call. Icon was upset, but didn't show his emotions outwardly. He had seen the article in the Long Island Newsday. The caption above the picture had read "Trigger Happy Diva." It went on to go into detail about Jakes murder, her shooting two Agents during her arrest and conspiracy to distribute crack charges.

O'Connor really didn't know how to deliver this news, so he figured the best way was to just spit it out.

"Well, you remember I told you there was more to this situation than we were seeing? There was and you are not going to like this at all."

Icon stiffened.

"What are you talking about?"

O'Connor shook his head and dropped it.

"Look I don't like all of this suspense shit and-"

"Jake was working for the Feds Icon. He was a confidential informant and he made buys from a lot of people. Destiny Love and Darron Archer, now both locked up were two of them."

Icon's jaw dropped in disbelief. No, not his son. Not his blood. A snitch? This can't be.

"When did you find this out?"

"This morning. The Feds just let us back in on the investigation. Apparently they need us to help them locate some of the other dealers on this conspiracy."

Icon was literally sick to his stomach. He despised absolutely nothing more than a snitch. And now the reality that he had helped to create and bring one into this world was too much for him to bear.

Then he remembered the $5000 that he'd sent after he made that phone call. Icon had gotten a guarantee that they would rid the world of Destiny Love forever.

God, he hoped it wasn't too late to save this young lady who he had tracked halfway across the country to eliminate for killing his son. A snitch?

"Thank you O'Connor. You can go now. I have to make a phone call. Fuck...I hope it's not too late."

* * *

Destiny was just about to take a shower when she heard her name being called for a visit. She really wasn't expecting Donovan and Jayonne to come this early. Not at least until she had talked to them. On her way out she walked past a group of women who were giving her angry stares. She had kind of learned how to ignore them. Iman had already told her about the click of MS-13 chicks who were known to do some crazy shit. But she didn't have to worry about them unless she crossed them or stepped on their toes, which she had no intention of doing either.

Destiny had tried to call the number Donovan had given the officer to give to her but she didn't know that the number had to be approved and added to her phone list. She started to get excited thinking that it was probably them anyway. She checked herself in the mirror and realized she probably looked as good as she was going to.

The visiting room was kind of crowded and the CO directed her to one of the two empty seats behind the thick glass. It was the sixth seat down and Destiny made eye contact with all visitors on the opposite side of the glass as she made her way to her seat. She knew most of the girls back in the cell block had drug charges that they had taken for or got caught up in by their man. She wasn't surprised though, when she saw what she guessed were probably mothers visiting with their daughters.

She approached the glass where the officer had told her to sit. She stopped and froze. She couldn't believe her eyes. What are you doing here? She thought to herself. Benzino was still bandaged up and his arm was in a sling to take the pressure off of his shoulder. He motioned for her to pick-up the phone and sit down. She was still as beautiful as he had remembered. Destiny sat down and picked up the phone.

"Hi Lucky. What are you doing here?" Destiny asked Benzino.

Dam! He thought. He hadn't heard that alias in so long. After Destiny had told him that she was pregnant and he found himself falling in love, which he had no intention on ever doing, he abandoned her, the alias and fell off the face of the earth. She could tell he was stuck for a response and all those painful emotions she had burned connected with him resurfaced. She quickly became angry with herself for letting her heart hurt again for this bastard. He hurt her like no one else ever had, and vowed to never let herself be hurt like that again.

"I know that I'm the last person you want to see right now-"

"Exactly so let's make this quick as possible. My man and my son may be here at any moment and I don't want either of them to see you."

Ouch. OK, I deserved that and much more, he thought to himself.

"Well first off, I want to apologize for how I acted when you told me that you were pregnant." He paused. "My life has been more complicated than you could ever possibly imagine. I've seen, done, and lived through some things that turned me into a coward in thugs clothing. Any man or so called man that can turn his back on his woman and unborn child because he's too immature to face his responsibilities is nothing but a coward. I'm truly sorry for everything that you have been going through. I tried to control all of this when I realized it was you, but-"he trailed off at a loss for words.

She took in his words and watched him as he dropped head as his words trailed off. He had just said a mouthful and although this was really late in the game, it was still good to hear. Destiny had also been introduced to the Bible by Iman. She recalled a scripture that referenced forgiveness. She couldn't remember the scripture word for word but it was something about, if you don't forgive others then your sins won't be forgiven either. He looked nothing like the Lucky she'd known. The confidence and cockiness that had attracted her to him. Now as she looked at him she saw him as a regular human being who had made some mistakes and bad choices. But she was still struggling with the forgiveness.

"Look, Lucky-"

"Benzino. My real name is Benzino."

"You even lied to me about a nickname?" she said becoming frustrated again.

"I've got some things I need to tell you," he started and for the next half hour she sat there stunned and speechless as he told her about his parents being killed, to him working for the man who's son she'd killed.

"I could have tracked you down easily. But when I saw the picture of you and my son that Icon had shown me from your apartment, I started to focus on other things. Your son. He looks exactly like my sister as a baby. It really fucked me up."

She didn't know how to react to the new information. It was too much with everything else that was going on.

"OK, people let's wrap it up. Visitation is over!" shouted the officer in charge of visitation.

"Look, I'm going to be in touch. I'm going to write you and send you a phone number that I can be reached at," said Benzino.

She nodded and slowly stood up, replacing the phone on the wall. She would go back and sleep on this. She needed to process this new information.

* * *

Destiny had every intention on going to sleep. But she felt unclean with the sweat from the nervousness of the courtroom sticking to her skin. She also felt a lot of muscle tension which she felt that a nice hot shower would help to relieve. She began to gather her jail issued underclothes that she planned on changing into when she got out of the shower. She looked over to her pillow and saw her new best friend, outside of Iman, her Bible. A spirit inside of her compelled her to pick it up. Using her spirit as a guide she opened her Bible which led her to scriptures referencing all sins being forgiven by the blood of Jesus who was crucified on the cross. Right then and there, she dedicated her life to Jesus Christ.

Five minutes later Iman came in looking around nervously. But she stopped when she saw Destiny sitting on her bunk with her Bible in her lap. Iman thought to herself how strangely serene and at peace Destiny looked.

"What's wrong?" Destiny asked noticing Iman's nervousness.

"Something big is going on. Lucy and Trish are in a corner cell having a meeting. They only have meetings when they are about to move on somebody."

"Well you didn't do anything to get in their way, right?"

"No."

"So what are you worried about?" I heard somebody say your name, Iman wanted to say but couldn't get it out fast enough.

"I'm going to take a shower. Just relax, everything is going to be fine," Destiny said grabbing her clothes and walking out of the cell.

Iman watched her in shock. She had to rub here eyes because she couldn't believe what she was seeing. As Destiny walked out of the cell Iman saw a small white ring hovering just above her head.

"Oh my god," she whispered to herself knowing that she was witnessing a sign from God, that was only meant for her to see.

It was her acknowledgement that she was doing his work by bringing him saints. But her tears slowly began to fall realizing what else it meant. She closed the cell door and got under her covers.

* * *

Destiny hung her clothes and towel on the wall turned on the shower. She took off her clothes as the steam from the hot water began to fill the shower stall. She was still trying to get use to taking showers with flip-flops on, but she had learned soon after she'd gotten locked up that it was dangerous health wise to take a shower barefoot. She grabbed her soap and washcloth and stepped into the stream of hot water.

She soaped up her body and threw her head back letting the water run through her hair and the drum of the hot water relax her muscles. Her mind took her back to when she was younger. She had been somewhat tomboyish and played with a group of little bad ass boys. Her mother never really liked that idea but accepted it because her child seemed to be a happy child. But what her mother did have a problem with was that her beautiful daughter would give her such a hard time about taking a bath after running the playground for hours at a time. She actually smiled at the recollection of how stubborn and silly she was.

She heard two quick footsteps splash approaching her from behind and felt the excruciating pain of a sharp object tearing into her back. The first stab wound tore a hole in one of her lungs.

"Icon said this is for Jake bitch," whispered Lucy pulling the shank from Destiny's flesh and stabbing her again.

Destiny tried to scream but couldn't find her voice. Again the knife went in. And again. And again. God it hurt so much and she couldn't catch her breath. Her legs gave out and she hit the floor hard. She saw all the blood. Her blood. She looked up and saw the Mexican girl standing over her holding the 8 inch hunting knife. Her eyes began to force themselves closed. And her spirit left her body.

Chapter 36

As Destiny's spirit left her body an ice cold chill shot through Donovan. He instantly knew something was terribly wrong with Destiny. They were sitting in a barbershop in Brooklyn called 'Butta Cutz' waiting to get their haircuts. They had a funeral to go to as well as going to see Destiny tomorrow. Buck was in the chair getting a line-up by a big brother named Byron, while Jayonne sat on Donovan's lap sleeping in his arms. Donovan had finally got oney to stop crying after seeing his mother in court, sadly enough at which time he could not make contact.

Donovan would have left Jayonne with Shay's family while they went to court but when he tried to, Jayonne began to cry hysterically. What Donovan didn't know was that Destiny didn't really associate with that part of her family since her son had been born. To Jayonne, they were really just strangers.

The barbershop was fairly empty and Byron had started a conversation with Buck.

"That's a fly caddy you pushin out there playa. I don't think I've seen them rims around here before," said Byron.

Buck was somewhere lost in thought reflecting on his lost love, when the question brought him back.

"Oh, thanks potna. I had em' custom made by a company out of Cali. A couple of dudes down my way ordered them from my shop after they seen em' on my caddy."

"I could tell by your slang and swagger you wasn't from around here. Where you from?"

"I'm from Tennessee. Me and my brother came up on personal business. We got a funeral to go to tomorrow."

"Damn, I'm sorry to hear that, "said Byron dropping the conversation. A cute girl entered the barbershop and headed to the back.

"You know I got a tight schedule Iyana. You were supposed to be here ten minutes ago," said Kim the hair stylist at 'Butta Cutz.'

"Come on Kim with dat bullshit. I got caught up in traffic coming from Manhattan. Plus my boss really didn't want me to take off early. And , ain't nobody else in here no-way," said Iyana.

She was right. Kim knew that Iyana worked in Manhattan as a paralegal for a large law firm and she had called her yesterday for an emergency appointment. Iyana had a funeral to attend, of a good friend who'd been killed out of town and her body had been flown back home to be buried.

Once Iyana was situated in the chair to have her hair done, she recognized the guy that was sitting in the barber's chair. She had rushed in so quickly that she hadn't even noticed any of the people in the shop. They made eye contact and she smiled and waved at him. It was clear to everyone who was at the get together at Shay's mother's apartment in the projects after the wake last night, that Buck was having a difficult time dealing with Shay's death. Buck gave her a polite smile that quickly faded as Byron spun him around in the chair.

"I'm still trying to make some sense out of all this craziness. Destiny and Shay were the last two girls from the hood likely to end up in the situations they were in. Shay, shot in cold blood by FBI agents? Destiny locked up for killing Jake Wallace and BG? It just doesn't make sense," Iyana said to Kim.

"Oh, that's the funeral you have to go tomorrow? Now that Destiny chick? That bitch is gangsta! Icon would have my ass fired in a heartbeat if he heard me say this, but that goddam Jake had it coming sooner or later. I was fuckin that pretty muthafucka on the low until he got this strange phone call one day. After I found out what it was about, I had to shut that affair down," said Kim.

"What was the phone call about?"

"Now, if I repeated that, even though Jake is dead, Icon would kill me!" They finished getting their haircuts and went back to the hotel where Buck had rented a suite for them all to stay in.

"I'm gonna go down to the bar and have a drink Don. Ya'll cool?"

"Yeah we aight. I think we gonna watch Spiderman again on Pay-per-view or watch cartoon network. I gotta check the phone messages to see if Destiny called yet."

"Don't worry you'll be able to see her tomorrow after the funeral. I know how much you two wanna see her."

Donovan's heart leaped at the thought of seeing her again. But what he didn't realize was the course of his future and his Destiny had been changed forever.

* * *

Icon was making arrangements for the monthly card game with his international associates when the call came through.

"It's done. We tried to stop it, but the wheels were already in motion," said the voice on the other end.

"Thank you, for your attempt. The rest of the funds for your services will be sent the same way. I'll be in touch."

Icon slowly pushed the end button on his phone and sat it down. He'd put out more hits than he could remember, but this was the first that he felt was truly unjustified. Fuck it, he thought. What's done is done and his wife would finally be satisfied.

By now Icon was truly furious with that ungrateful bitch Columbia who had disappeared with his daughter without having enough respect for him to call and at least let him know that they were safe. Fortunately, he was a man who made back-up plans for all situations.

His primary concern at the moment was making sure that his monthly game ran smoothly. Everything else was of little importance.

Chapter 37

The funeral was difficult for everyone. The same girls who had watched Shay go through her trials and escape the trappings of the projects, came out to give her a hood soldier's sendoff. What Shay didn't know was that when she would come back and ride through the hood, to a lot of the girls, she had been a sign of hope and motivation that they could make it out in spite of their circumstances.

Donovan, Buck, and Jayonne had left the burial site right after they lowered the casket into the ground. It had been too much for Buck to handle. He was now sitting on the passenger side of the Caddy as they pulled up to the jail to go visit Destiny. Donovan had continuously checked the messages, but there had still been no call from Destiny.

"I'll be right out. I just want to make sure we can visit before we park." Said Donovan double parking in front of the jail.

Buck was so out of it, he just nodded.

Donovan ran up the steps and into the front door. He looked around at the high ceilings and sparkling floors. It looked more like an office building than a jail, he thought. There were two corrections officers standing at a guard post holding a conversation as he approached.

"Good afternoon, how can I help you?" asked one of them.

"I'm here to visit an inmate. Destiny Love. This is my first time here, but you can expect to see me a lot. I just wanted to make sure that we could visit. My brother and her son are outside."

"Excuse me sir, but I can see that you haven't heard."

"Haven't heard what?"

"There was an incident here yesterday involving Ms. Love. No one contacted the family?"

"What kind of incident-contacted the family? What are you saying? What happened?

"She was killed in the shower by-"

And that was the last thing Donovan heard. He mentally shut down and could no longer hear anything the officers said to him. They believed that he had possibly went into shock by the expression on his face as he turned to exit the building. They had no idea his state of mind was something far more dangerous than shock. There was only one name that constantly reverberated in his thoughts. Icon. He remembered the name that induced fear in Destiny when she spoke it and knew that somehow, someway, he was the hands pulling the strings behind her death. As he stepped out into the sunlight on the front steps of the jail, Donovan believed he could feel Destiny's presence. He smiled as the tears stung his eyes and covered his face. He looked up to the heavens, where he knew she was and said ,"Baby-I gotchu."

Chapter 38

Benzino was sick with regret as he sat off to the side watching Icon's monthly Poker game, Icon had informed him of the hit that he had put out on Destiny and that he'd received confirmation that the deed was done. He also conveniently omitted the information the he received from O'Connor about the other role that his son Jake had played in all of this. That would have been too embarrassing to disclose. That all this madness had been over a snitch.

The game had a much different feeling though on this particular night. It wasn't the physical void of Simpson being missed, because there was always enough old-timers with big money to fill the seats. But Simpson had become just as much a part of the monthly game as Icon, and his witty humor would sometime set the mood of the players at the table.

Icon also noticed the heads turning looking for his showpiece. Columbia's presence had become a part of the atmosphere as well, for the old-timers knew that she belonged to Icon. Icon use to call her his good luck charm, but to the other players at the table she was eye candy in her skimpy and most revealing attire. There had still been no word from her.

But Icon being the man and entertainer he was, he put in a call to an exclusive service that provided unique and exotic women of all races. Even though the presence of the beautiful women was appreciated, the vibe was still different.

The vibe was different, but the heavy piles of hundred dollar bills that stayed stacked in the middle of the table were the same. Well, almost the same.

"I'll see ya'll fella's came to play tonight," Icon stated noticing the pots and bets becoming bigger.

"My son's said they had a good month. They know I come to N.Y. once a month to play poker and dropped $150,000 in my limo before I left Houston," said old man Reggie whose sons were heavy weights in Texas.

He'd passed on his empire to them once he got his foot in the door of the oil business. Icon should have known something was up when he came in with a small duffel bag.

"Yeah I brought some extra too," started Glen Cove George. "I just locked in a couple of big contracts with the Government and brought 5 new dump trucks. So I had a few extras to play with too."

Icon figured George had already lost about $40,000, and that hadn't put a dent in those stacks that sat in front of him at the table. But he was cool with that. If they wanted to toss some paper around, so be it. That was the reason he had sent his driver to take Benzino to get him $200,000 out of his stash. On Benzino's way back into the building, he decided to use the rear entrance. As he had approached the rear entrance, Benzino had paused to acknowledge what a nice night it was. The moon was full, lighting up the sky and combined with the stars to make a beautiful sky. He thought that he had heard some movement off in the shadows. He was on his way over to investigate but then considered the 200 g's he had in the bag hanging over his shoulder. Nah, that wasn't really a good idea he thought. When the large alley cat came out of the shadows, he smiled to himself. Too paranoid. Nobody would try Icon, he thought. Well, almost nobody.

That dam alley cat almost blew my cover, Donovan thought. It wasn't like it made much difference. He was a man with a mission, and noone would come between him and his mission. He stepped out into the moonlight in fatigues and black combat boots as soon as Benzino was let in the heavy steel door by the huge brotha with braids that hung to his shoulders. Security he figured. Hova had told him that he was up against some unbelievable odds. But Donovan gave less than a fuck about what he was up against.

He had been up against unbelievable odds for real against radicals at war willing to die for their cause. And he was still breathing. He'd gone to see Hova after he was able to organize his thoughts. He knew the who and the why, he was pretty sure of the how, but he needed the where and the when. Once the shock wore off from receiving the news that Destiny had been murdered, he gave Donovan the name of the barbershop where Icon set up large poker games once a month and he was sure that there was one in the very near future. Donovan knew exactly where 'Butta Cutz'was located. He just had to make a trip back down the highway to get the weapons he needed.

Hova had given him a number to call, a password, and a coded message. After the brotha with the Jamaican accent on the other end of the phone answered, Donovan said" when Kingdom come, thy will be done."

"On ert asitis in eaven," the Jamaican cat finished the statement. They made arrangements and hooked up. The Jamaican cat had led him to a basement of a rundown building in Southside Jamaica Queens. When they entered the huge room lined with everything from two .22's to grenade launchers, Donovan whispered, Holy shit!"

"Look mi bregren. Ova like a bruddah tu mi. You tek whateva you need. I owe de mon more dan me could eva repay im."

Donovan left with enough artillery to take out a small army. Now as he stood in the alley reevaluating his escape route, he figured that it was time to make his move. As he got his mind ready to go in, he thought, killing machine-murder everything moving. He climbed up on the dumpster and threw his bag of weapons on the roof.

Once he was on the roof he heard sirens and saw flashing red lights approaching quickly. He ducked down in the shadows as the fire engine raced past the building, sirens blaring headed towards its destination. As the sounds faded he removed tools from his bag and began to open the vent leading into the roof of the building.

* * *

It had taken her a few weeks, but Columbia had finally gotten herself settled. She figured the best way to work through her situation, was to get her and her daughter as far away from New York as possible. She had comtemplated relocating to a few different places, but finally came to the decision that Houston, Texas was a perfect spot for her to start over. When she went online to a search for a new condo, she was overwhelmed with the possible selections.

Columbia and Aliyah had flown out to California for the few days following her killing Simpson. She had immediately destroyed her phone, but she desperately missed her brother. For the short period of time that she hadn't seen him, she had no idea that she would miss him this much. But it was necessary. Benzino's loyalties laid with Icon and in her mind it was time for a change. Her sanity and survival depended on it.

But as she sat in her new place two days ago, she thought that if she got Icon out of the way, that she and Benzino could both start over. She also knew with Jake dead, that her daughter Aliyah was the only child heir to Icon's empire. Sure his wife would beef and contest it, but fuck that bitch. Icon's name was on her birth certificate and Aliyah was in his last will and testament. Yes, getting rid of him would make the situation better for everybody involved.

So she made reservations on a flight out of Houston that would put her in New York the same day as Icon's poker game. Benzino didn't attend these games and would generally only stop by for a hot minute, and then be off to tend to business. But as she sat in the rental off in the darkness of the alley behind 'Butta Cutz' and watched her brother go in the rear entrance with his shoulder bandaged up, her heart sank. He'd been hurt, and from the looks of it, pretty badly. In all their years, she had never seen him show any sign of weakness. He had been trained with more combat skills than she had. What could have possibly happened?

But as she sat there her thoughts racing after Benzino went inside, she caught a glimpse of someone moving in the shadows. She thought it was a bum until she saw the man climb up on the dumpster and onto the roof. Oh, hell no she thought thinking that she might be about to loose her brother. She pulled down her mask, checked the security of her knives and slipped out of the rental dressed in all black. With her back against the wall, she slowly crept towards 'Butta Cutz'. Whatever was about to go down, she had to stop it.

* * *

Benzino had downed a couple of Heinekens and felt the effects on his bladder. He was conversing with one of the ladies from the service. Her island tan and greenish-brown smiling eyes caught his attention and kept it. She said her name was Monique and she was born of parents from the Barbados.

"Look beautiful. Don' you move a muscle. I'll be right back," Benzino told Monique.

It had been a few weeks since he had been with a woman and figured this one would be perfect to get his nuts out of the sand with. She smiled and stayed put as he headed towards the bathroom. The mood had changed considerably. Everyone, all 27 people present seemed to be enjoying themselves. A smooth groove from Smokey Robinson floated in the background as alcohol filled and disappeared in glasses at a rapid pace. Benzino smiled. Hopefully things would be back as close to normal as possible very soon. As he walked out of the area where the gambling was going on and into the front to use the barbershop bathroom, he thought to himself, that he didn't like change very much. Especially when things were going good. He made it to the bathroom and closed the door. He looked in the mirror and with his good arm splashed cold water on his face. He was staring deep into his own eyes wondering yet once again, where is my baby sister when he heard an explosion rock the building.

* * *

Donovan had watched the scene through the ceiling vent long enough. His keen senses also shot off warning signals that he was not alone. He had three grenades, an m-16, and two Ruger 9mm with extended clips. He had two extra clips for the m-16 and the extended clips on the Ruger held twenty-two shots. He saw the guy who had went in the back entrance leave the room after talking to some woman. Ready to get this all over with, he removed the grate from the ceiling. He removed the pins from the grenade and dropped all three in simultaneously. He already had one of the Rugers cocked and aimed at the head of the man in the wheelchair. One of the grenades landed dead in the center of the poker table. As the men at the table realized exactly what is was and started to take cover, Icon looked up and into the barrel of Donovan's gun. Two shots hit Icon in his head and mouth causing him to back flip out of his chair at the same time as the grenades ripped through the entire room. The force from the explosion sent Donovan tumbling out of the attic and halfway across the roof. But he knew for sure Icon was dead.

As he tried to shake off the impact of the explosion, he saw the silhouette of someone on the roof with him, but before he could respond, he felt a sharp pain rip through his thigh. He looked down and saw the knife. The blast had thrown him away from his guns and as he saw the figure draw back it's arm, the moonlight flickered off the knife. Only one thing he could do....Run! He turned and headed towards the front of the roof and took off running as fast as he could with a knife in his thigh. But just as he was about to jump, a second knife entered the back of his arm. He landed hard but was glad to see Buck sitting where he was suppose to be.

Buck pulled up, picked up his brother and got the fuck outta there.

* * *

Columbia watched from the roof as the green Cadillac sped away into the darkness but she couldn't worry about that now. If there was a chance at all to save Benzino, she had to take it. Columbia ran back across the roof to where the man had been standing. There were streams of smoke pouring out. Oh my God, the place is on fire. She thought. She looked inside and saw all the dead bodies. She dropped down inside. She was turning bloody bodies over left and right. Her heart was hammering in her chest. When she saw Icon, the man that she had actually come to kill, her whole body stiffened. It was only then that she realized that there was a possibility that she would not have been able to do it herself.

Find Benzino! A voice screamed out in her head reminding her what she was up in the middle of all this mess for anyway. That's when she heard a pounding on the wall coming from up front. She stepped over more dead bodies and body parts. The sound was coming from the barbershop area. She still hadn't seen her brother and she hoped and prayed that it was him. As she pulled the door to go into the front, she realized it was jammed.

"Benzino!" she cried out in hope.

"Yo, who dat?! What's going on? I'm stuck in the bathroom."

"It's, me Columbia. Hold tight. I think those explosions shifted the framework of the building."

She turned to see that the fire was spreading quickly. Thinking on her feet she went and searched the dead men that had been playing cards. One of them had to have a gun. Once she found one, she ran back to the door.

"Get away from the door, I'm going to shoot out the hinges."

Two minutes later, they were free and she was pulling him towards the front door.

"But what about Icon? He's still back there."

"He's dead and this place is gonna burn to the ground Benzino. Let's go." It took a few seconds for him to catch on, but the crackling flames and smoke told him if there was anyone back there, they were well done. They ran out of the barbershop and to the rental in the alley. Columbia had some serious explaining to do. But right now they had to put as much distance between them and this scene as possible.

Kelvin F Jackson

COMING SOON FROM KELVIN F JACKSON

I WON'T TELL
(YOUR SECRETS)

Traffic was moving well on this clear winter night. Demitri Howard had just under an hour ago left yet another industry party in Manhattan. They had begun to become monotonous after about a year ago. But in the business of entertainment, it was absolutely necessary to attend these functions. At one point in his career he would have done just about anything to be invited to one of those industry functions, where everybody who was anybody would be in attendance. But that was before his incredible success story.

Demitri had learned years earlier that you don't forget where you come from. The same people you see on the way up are the very same ones you gonna see on the way down .So after that five and a half years he spent in Federal and State Institutions, he'd become a much wiser individual. He had learned quickly who his friends were and the important role that family plays when everybody else forgets about you.

The Midnight black stretch chauffer driven Maybach cruised at a smooth eighty-three MPH on 495 east headed to one of his many luxurious homes located out in the Hamptons. The custom made chrome twenty-four inch DAVINCI rims riding on shiny black Pirelli tires made the vehicle look similar to a mini spaceship. Demitri poured himself another drink from the bar as he reflected on the events of this past evening. He had to laugh at himself, but there was no humor in it. He couldn't believe that he had let himself be subjected tó this woman's bullshit. But that was what he got for going against his own rules.

Demitri had already won numerous Black Film awards and was one of the first few African Americans to secure an exclusive deal with Time Warner Home Video as well as being the owner and CEO of one of the largest Black Film production companies in the country. There were women of all races, shapes, and sizes, beating a path to lay claim on one of the most eligible bachelors in America. So how the hell did he get caught in Michelle's spider web? He had been conversing with an up and coming actress that he had considered casting as the lead in one of his future films, when he heard Ms. Michelle Malone's distinctive voice.

"I was just sent a script to read for an upcoming lead in Quentin Tarantino's next movie," She was telling one of her model girlfriends.

Demitri knew that she was putting on this show for his benefit. Sure it was possible that she had been sent the script. Especially after she had reached stardom floating on his coattails from major roles in his last three films.

"Oh Demitri. Hi.I didn't know that you would be here," she lied.

"What's up Michelle?"He asked turning to face her.

It had been about a month since he'd seen her and the official end to their relationship, but her breathtaking beauty hadn't lost any of its affect on him. Keep your game face.Dont let her see you sweat, he told himself. Her stunning likeness to Alicia Keys which initially attracted his attention was part of the reason that ending the relationship had been so difficult. The other part was that he'd let her into his innermost world.

"I've been good. Haven't seen you around much lately," said Michelle.

"I've been spending a lot of time at the house out in Malibu, working on a few projects that have upcoming deadlines," and so I don't have to see you parading around with your new boyfriend that plays for the New Jersey Nets, he thought to himself. "I don't see um- what's his name."

"Oh, Warren is out in San Antonio. He'll be back in a couple of days she quickly volunteered.

Demitri would never forget that first time he'd seen superstar shooting guard Warren Irving with his recent ex. He was sick, as he saw Michelle clinging to Warren entering the premier and private showing of Martin Lawrence's latest movie. Demitri pushed the memory to the back of his mind.

Michelle had given him her inviting come fuck me eyes that he knew so well. But he refused to give in to his hormones and emotions that were screaming for her familiar sensuality. He was also sure that this was probably the same look that she'd shared with her new man more times than he cared to imagine.

"Demitri we really need to talk," she said moving close and whispering in his ear.

He recoiled as if she were a snake.

She frowned.

"Michelle, we have absolutely nothing to talk about. You said everything you had to say the night you- As a matter of fact I'm out!"

He had spun on his heel and left her standing there with her mouth wide open. Of course everyone was in their business and watched in amusement. Their soap opera of a relationship had become a main topic of conversation in the tabloids and Demitri despised the negative energy and attention.

Fuck it, he thought as he turned on his laptop and began to type in ideas for one of his new productions. He would be on his private Jet headed back out to Cali in the morning anyway. With all of his current obligations and responsibilities the last thing that he had time for was drama.

He was just saving his ideas to one of his files as the Maybach turned into the long driveway that led to his lavish estate.

Demitri was still awe at his seemingly overnight success as he looked at the sprawling 20 room, 8.5 million dollar mansion, on beachfront property that was illuminated off in the distance. It had been a long time coming, but God had blessed him for being a faithful servant. He would have never thought that the same man who had run up and down the interstates of the east coast selling guns and drugs, would achieve such a level of success; producing movies that his people could relate to. Demitri had initially started with straight to DVD movies from storylines of novels he'd written in prison that brought a new dimension to the urban literature game. Eight bestselling novels and five movies later, he was worth somewhere in the ballpark of 80 million.

The limo rounded the huge multicolored waterfall-fountain that was the centerpiece out in front of the estate. Once it came to a stop at the double front doors, his driver Maurice was at the limo's rear doors seconds later. As soon as Maurice opened the door Demitri felt the significant difference in temperature between the city and the open waterfronts of the Hamptons. With the chill blowing in off the ocean it couldn't have been more than just above freezing.

"What time we pullin out in the morning Meech?" asked Demitri's driver and close friend of the past twenty years.

"I was thinking around eleven. That way I will be well rested and the time change won't affect me that much," Demitri said gathering his laptop and other belongings.

Demitri stood 5ft 11inches in his handmade full length chinchilla, wearing a stocky 245 pounds well. His chocolate complexion and winning smile were highlights that accented his magnetic personality.

"Why do you ask? Did you have plans?" Demitri asked already knowing the answer.

"Well you know I like to swing by the spot and check on ole girl when I come to town. But we been runnin non stop since we hit NY."

Maurice was relating to his latest fling, a drop dead gorgeous Native American exotic dancer nicknamed Pocahontas, who also worked as a bartenderat6 one of the local clubs.

"Go ahead and do ya thing playboy. I still got some ideas bouncing around in my head that I wanna put on my laptop while they still fresh. Just make sure you back in time for our scheduled liftoff."

"You sure you don't want me to bring back a freak for you?"

"Niggah please! The last thing I need is another chick thinking she gonna get her Pac-Man make it rain game on with me. Not to mention I need to get some rest before we get back to Cali. We start shooting the film starring Angela Basset in two weeks," said Demitri punching in the code and disarming the security system.

"Well it's a quarter after two now. I'll be back by seven, no later than eight," said Maurice getting back in the limo and pulling off.

Demitri entered the mansion and ascended a set of steps to the right of the large luxurious transparent elevator that was lined with brown and tan leather from one of the finest shops in Milan. He reached the top of the steps and took the east corridor that had been decorated with exclusive works, African oil paintings and sculptures,that led to the master bedroom. He crossed the threshold through the double doors, walked over to the floor to ceiling window that gave him the view that sealed the deal when he first purchased the property.

As he looked out across the quarter-mile stretch of sand that covered the distance between the house and the Atlantic Ocean, he could see the waves rolling up to the shore under a magnificently clear, star and moonlit sky. It was additional confirmation of the greatness of the creators creations. Once he was eventually able to pull himself away from the magnetic visual, he kicked off his shoes and sat on th bed opening up his laptop. He began pecking away at the keyboard and before he knew it an hour had passed.

He realized that he'd once again gone into a zone and more than likely laid the foundation for another prospective award winning production. He stood up and stretched his legs which were beginning to fall asleep. In
his peripheral he spotted something out on the beach.

A fire?!

It was about 200 feet away from his back deck. That hadn't been there before, he thought to himself. It wasn't a big fire, but just big enough to make him put on his coat and go investigate. He reached under his mattress and pulled out his 10mm and slipped it into the small of his back. He had been long out of the streets and didn't carry guns out in public, but he would always have hardware close by to protect home base. There were some crazy people in this world that we lived in. He put on his coat and exited through the door that led down the steps and to the beach. The cold seabreeze coming off the water nipped at his bare cheeks as Demitri trudged through the soft sand headed towards the fire.

He saw a balled up blanket.

What the fu-?

He heard a sound.

It was non-threatening, but his instincts made him reach for his gun. He could hear the sound clearly now.

A baby crying.

He put the gun away and knelt down next to the blanket. It couldn't have been more than thirty degrees on the beach. There was a note sticking out of a small opening in the thick pink blanket.

He looked left.

He looked right.

Nothing but darkness as far as the eye could see in either direction. Demitri unfolded the paper that had been folded once and it read:

I am an addict and I don't have the strength to kick my habit to take care of my daughter. I stayed clean through my pregnancy, so she is in perfect health. I want her to have a chance at life that I can't give her. Her name is Tianna Nicole I believe god led me to you for a good reason. Please see that she finds a good home.

The baby was crying louder now, probably sensing someone near. Demitri opened the blanket only to find that the baby was wrapped in two more blankets lined with four bottles and six diapers. He opened a slit in the last blanket to see two tiny wet brown eyes staring back at him curiously. She couldn't be more than six or seven weeks old. She was adorable.

"Hey cutey," he whispered smiling.

Tianna broke into a toothless grin and his heart melted. He scanned the area again. Tucking her inside his chinchilla to keep her warm he turned around and headed back to the mansion. Little did he know, neither of their lives would ever be the same again.

* * *

"Come on bitch! The Niggah got that lil crumb snatcher. So now we can get the fuck up otta here and get my money," said Lex to Anita as they watched Demitri take Tianna inside from up the beach.

Tears made tracks down Anita's face as the emotions hit from the thought of never seeing her daughter again. But she knew that this was what was best.

"Aight Lex, dam. Calm down-I'm comin," she said forcing herself to leave the scene.

Anita was a twenty something year old crackhead prostitute that had been a beautiful young lady with a future, before she was seduced by what she referred to as *the god of crack cocaine.* Some six years earlier she'd come to New York from Alabama to attend Hofstra University. Her beauty and naivety made her a much sought after prospect for predators. One night after a frat party in the first semester of her second year, she was intoxicated and got invited to the apartment of a young brotha on the football team that she found attractive. Her acceptance of this invitation would be the beginning of the end of life as she knew it.

She had already been doomed by genetics due to the fact that alco0holism and addiction ran in her family. So Mark offered her the pre-rolled blunt laced with crack cocaine and she hit it, school, her dreams, and ambitions all went up in smoke.

Anita met Lex at her lowest point, after losing contact with her family and close becoming homeless. Lex was a combination of the worst; a dealer-pimp-addict, that catered primarily to the rich in the Hamptons Underworld. But once Anita became pregnant with a baby that only God knew who the father was, Lex locked her away in their apartment and absolutely forbid her to get high.

It had been a financial strain taking care of her; her checkups, and feeding her, the baby and his habit. But after some investigation of this big-time movie cat, they both figured they'd found a home for Tianna.

"Do you really think he'll keep her?" Anita asked as they made it back to the car.

"Sheeeiit, I don't know. I just know that we couldn't," said Lex ending the conversation.

Before they pulled off Lex pulled out a crack pipe and loaded it up. Watching him Anita immediately forgot about her daughter which Lex knew she would. After they both filled their lungs with poison and filled th car with the acrid smelling smoke, Lex pulled away from the beach headed towards the next trick. Anita had put on weight during her pregnancy and had recently been pulling in a lot of return calls from tricks. Lex needed to literally milk this cow while her tits were heavy and had every intention of doing so!

Kelvin F Jackson

ORDER FORM

BIG STAXXX ENTERTAINMENT
8972 Quioccasin Road
Suite 128
Henrico, VA 23229

NAME: _____

ADDRESS: _____

CITY/STATE: _____

ZIP CODE: _____

INMATE #: _____

TITLE _____

LOOK WHAT YOU MADE ME DO
BOOK PRICE $15.00
SHIPPING/HANDLING (Via U.S. Media Mail) $3.95

FORMS OF ACCEPTED PAYMENT
Institutional checks and money orders, all mail in orders Allow
5-7 business days to be delivered
(All inmates receive 20% discount)
Every copy purchased from BIG STAXXX ENTERTAINMENT will
be personally signed by author